Traitor's Legacy

by

Beth Trissel

Traitor's Legacy Series

This is a work of fiction. Names, characters, places, and incidents are either the product of the author's imagination or are used fictitiously, and any resemblance to actual persons living or dead, business establishments, events, or locales, is entirely coincidental.

Traitor's Legacy

Cover Art by *Debbie Taylor*

The Wild Rose Press, Inc.
PO Box 708
Adams Basin, NY 14410-0708
Visit us at www.thewildrosepress.com

Publishing History
First American Rose Edition, 2014
Print ISBN 978-1-62830-477-0
Digital ISBN 978-1-62830-478-7

Traitor's Legacy Series
Published in the United States of America

She dashed between them, followed by a wiry slave who made for the stables. "I am truly sorry for your violent reception at Thornton Hall and beg your forbearance," she blurted, and flung herself at Vaughan's feet just across from the wounded guide. "Spare my foolish brother, I beseech you."

Hardly in a position to indulge her notions of chivalry, as he was stained with blood and constrained by the need to apply pressure to Percy's wound, Vaughan scowled at her in bemusement. "Get up, woman. I shall consider your request."

She raised her head and met his annoyance with a plea in her earnest gaze, like sunlight on water lilies. So clear, her hazel eyes, cast with a greenish hue, and her face was really rather pleasing. Remarkably so.

What on earth was he thinking? Vaughan wrenched his attention away from the distracting girl. "Might I have clean cloth to stem the flow, Miss—"

"Monroe," she supplied, and reached into her bodice. "Claire Monroe."

Lovely name.

Too bad it belonged to a Rebel.

Traitor's Legacy is the sequel to award-winning historical romance novel, *ENEMY OF THE KING,* also available from The Wild Rose Press, Inc.

Dedication

To my enthusiastic friend and supporter,
Ann See,
without whose help this novel would not
have been possible.

And to the fine folks in North Carolina,
dedicated to preserving their rich heritage.

Acknowledgments

It was my privilege to feature Person's Ordinary,
still standing outside of Historic Halifax
in what is now the town of Littleton, NC.

I'm also grateful for the valuable assistance I received
from Williamsburg historian Taylor Stoermer.

For more on Historic Halifax, visit:
http://www.nchistoricsites.org/halifax

Chapter One

May 1781, countryside near the Town of Halifax, North Carolina
The American Revolution Rages On

Spies were the devil to catch. This time, British Captain Jacob Vaughan had the advantage. Sweltering in his scarlet coat, he and his sharp-eyed scout, Percy, galloped after the Rebel. If Vaughan's informant was correct, and he'd better be with the guineas he'd given him, the rider tearing over the dirt track ahead of them on a fine bay gelding was Lieutenant Stuart Monroe and he carried a valuable, treasonous letter. Clues in the message led to the stash a band of Patriots had secreted for a bounty on now *British* General Benedict Arnold's head.

Vaughan's orders: thwart the Rebel scheme to bribe a weak-willed Loyalist into betraying Arnold's whereabouts. His own contempt for the General's treachery mattered not a jot.

Percy, the slave Vaughan had liberated from a reluctant planter, glanced over his shoulder. "Fellow's headed for Thornton Hall, Captain! Home to the Monroes."

"We've got him!" Vaughan would be back in *Person's Ordinary* quaffing ale in the local tavern before the day was done.

So confident of Monroe's capture he could crow, he urged his mare past the flagging guide. La Belle's chestnut-colored neck glistened in the late afternoon sun, but the hunter's endurance had grown since he'd taken her from Patriot Captain Jordan's stables last August. Now, he'd catch that blasted spy with the very horse Jordan had bred for speed.

"Why you reckon he's risking a homeward race?" Percy called from behind him.

"Beyond me." Vaughan figured Monroe would run to ground after their arrival at the Ordinary.

He barely had time to wet his lips before heading out after the Rebel who bolted from the tavern and sprang onto his waiting mount. With Crown forces gathering in Halifax, Monroe couldn't return there. Whatever the spy's reason for making this mad dash to his den, Vaughan was on his tail.

"I'll have Monroe and that letter by nightfall!"

"How you gonna read it?"

The ingenious cyphers Patriots contrived to safeguard their messages could only be broken by the one with the book they'd used to create it, or knowledge of invisible ink, or whatever craft they'd employed. Maddening.

"First the letter!" He'd worry over deciphering it later.

"There!" In the blue coat and white facings of the Virginia Light Dragoons, their quarry bent low over the horse's straining neck. The bay's long legs were fast covering ground.

Percy gave a low whistle. "Hell of a rider."

"Let him fly. No man outrides me."

"Heard tell there was *one*."

McCray must've blabbed, blast him. Captain Jordan had the swiftest mount, bar none, and Vaughan nearly caught the rogue, useless justification he didn't bother to voice.

That particular humiliation occurred last summer in Backcountry followed by a string of Crown setbacks. Loyalists needed encouragement to rally round the king's banner. The Patriot plot to catch General Arnold and hang him from the highest tree would dampen Loyalist support.

"Captain!" Lieutenant McCray, the hardened dragoon who'd accompanied Vaughan through the Carolinas, pounded up to them on his blowing mount, the rich scent of horseflesh strong in the heat. A hair behind him rode Ensign Anderson, the young Loyalist Vaughan had taken under his wing.

"Monroe's just out in front!" Vaughan yelled.

Evergreens were thick along this stretch of road. Further ahead, oaks and poplars arched lofty branches over them in a shady bower that enclosed their small party, then parted to reveal a tree-lined approach to the house. At the end of this finger of refinement in the rustic landscape, stood Thornton Hall. The two-story frame house built in a T shape with wings on either side rose from the countryside like a modest English manor, a welcome sight to his battle-weary eyes.

Despite Vaughan's aristocratic upbringing and the vast estate he was to inherit, he was impressed. Especially when he compared Thornton Hall to the crude cabins he'd passed earlier. It had been months since he'd seen opulent Charles Towne homes.

A wrench in his gut accompanied the memory of Jordan's lavish plantation where he'd found *her*,

Meriwether Steele, the Carolina peach. Now Mrs. Jordan. Her marriage was of no consequence, he reminded himself. She'd made her choice and—

Damn it all. "Where's Monroe gotten to?"

"Must've run to cover!" Percy shouted.

How? When? He was just under their noses. "Confound it. "We'll flush out the cunning fox!"

In spite of grinding fatigue, Vaughan charged ahead. It had been a punishing day on top of a hellish year, but there'd be a promotion in this assignment. He'd damn well make major, would've already if not for the elusive Captain Jordan. While still a favorite with his superiors, Vaughan had lost some of his shine in the Jordan debacle and must make amends.

He cantered up the *allée* fragrant with cedars on either side. Wheat greened the surrounding fields and reddish Devon cows grazed in lush pasture, reminiscent of home. A thoroughbred mare and yearling filly threw their heads up and nickered from a grassy meadow gilded with buttercups, an increasingly rare sight when so many animals were confiscated or slaughtered.

Not only by British troops. Hungry, sometimes greedy, Patriots also spoiled the land. Men were men. Unless sternly held in check, mayhem was inevitable.

As Vaughan drew closer, he admired the embellishment carved beneath the arched roofline and above the doorway of the gracious home. Pity he could expect scant hospitality in this nest of Rebels. The ever-present wariness he carried with him heightened as he trotted La Belle into the cobbled yard.

Halting his winded mount, he scanned the great stone at one side of the house. Unusual. Too large to move, the builder had simply left it, trees clustered behind. Outbuildings were arranged near the house. He ran his gaze over the smokehouse, dovecote, stables…the kitchen must be around back. Pecan trees graced the lawn, and he glimpsed an orchard beyond the home.

A charming scene. Why did these people risk all?

The tenacity of Patriots perplexed him, but dispirited folk were coming to their senses and siding with the Crown as the war dragged into its seventh year. Victory lay within Great Britain's grasp. Finally.

Percy reined in at Vaughan's side. Hooves clattering on the cobbles, McCray and Anderson trotted up behind them. Not a soul in sight, though Vaughan had no doubt they were observed.

"Look sharp. Search every inch of the—"

"Captain! Watch out!"

Vaughan ducked. Percy's body jerked to the report of gunfire. He yelped and slumped in the saddle. Blood streamed from between the brown fingers he clasped to his side. That shot came from the house and was intended for Vaughan, he was certain. Outrage at the attack overshadowed any concern for his personal safety.

"Steady. I've got you." He reached over and grasped the big Negro to keep him from toppling to the cobbles.

Lieutenant McCray rushed to their aid. Eyes searching, Ensign Anderson aimed his musket at Thornton Hall. McCray lowered Percy, groaning, to the yard. Vaughan had lost too many good men to these sneaky Patriot tactics and wasn't about to let this one go without a fight. Not only was the former slave clever, he just plain liked him.

"Find whoever did this and shoot the bastard!" He was angry enough to do the deed himself, but must see to Percy. His medical knowledge surpassed the others.

He slid from the saddle in fitted buckskin breeches. His black top riding boots crunched on the stones. Laying his musket down, he crouched near the fallen man and thrust his gloved hand over the wound to stem the tide—pulling off the second glove with his teeth for the makeshift compress.

Ahead of him, McCray and Anderson advanced on Thornton Hall to bash open the door and search room to room for the culprit. Bayonets glinted at the end of leveled muskets and sabers hung from scabbards in a sling around their shoulders. Lieutenant Colonel Tarleton wouldn't protest a swift reprisal. He'd cheer them on. Vaughan was even tempted to torch the estate and teach these defiant—

"No! Wait!" a woman shrieked.

"What the—" *Hell* died on Vaughan's lips as the double front doors opened wide and a slender figure in a froth of turquoise flew out.

Snatching up her petticoats, she ran down the stone steps. "Captain, please, I would speak with you!"

Loose brown hair, streaked gold in the sunshine, cascaded over the young woman sprinting toward him. "'Twas a rash act by a mere boy bent on avenging the death of our father!"

The startled dragoons placed their bulk between her and Vaughan, kneeling beside Percy. She wasn't deterred in the slightest. "Allow me a word, sir. I beg you."

Was she actually leaping up in the air to see past the officers? Preoccupied as Vaughan was, her desperation and feminine appeal caught his attention. So totally unexpected. His temper, inflamed only moments ago, cooled to a simmer.

"If you desire leniency, Madame, bid your servants to fetch warm water and fresh linens and tend to my man."

"Do as he says!" she called over her shoulder at unseen onlookers. "Send Joseph for Doctor Phillips."

Vaughan sensed the flurry of activity in the seemingly unprepared household. Perhaps she spoke the truth and no foul play was afoot. No stealthy ambush awaited them.

How could he be sure? Snipers might lurk at every corner. Hidden and deadly, like a crouching panther ready to spring.

Still, she seemed sincere, and Vaughan was an astute judge of character. Percy needed a skilled surgeon to remove the lead ball. With an able hand at the job and proper nursing, he should live, if infection didn't set in. So many *ifs* with a gunshot wound, and this forthright female completely took him aback.

All these considerations ran through Vaughan's mind in an instant. Accustomed to making sudden decisions based on hurried assessments, he determined in this matter, at least, he must trust her. An order swiftly followed.

"McCray, let her pass and one other to fetch the doctor."

"Yes, Captain." McCray and Anderson stepped aside.

She dashed between them, followed by a wiry slave who made for the stables. "I am truly sorry for your violent reception at Thornton Hall and beg your forbearance," she blurted, and flung herself at Vaughan's feet just across from the wounded guide. "Spare my foolish brother, I beseech you."

Hardly in a position to indulge her notions of chivalry, as he was stained with blood and constrained by the need to apply pressure to Percy's wound, Vaughan scowled at her in bemusement. "Get up, woman. I shall consider your request."

She raised her head and met his annoyance with a plea in her earnest gaze, like sunlight on water lilies. So clear, her hazel eyes, cast with a greenish hue, and her face was really rather pleasing. Remarkably so.

What on earth was he thinking? Vaughan wrenched his attention away from the distracting girl. "Might I have clean cloth to stem the flow, Miss—"

"Monroe," she supplied, and reached into her bodice. "Claire Monroe."

Lovely name. Too bad it belonged to a Rebel. Even so, he couldn't stop his eyes from following the curves mounding up out of the lace-edged cloth as she withdrew a square of embroidered linen.

"Please. Take this, sir." She passed the handkerchief into his free hand.

Her smooth fingers brushed his weathered skin and sent a jolt pulsing through him. He almost jerked up his head and stared at her, so violent was his reaction, but restrained himself from such blatant notice. Claire Monroe was leaps and bounds ahead of the camp followers he was used to who did laundry, cooked, tended the sick and wounded, bearing their children along the way. Apart from the higher born officer's wives—and she outshone them—these hardy camp women were common. Despite her incomplete attire,

Miss Monroe was a lady.

Shaking off the unnerving sensation she evoked in him, he replaced the soiled gloves with this unlikely bandage. The blood flow had lessened slightly from his ministrations, and he pressed her spotless handkerchief to the wound.

"Claire! Git away from that vile officer, ye wanton strumpet!" On the heels of the gravelly boom accented in a Scottish burr, an elderly man in a dusky dressing gown stormed from the house. Silver hair flowed over his shoulders, and a gray beard covered his chest.

She startled in marked alarm. "Grandfather—no."

"Let me pass, defilers!" Waving her aside, the old gentleman railed at the dragoons.

Vaughan snapped an order. "McCray. Remove him at once."

"Not easily done," she said under her breath. "Mister Monroe's gone off his head." She leapt to her feet and flew back toward the fuming gentleman. "You mustn't interfere."

Lieutenant McCray seized the newcomer's arm.

"Unhand me, foul demon!" Battling to wrench free, he hurled venom. "Swine! Lucifer's archangel!"

Red-faced, McCray glowered at the insults.

"Leave me be, ye stinking lobsterback!"

"Not another word from you," warned the irate officer.

"Grandfather, you must desist." Miss Monroe grasped her incensed relation's other arm in an attempt to restrain him.

"Shame on ye, Claire! Closing ranks wie redcoats!"

He threw her off, as one might a child, and she

reeled to the side. Vaughan cringed to see her go down onto her knees on the cobbles like an urchin cast into the street. She should be petted and adored, not suffer this rude treatment.

Then the infuriated man rubbed salt into her wounds. "Devil's handmaiden! Defy this monster from the bowels of Hell, not yer own flesh and blood!"

Undeterred, the spirited girl scrambled to her feet. "Stop this now, before you're punished!"

She might as well try to contain a mad bull, and McCray wasn't known for his patience. The pistol stuck in his boot would come out next. It goaded Vaughan to see the old man felled, especially as he was evidently mad. And particularly not in front of his granddaughter, doing her utmost to save him despite his abuse.

Vaughan interceded. "Wait, Lieutenant! Take over here, Ensign."

Agog at the unfolding scene, the young dragoon didn't heed him. "Ensign!" Vaughan rapped. "Attend to Percy."

"Yes, sir. Sorry, sir." Anderson knelt by the injured guide and pressed his hand over the reddened cloth.

"Keep it exactly like that." Vaughan straightened and strode toward the glittery-eyed patriarch whose fiery glare smote his granddaughter.

Heightened desperation creased her face. "You are not yourself, Grandfather. Cease your ranting and accompany these soldiers peaceably."

With the visage of a wrathful prophet, he stabbed an accusing finger at her. "Scold me, will ye? Cavorting half-naked, bare-headed, with yer hair shamelessly displayed."

"Dire circumstances required my attention before I

finished dressing."

Like dew-kissed petals, her freshly bathed appearance made a stark contrast to Vaughan's gamey state, not to mention his men's. She'd donned a snowy shift, stays embroidered with a garden of flowers, and the eye-catching blue petticoat, but the remainder of her ensemble was missing. Not that he minded.

Did the sweetness of roses emanate from her? It could hardly be from anyone else. He briefly considered how long it had been since he'd inhaled anything quite so pleasant.

Very briefly. Her reasoning fell on deaf ears.

"I'm here, am I not, lass? No call for you to rush out of doors in such a state. Ye wanton hussy."

Not only did Vaughan resent the tongue lashing unleashed on Miss Monroe for her heroic action, but a familiar warning tolled in his head, one he'd learned to heed or he would have perished long ago. Then he spotted it—the glint of metal shining from beneath the man's black silk robe. He also wore breeches, stockings, shoes, and a blasted sword at his waist. The reprobate was clothed and armed.

Damn it all! Before Vaughan could prevent him, he unsheathed the blade in a whistle of steel.

"Jezebel! I'll rid ye of yer temptress locks!" Wielding the sword with a will to punish the wicked, he grasped his granddaughter, screaming, by the hair. Twisting the lengths, he hacked off her glorious mane.

A vision of Meriwether as she'd been when Vaughan saw her at Captain Jordan's home flooded back, her blonde hair cut from fever, and then later, lying on the battlefield with the bloody wound at her throat. Horror rushed through him.

"Turn her loose!" He lunged past the astonished lieutenant. Out came Vaughan's own saber—a favorite weapon—and he clashed it against Mister Monroe's upraised blade.

Forced to release his granddaughter and fight, he sent her spinning into McCray who caught the dazed female and held her fast. "Don't harm him," she begged Vaughan.

"If it can be helped." He had no intention of sacrificing himself or anyone else for this lunatic.

Pivoting his boot in the shorn tresses strewn over the cobbles, he dodged Mister Monroe's blade. Poor girl. What must her life be with him at the helm?

An expert swordsman, Vaughan swung his blade at the zealot. Steel clashed against steel as he parried that enraged stroke and the next. In his experience, religious fanatics were tedious at best. At worst, deadly. The next thing he knew, this crazed man would be calling her a witch and strapping her to a dunking stool.

Even lit with righteous fervor and strengthened tenfold, the senior Monroe was no match for Vaughan. A skillful twist and he disarmed his antagonist. The sword clattered to the stones with a satisfying clink.

He snatched up the weapon. "That is quite enough from you, Mister Monroe. If you weren't an old man, I'd have you flogged. You *yield* to an officer of the Crown."

His unrepentant opponent snarled. "I yield to no king's man. Makes no difference what punishment ye meet out to me, Captain. 'Twill rain hellfire on ye all."

A chill ran through Vaughan, as though someone had tread on his grave. "It already has," he shot back. "In Backcountry. Attacks out of nowhere, men sniping from every tree, Rebels and Loyalists at each other's throats in a bitter civil war." Only the presence of a lady kept him from swearing.

Monroe rewarded him with a sneer. "A mere foretaste of the brimstone awaiting ye."

"And you, sir, if this strife continues unabated. Or do you prefer to wade through rivers of blood in an everlasting quest for freedom?"

"If we must."

This hell-bent Patriot wasn't the only one willing to slog through gore and they couldn't all plead insanity. For the hundredth time, he wished himself done with these Americans and back in England. Lord General Cornwallis had likened battling them to sitting on an anthill. Vaughan heartily agreed. He should've achieved the rank of general by now for all his pains. As it was, he wielded authority beyond his rank and had the unquestioning respect of his men.

He gripped the fallen blade. "Lieutenant McCray, restrain this gentleman. Escort him to his chamber and secure the lock." He glanced at the white-faced young woman and gentled his tone. "Are you hurt?"

She shook her head, winking at tears. "Only a little."

More than that. Her petticoat was torn, knees scraped, and her slashed hair must greatly distress her. Most females would wail over the loss of such lustrous tresses in loud lament, like an Irishwoman at a wake.

He declined to remark on her hair, though, and increase her discomfort. Instead, he offered what solace he could. "You shall be tended to as soon as may be. Have you the key to Mister Monroe's chamber?"

"Our housekeeper has all the keys in her

possession. A distant cousin of my mother's, a widow, Mrs. Jenner."

Vaughan firmed his tone. "Advise Mrs. Jenner of the need for cooperation."

"I did so, sir, in passing. She will do as you bid."

A glimmer of sense. "Good. Ensign Anderson, remain with Percy until assistance arrives. Miss Monroe, summon a stable boy to tend our mounts. I expect them properly seen to."

She nodded. "Jim!"

At her call, a lean Negro darkened the stable doorway. He appeared to be in his mid-teens. "See to the horses," she instructed him, then returned her focus to Vaughan. "He's an able hand, Captain."

"Excellent. You will accompany me—" Vaughan broke off at the cry of a woman coming from the upper story.

"The Saints preserve us, the scarlet devils have come and we're ruined! All ruined," she proclaimed, her slurred tones those of a drunk or drugged woman, painfully reminiscent of his own laudanum-addicted mother.

A boy of about age twelve stuck his curly blond head out the window, the barrel of a pistol visible in his hands. "Let me at 'em, Mama! I'm not afeared."

Miss Monroe brandished her arms at the youth. "You should be, William! Get back inside and do not stir."

"Let the lad alone!" their grandfather bellowed. "He knows what's wanted. Not like you."

Such furious accusation. Vaughan stared from the unhinged man struggling in McCray's meaty grip back to Claire Monroe. Curling tendrils framed her pale face

14

and enhanced her tear-blurred gaze. "Are all your family quite mad, Miss?"

"No, sir. Not all." Her tremulous honesty was telling.

In that moment, Vaughan knew exactly whom she meant. "I shall require your assistance. We will conduct a thorough search of the premises for your errant brother."

Her liquid eyes widened. "Oh no. Stuart's not here."

"Is he not?" Vaughan discounted her attempt to protect her sibling. He'd expect nothing less. His saintly sisters would lie through their teeth for him on bended knee before the altar rail in church and not bat an eye. While sympathizing with her devotion, he couldn't allow her to influence him in any way.

"McCray, get the pistol and lock the boy in with his mother. Confine every person to their chamber except the servants and keep a close eye on them." Annoyance flashed through Vaughan. "I hadn't thought it necessary to bring a company of dragoons to secure one poorly defended household."

Out jutted McCray's jaw, the bulldog. "Nor is it, Captain. I shall see to matters. There will be no more trouble."

"I'm gratified to hear it. I've a spy to catch."

At the very least, he needed that letter. He'd wager Lieutenant Monroe did not yet know its contents. Only the Patriot who could decipher it held the key. Rumors were rife that a master spy dwelt in this region of North Carolina, though his identity remained elusive. These conjectures were heightened by the conversation Vaughan's sly informant had overheard and related, for a price.

This information led to his interception of Monroe at *Person's Ordinary* today. By the barest thread, he'd thwarted a rendezvous between the spy and some mysterious individual known only as *the Patriarch*, to hand off the letter. The Rebel scheme had faltered, and Vaughan meant to see it fail entirely.

He laid the confiscated blade beside Anderson. "Mind this and my musket. Do not lose the gloves."

"I shall give orders to have them cleaned, sir," his shaky hostess offered.

"Thank you." He had to give her credit, she truly was trying.

Leaving the weapons with Anderson, Vaughan strode to his mare and patted her on the neck. A lesser mount would have bolted in all the confusion. Not La Belle. Captain Jordan had trained her well, and Vaughan built on the solid foundation. Taking the pistol from the bearskin covered saddle holster at the horse's side, he stuck it in the top of his boot, the cartridge box ready at his belt. The curved grip of the embellished pistol fit perfectly into his hand, and his aim was one of the best in the army.

"Captain."

He glanced around at the soft summons. "Yes, Miss Monroe?"

She fixed those wonderful eyes on him, more lethal than a backwoods rifleman. "Shall I lead the way, Captain?"

"Certainly." He'd be tempted to follow her anywhere. A most unsettling thought.

Nothing about this fetching young lady struck Vaughan as calculating, but for the sake of her adored brother and sacred revolution, he strongly suspected she'd try to deceive him. He'd hate to have to make her arrest. In fact, he should loathe it to his core. And he'd only just met her.

Why did she have such a potent effect on him, and why did it seem his fate to encounter beguiling females on the wrong side of this infernal conflict? If they weren't Rebels to begin with, they inevitably adopted the cause.

Could he persuade Miss Monroe of her duty to the king, to him, and win her allegiance? Perhaps. She'd conducted herself splendidly thus far, and for such a prize he was willing to give his all.

With the deportment inherent in his breeding, he gallantly gestured her ahead. "After you, Miss. McCray, follow shortly with the prisoner."

"Nae!" Mister Monroe erupted. "I'll not be held prisoner in m' own home, aided and abetted by that traitorous wench! What say ye fer yerself, Claire?"

Vaughan pivoted at the outburst and glared at the older man. "It matters not what she says. You are on a very short tether with *me*, sir. There's a sound jail in Halifax. Do not further tempt me to lodge you there."

He glowered back at Vaughan like a baleful rooster ready to fly in attack. If the intractable Patriot thought to intimidate him, he was sorely mistaken. No man intimidated Vaughan, as Mister Monroe would shortly discover.

"Please, Captain. Take my arm and let us proceed."

He turned to see Claire extend a trembling hand. This endeavor to deflect the clash between him and her infuriating relation didn't fool him, but he silently applauded her all the same. "Much as I should enjoy assisting you, dear lady, I fear I am stained."

"No matter." She waited as if in expectation he would escort her up the stairs to a dinner party.

If only he were. What an agreeable prospect.

"As you like." Endeavoring not to soil her sleeve, he circled his arm around hers. Tingles pulsed through him.

He felt her fear, also her resolve. Admiration for Claire only grew, and his distraction with it. Her lovely name slipped insistently through his mind. He wished she might slip into his arms and—

Stop! he ordered himself.

He must attend to the urgent reason for his arrival at Thornton Hall and not dwell on its young mistress, or the coveted promotion would pass him by again. And he'd have to answer for yet another misadventure.

'Damn foolishness. Rein yourself in, sir,' his father would chide.

And he'd be right. But even that old warhorse would be hard-pressed to withstand the charms of Claire Monroe.

Chapter Two

Lord help her. Claire swept through the front door with the most handsome, potentially dangerous man she'd ever met, feeling like a shorn lamb by comparison.

All her hair gone! She fingered the drastically shortened lengths. Both knees were skinned, and she was only half-dressed. What a disgraceful state. She could weep, but this was no time for self-indulgence. Others had endured far worse trials for the cause.

Despite her distress, she couldn't keep her eyes from the striking officer. She'd never been irresistibly drawn to risky men before, and abhorred unsettled circumstances, yet he lured her like no other. Though not outstandingly tall, he was above medium height and appeared disarmingly youthful for a hardened dragoon. Blond hair, streaked by the sun, showed beneath his helmet and his skin was lightly browned.

He reminded her of a golden knight. But his soul was hidden in shadows. Secrecy ringed his blue eyes.

The silver crescent shaped *gorget* engraved with the Royal coat-of-arms and worn at his throat like a piece of medieval armor, the silver epaulettes on his scarlet shoulders, the extra braid at his sleeves, and the crimson sash around his waist, all signified his rank. But she didn't know his name.

Should she inquire, or wait for him to offer? What

were her duties under such unusual circumstances?

Normally, he'd be announced upon his arrival at Thornton after an introduction to whomever opened the door, usually Mrs. Jenner. And they had few callers these days.

The Legion's invasion of Thornton was the last thing she'd anticipated this afternoon. Only a seer could have foretold that momentous event. Before the dragoons coming, she'd pondered how she might while away the evening, assuming her fitful relations allowed her any free moments.

Now, she must shield the older brother who'd led these soldiers here and the younger one who fired the untimely shot. She had no idea how to accomplish this, except to stall for time while she plotted, and pray Stuart had squirreled safely out of sight. Above all, she must attempt to atone for her family's outrageous behavior.

By offering the captain her arm, she hoped to establish herself as the courteous hostess, and this British officer, a guest in her home, knowing full well he could make life exceedingly difficult for them if he chose. In fact, he held their lives in his bloodstained hands. A point seemingly irrelevant to her addled grandfather, who'd only be satisfied if she attacked these redcoats. As for her mother, she wailed upstairs like a banshee keening an approaching death.

What wouldn't Claire give for some sanity in this home?

As if in answer to her unspoken prayer, the housekeeper met them in the entrance hall. "Mrs. Jenner. Thank you."

The able woman held a brown stoneware basin

wafting an herbal scent. The healing tincture mixed with the steaming water was comfortingly familiar. Reddish curls escaped her cap and clung to her flushed face, evidence of the frantic activity preceding Claire and the captain's arrival.

She panted from exertion. "Glad to be of service."

Stooped, gray-headed Ezekiel, partly obscured behind Mrs. Jenner's plump figure, bore fresh linens and a blue woven blanket tucked over his white sleeve. Clutched in one dark hand were green yarrow leaves from the kitchen garden out back. The pungency from the crushed herb also scented the air.

Thank God these two had their wits about them. Claire's were sorely scattered, and the captain seemed inordinately fond of this Percy. "Ezekiel has much skill with herbs, Captain. Woundwort is curative and 'twill ease the pain. The wash also contains the essence of thyme, plantain, knitbone, and rosemary."

"Yes. A wash of these plants and the poultice is well-advised." He dropped his arm from Claire's and waved Ezekiel and Mrs. Jenner toward the yard. "Return at once, Ma'am. Lieutenant McCray requires your assistance."

The elderly Negro shuffled ahead as rapidly as his rheumatism allowed, but Mrs. Jenner paused to bob her capped head. "Yes, Captain."

"And send someone to tend Miss Monroe's battered knees at your first opportunity."

This marked courtesy didn't go unnoticed by Claire, or Mrs. Jenner. The harried woman arched reddish brows at the commanding officer. "Very decent of ye to think of her, sir."

He gave a nod. "Have you a healing salve?"

"Indeed. Made of sumac, slippery elm, and woundwort by Ezekiel."

"Excellent."

"Most kind, Captain," Claire murmured.

He waved aside their appreciation.

Mrs. Jenner dipped her rotund frame in a short curtsey then hastened out the door to the Loyalist in the green coat called Anderson and the wounded former slave lying prostrate on the ground. The captain's judicious gaze assessed Ezekiel who bent over Percy and slipped the folded blanket beneath his head to cushion it from the cobbles. Mrs. Jenner passed him the basin and linens, clearly entrusting him with the nursing.

"Your man has a ministering touch with the wounded," their keen observer commented.

"Yes. Ezekiel is gifted in this regard. Also with the sick."

"Following the doctor's visit, he may attend Percy."

"An ideal course of action, Captain."

"When all is secured and a bed prepared, see to it he is gently borne to sheltered quarters."

"As soon as may be, sir." Claire pondered where to house the invalid. The site must allow the least exposure to family secrets while satisfying the captain as to his proper care. And how long might this stay extend, for that matter?

"Army of Pharaoh! God will smite ye!"

Once more, her grandfather's raving intruded.

Oh, how she wanted to stop her ears and his crazed tongue. Sometimes it was more than flesh and blood could bear. She fought to steady her nerves while the brawny lieutenant strong-armed her protesting relative into the house. As hale as the older man was, she had no fear his bones would break, but his haranguing was upsetting in the extreme, not to mention perilous. And here she was trying to make amends.

Again, she implored the captain. "Jail would be intolerable for Mr. Monroe, sir. Mrs. Jenner is competent. I beseech you to allow her to attend him."

Their rosy-cheeked housekeeper skirted back inside and the senior officer motioned her ahead. "Very well. He may remain secured and subdued in his chamber. Will you see to him, my good woman?"

"Willingly. You can rely on me, sir. This way, Lieutenant, if you please."

Her ample bosom heaving, Mrs. Jenner sidled past the tussling pair and knocked over the brass candlestick on an oval stand. Fortunately, the wick wasn't yet lit. Unsinged, she righted the candleholder and sailed down the hall, her striped skirts brushing the heart pine wood floor.

"Not to fret, Miss Claire. I'll dose him proper!" she called over her shoulder.

Claire could do with a dose herself, particularly with the rabid man spewing protest. "The brew's not fit fer slops! I'll have none of it!"

Mrs. Jenner rounded on him breathlessly. "You heard the orders, same as me. You're to have a goodly dose, Mister Monroe, and no mistake."

The captain turned those blue eyes on Claire. "What does she give him?"

"Valerian, betony, camphor, and a few drops of laudanum. 'Tis Ezekiel's sovereign remedy for nervous hysteria, though more often than not Grandfather refuses it."

"Lieutenant McCray will assure he takes his medicine, if Mrs. Jenner doesn't. But I rather think she will."

"An indomitable woman," Claire agreed, amid the scuffling and curses coming from her belligerent relation. "But Mrs. Jenner practically has to kneel on his chest and force it down his throat. He is far too strong for Ezekiel to manage. We need more assistance with him."

"Damnation shall come on ye all!" trailed in his wake.

Dear Lord. Claire pressed trembling fingers to her temple and bowed her head. Cropped tendrils curled around her hand, and she blinked at the tears stinging her eyes.

"Does Mister Monroe always behave in this manner?" the captain asked.

She raised her tremulous voice to be heard above the hubbub. "Since the madness came. He was a different man before. Some days are far worse than others. Then we can do nothing, except pray."

"Poor lady."

His sympathy seemed oddly genuine, as it had when he'd asked if she were injured and instructed Mrs. Jenner to tend her scrapes. Not at all what she'd expect from a dragoon officer, and she studied him through the sheen of tears.

He seemed pensive. "To lose a beloved relation to madness is a different form of death."

"Worse, I believe," she found herself confiding.

"Quite possibly." He spoke as if he knew. "What of your mother?"

Claire shrugged helplessly. "She took to imbibing patent nostrums that left her muddled even before Father died. The war taxed her delicate constitution. Now with Grandfather's illness, she's further declined."

The hint of empathy in his steady gaze spurred her to deeper revelations. "Had you not ordered Mister Monroe to his chamber, I should have sought refuge in my own."

"I am in charge now and that lunatic shall remain as he is for the duration of my stay, with sufficient provision," the captain added, addressing her concern before she even voiced it.

Already staggered by the sudden happenings, Claire didn't think she could possibly be more thrown off balance. But she was, and fought an impulse to burst into tears. Most unseemly.

Battling to steady her reply, she voiced her gratitude. "Thank you, sir. 'Tis most forbearing. And I'm obliged to you for your aid to me when Grandfather was wild with rage."

His gaze hardened. "It could have been your throat he cut. Your elder brother should assume his rightful place in this tumultuous household and take you under his protection."

"A welcome relief, and I have every assurance Stuart will do so, if the war ever ends."

"Aye. I've fought it almost from the start."

But he appeared so young.

"Experience heaps on decades," he said, as if reading her thoughts. "Contrary to what you may believe, I am not your enemy, but your liberator. Not only because I intervened in the attack by your grandfather. I speak of my capacity as an officer in the

25

service of His Majesty King George."

She stared numbly at him. Britain's idea of liberating America wasn't what her adored father had died in rebellion to, and dearest Stuart risked all carrying on the revolution. The freedom Patriots ardently desired was not to be found under this king, or any other.

"You will understand better in time." The captain exuded confidence for one so war-weary.

Removing his brass helmet, he set it on the drop-leaf walnut table at the right of the hall, the red horsehair plume fluttering from its crest. The black brim emblazoned with the white skull and cross bones death-head and the words, 'or glory,' was the grim motto of the Seventeenth Light Dragoons, a swift, rigorous cavalry, respected and feared by Rebels. Detachments from this regiment also served with Colonel Tarleton's infamous Legion.

"*Bloody Ban* is paying Halifax a visit," Stuart had hastily informed her, and sent Claire's heart into her throat at Banastre Tarleton's dreaded nickname. "A small party of dragoons out in front of the pack reached the Ordinary first. But more are coming. And beware. That captain's a sharp one."

After rattling her with this revelation, he'd ducked through the door hidden in the wall of the west parlor and secured it behind him. Providentially, the builder of Thornton Hall, their great-grandfather, had been beset by fears of attack from every quarter. Consequently, he'd constructed a passage within the house. Extremely fortuitous now. From the parlor, it led to various levels with access to the second story, the attic, and cellar. No outsider knew the rough entry, disguised as part of the cellar wall, opened into an earthen tunnel that ran to the great stone in the yard. A small copse of trees further obscured the exit and allowed retreat to the meadow behind the house.

Stuart had arrived by this furtive route, but he dared not flee through it yet. He must remain concealed within Thornton until Crown forces left Halifax. If Tarleton's Legion was at hand, could Lord Cornwallis be far behind? The dragoons were the eyes and ears of his army, and he, its head.

These were dark days for the revolution. Claire couldn't imagine their local militia had put up much of a fight.

As for her, she'd smuggle provisions to Stuart and guard the mystifying cypher he'd thrust at her. His suspicious mount was hidden behind the false wall in the stable. If Bryan remained quiet, they just might get away with the deception. But the captain did, indeed, have a shrewd look about him, and the letter he sought was tucked in her bodice.

Would he think to search her?

She'd barely had time to glance at the folded parchment before concealing it beneath the handkerchief she'd handed him to staunch his guide's blood. The absence of the hankie left a gap she must take pains to obscure.

Again, her unlikely escort gestured her ahead. The black onyx ring on his middle finger caught her eye. The stone in the broad gold band was emblazoned with the head of a stag, likely a family crest.

He cleared his throat. "I regret I cannot yet permit you to retire to your chamber to complete your toilette as I am in want of your assistance. Pray be so good as to show me your gracious home."

Not yet. Stuart mightn't be safely in place, or a secret door left ajar. Any number of potential pitfalls lay before her. She must delay him.

A thought occurred. The captain seemed parched, as though he'd been months in a dry land. Partly to waylay him and partly from a genuine desire to ease his thirst, she dangled a lure before him. "Surely you will take some refreshment first, sir?"

A faint smile told her he was aware of her ploy. "That would be most welcome. The moment I apprehend your brother."

"You may be hindered in your purpose for some time. Lieutenant Monroe is seldom at home. Preferring Virginia."

"The devil take ye, Lieutenant, and you with him, ye wicked hussy!" Her grandfather's muffled wrath sounded beyond the door shut against him.

The forceful newcomer glanced upstairs. "I can see why."

"Quite so. Meanwhile, might you not seek my brother, if you must, and drink all in one? If he is here, as you suspect, he will not simply vanish."

"That is precisely what I expect him to attempt. However, it's a difficult act to carry out with us on the premises. Perhaps I might accept your charitable offer and stop for a draught of ale and water to wash my hands."

Relieved at this slight concession on his part, Claire beckoned to Minnie. The dark mouse-like girl swallowed in a white cap and apron, quaked at the side of the entrance hall. "Did Sally send you?"

"Yes, Miss."

"Tell your mother we have guests and shall require an ample supper. Sally is the household cook," Claire explained to their onlooker. "And, Minnie, bring plenteous refreshment for Captain—" she paused with a questioning glance at him.

"Vaughan," he answered.

Her mouth fell open, and she could not keep herself from gaping at him. If he'd forcibly struck her, she'd scarcely be more taken aback.

In turn, he arched sandy-colored brows at her. "This title is of significance to you?"

So thunderstruck she could scarcely speak, she pressed balled fists to her chest and gulped. "Are you perchance any relation to the local merchant, Mister Thomas Vaughan?"

"My cousin."

Good heavens.

"Are you well acquainted with the gentleman, Miss Monroe?"

"Ummm…yes. Somewhat." This didn't seem the moment to divulge her recent proposal from Thomas Vaughan.

Conscious of having gained the captain's close scrutiny, and wishing she might beat a hasty retreat, she shifted uneasily and her cheeks warmed. Her scrambled thoughts spun as she addressed the waiting girl. "Fetch Captain Vaughan some ale and a basin of fresh water. Do not neglect the towel."

Minnie appeared addled enough to forget her head, and Claire wasn't faring a great deal better.

"Also for my men. Not neglecting Percy. He must be perished with thirst," the captain directed.

His mindfulness of those under his charge was

commendable. A British dragoon he might be, but not one utterly absorbed in himself. And he'd had thought for her, hadn't he, and allowed her afflicted grandfather to remain under house arrest. Not in the least what she'd expected.

The lack of movement caught her eye. "Minnie, don't stand there gawping." Lord knows, Claire was doing enough of that for them both. "Get Maddie to assist you and bring sufficient provision." The girl bounded off like a startled hare and Claire spoke again to the captain. "Thomas—I mean, Mister Vaughan—has an uncle in England, I believe," she stumbled, scolding herself for her blunder.

Those vivid eyes were even more intent on her. "My father. Lord Edward Vaughan."

"Dear God in heaven." The outburst just came forth on its own. Too late, Claire clamped her thoughtless mouth together.

His lips twitched in seeming amusement. "Petitioning the Almighty is not required, Miss Monroe."

The flame in her cheeks intensified. "No. And Grandfather would accuse me of taking the Lord's name in vain. But—" Her impression of Captain Vaughan's noble appearance wasn't off the mark. "Then someday you will be—" she broke off, kicking herself again for her candor.

"The Sixth Earl of Carbery."

She gaped at him.

"The family seat's in Wales."

His educated English accent wasn't remotely Welsh.

Again, he seemed to discern her thoughts. "I reside

in Devon, when I am at home. My mother's estate."

"How marvelous it all sounds. And how bizarre to find myself conducting this conversation with you, sir."

"Why is that? Are you not a refined young lady?"

"Attired like this? I stand before you utterly disarrayed."

"Through no fault of your own, Miss Monroe."

"Indeed. Normally, I comport myself with decorum, but can lay no claim to the vaulted life you were born to." If he were decked out in full regalia, she couldn't have been more impressed, or felt less inferior by comparison.

"Even so." He swept reddened fingers at the entrance hall, divided from the stair hall by an elegant archway through which the staircase was visible, rising in a straight run against the far wall. Portraits of austere ancestors graced the pale blue walls. Their timeless gaze met his regard, and hers as she followed the focus of his attention.

"This is an admirable house. The finest I've seen in a donkey's age," he asserted.

"Gracious of you to say, and strange to be receiving praise from—" she faltered.

"An officer of the Crown and future lord?"

She nodded. "Your cousin, Mister Vaughan's, home is also admirable." The wealthy merchant always seemed to have plenty of money while others struggled in these challenging times. "He is a most amiable gentleman, his manners, flawless."

"Indisputably. No one more so."

"Regrettably, he has been ill of late."

Skepticism touched the captain's gaze. "Taken to his bed, has he, poor fellow?"

"Yes, well, possibly. We are not apprised of his current condition. Only that he has been unable to call."

"Ah. What a shame to be deprived of such diverting company."

Did Captain Vaughan resent this relation? The sarcasm edging his tone was unmistakable.

Aware she blathered on, Claire ventured a question, cloaked in an observation. "Mister Vaughan is most affable, and yet—"

"Yes?" the captain pressed at her hesitation.

"We sometimes conjecture whether he is—" again, she faltered.

"Inclined toward Loyalist or Whig sympathies?" her perceptive observer finished for her.

Uncertain why she'd voiced her query, aside from burning curiosity, she nodded.

His eyes narrowed. "As do I."

"Oh dear. Forgive me. I fear I've spoken rashly. A grievous fault, I owe."

"Do not distress yourself."

"But I never intended—I shouldn't wish—to see him come to any harm on my account."

"Fear not. Mister Vaughan is in no danger at present. Certainly not on your account."

"Because he is aligned with the Crown?" She must know.

A faint smile pulled at Captain Vaughan's bold mouth. "My esteemed cousin's position is solely dependent upon which side he deems likely to prevail at any given moment. The state of his business is all that concerns him."

A swell of indignation filled her.

Slight amusement crossed the captain's blue gaze.

"You do not approve?"

"I prefer he choose a side and remain true, whichever cause it may be," she asserted with a flash of her old spirit.

"A quaint notion."

She fell over herself in protest. "But there are so many turncoats these days."

"Unarguably. Yet Thomas Vaughan does not possess enough garments for his many changes of affairs."

In spite of her dire predicament, a short laugh escaped her at his dry wit.

To her continued surprise, Captain Vaughan regarded her with a blend of inquisitiveness, and something else, a glint of approval. "If you desire constancy, seek elsewhere, Miss Monroe."

Again, she'd inadvertently divulged more than she intended. Fortunately, Minnie appeared bearing a wooden tray with four tall mugs. The fragrant amber liquid reached to the brim of the gray vessels decorated with blue flowers. Their best stoneware.

Good. The girl remembered. The brown pottery was for common use. Pewter tankards had long since been melted down for shot, as had pewter plates, porringers, and any lead in the house. At Minnie's side, her twin sister Maddie held a basin worked in the same flowery design, filled with water, and a white linen towel. Maddie was by far the cleverest of the fifteen-year-old twins, and usually at her mother's side, though both tried the able woman.

"Here, sir." Maddie extended the basin toward the captain.

"Ah, heaven-sent. But first, clean the blood from

Miss Monroe's knees. Gently, mind."

With the manners of an earl, Captain Vaughan turned his head while Maddie lifted Claire's soiled and torn petticoat to lightly sponge her scrapes, then returned the basin to him. He immersed his hands in the water, turning it bright red, and dried them on the cloth and blotted his glistening face before returning the linen to Maddie.

He frowned. "Where is Mrs. Jenner with the healing salve I requested for Miss Monroe?"

"Distracted just now, sir," Maddie ventured, while Minnie stood, eyes bulging, her nose twitching like a rabbit's.

"As soon as may be," he directed the more composed of the pair. Then to Claire. "Will you join me in some refreshment?"

"Yes. Please."

He transferred one of the mugs to her hand. Grasping a second cup, he raised it in tribute. "To your most excellent health."

"Thank you, Captain." She swallowed the nutty brown liquid, noting his eyes on her and his cup upraised, as if he were waiting. What more invitation did he require?

"Will you not drink, sir?"

A smile curved his lips. "Now I shall." He emptied the contents in a few hurried gulps.

What in the world? Her gaze riveted on him. "Did you fear I would attempt to poison you?"

"Not you, sweet lady. Yet perhaps someone in your household. One cannot be too cautious these days."

"Heavens above. I should not like to answer to Colonel Tarleton for such an act."

"So, you know I serve under Tarleton?"

Another slip. "Or Lord Cornwallis."

He shrugged, but the furtive expression still furrowed his brow. "I should not wish for you to answer to either one and would do all in my power to protect you. Yet my party underwent an ambush on this plantation."

"By a rash boy. Nothing more. We want no trouble here."

"By *we,* I assume you refer to yourself and your elder brother who is by no means in accordance with the Crown."

What could she say? The remainder of her family were as unstable as shifting sand. Only Mrs. Jenner had any sense and her kinship was a distant one, though Claire had forged a close bond with the caring housekeeper.

"In as far as I am able to offer assurances, Captain, please believe we intend no opposition."

"Overt, you mean. Nevertheless, I shall accept your assurance and hospitable efforts." Restoring the vessel to the tray, he spoke to the waiting girls. "Deliver beverages and clean water to the others and fetch that ointment for your mistress. Then make up beds for me and my men."

His tone bespoke one accustomed to instant obedience, impressive and more than a little intimidating.

"Where, sir?" Maddie asked.

"Wherever Miss Monroe decrees."

"The enclosed porch at the back of the house will serve as a sick room for Percy, I believe. 'Tis sheltered from the weather."

Captain Vaughan inclined his blond head, and Claire continued. "Prepare bedding in the east parlor for the junior officers, Maddie."

"Lieutenant McCray alone," Captain Vaughan amended. "Ensign Anderson will sleep in the stable and watch over our mounts and the grounds. Provide him bedding out there."

"As you like." Claire prayed the youthful officer wouldn't overhear Stuart's horse hidden behind the false wall. But how could he not?

"Do not neglect Ensign Anderson. See he is served *plenteous* refreshment," she emphasized to the girls, hopeful he might heavily imbibe the ale. A drunken stupor suited her purposes.

Did Captain Vaughan guess her reasoning? Feigning innocence, she glanced at him. "We have a parlor upstairs that might accommodate you, sir, or perhaps you would prefer Lieutenant Monroe's chamber?" The height of irony if he were to occupy Stuart's bedroom.

And it wasn't lost on her astute companion. With a faint smile, he smoothed back hair worn in a queue at his neck and tied with a black ribbon. White facings set off his cuffs and the braid ringing the silver buttons on his red coat. Not a favorite hue in this Patriot home.

"The parlor on the second floor will meet my needs quite well, thank you, Miss Monroe."

"Would you like water for bathing readied in a tub before the fire in the hearth? The nights are still cool." Surely such luxury would be welcome after days in the saddle, especially to a gentleman of his elevated station who could only make his ablutions in a cold stream, unless water were heated over a campfire.

His smile widened. "Yes. Most thoughtful. Now, I must insist you conduct me on a tour of the premises."

She lifted her gaze to the knowing in his. "Very well."

He would endeavor to discover what she must make every attempt to conceal. Foremost, Stuart. And there was no opportunity to finish dressing or don a hat. Touching a hand to her once resplendent tresses, she sighed. She must resemble a sheared sheep, and a bedraggled one to boot. An unbecoming image. It took the utmost restraint not to bemoan her loss.

"Your hair is really rather fetching."

Startled, and admittedly pleased by the compliment, she stayed as she was, studying him closely. "How so?"

"The way it frames your face." He smoothed a curl at her cheek, sending quivers through her. "I once knew a woman with hair much as yours."

"Not hacked from her by a mad relation, I trust?"

"No. Cut from fever."

"Did she recover?"

Fondness touched his eyes. "Fully. In a small way you remind me of that lady."

"But I am not her."

"Indeed you are not. Your brother attempted to shoot me." He patted his right side. "She succeeded."

Claire gaped at him again. No scar was visible beneath his coat, but she detected the shadow of a wound in his eyes. "And yet, you care for her?"

"Oh, I was sorely vexed, make no mistake, but I admired her daring."

"Patriots can be so."

"She was a Loyalist."

Could this conversation grow any stranger?

He glanced away. "But she took the side of the man she loved."

"And that man was not you."

"Alas. No."

This woman, whoever she was, must have dealt him quite a blow. And Claire hadn't thought a dragoon captain possessed a heart to injure.

His gaze returned to hers, arresting her on the spot. "There are stranger things in love and war than your wildest imaginings, Miss Monroe."

"So it would seem." The insane tremors coursing through her at his touch, for one. And the quivering desire swelling in her for more.

Was she that deprived of engaging male companionship, or was it him? She suspected the latter. His stunning masculinity awakened every sense, rendering her nearly witless. If she didn't have care, he'd coax further admissions from her. That he appeared far kinder than she'd anticipated could be a ruse to put her off her guard.

For pity's sake, how could she vouchsafe this letter and her brother if Captain Vaughan led her astray? She must keep a level head and not fall prey to his allure.

Thoughts flashed through her like heat lightning.

Stuart had only a brief opportunity to apprise her of his near capture at *Person's Ordinary* before he could pass the letter to the man known only as *The Patriarch*, adding that he never would have attempted the rendezvous if it hadn't been prearranged. Not with Tarleton bearing down on Halifax.

As it was, Stuart didn't sight the individual he'd anticipated meeting. And it was this man who was to decipher the message. How Captain Vaughan knew of the meeting beforehand, Stuart couldn't surmise, unless someone in their small, trusted circle had betrayed them.

Not the Patriarch himself, surely? Stuart didn't know his identity, but he was said to be an unflagging Patriot.

No. It couldn't be him.

Moreover, Stuart had insinuated Claire might have the ability to decipher the message, penned by a fellow officer of their late father at his behest, with personal references to Captain Monroe that she might be familiar with given the closeness of father and daughter. To avenge their late father and others in Virginia and elsewhere who'd suffered at the hands of that fiend Benedict Arnold, considerable wealth had been collected for a price on the traitor's head. Given the scarcity of coins in the colonies, this treasure must be goods, possibly silver, and other valuables taken from Tories.

Where the stash was secreted lay in the letter. Only her father, now gone, and the author of this missive knew the exact location, assuming he still lived. With so many falling away, could she trust anyone, apart from Stuart?

"Miss Monroe." Captain Vaughan's voice, gruff with fatigue, broke into her scheming. "Lead on. Pray do not neglect a single nook."

"But of course." Just the hidden door in the west parlor, the passage beneath the stairs, and anything else that occurred to her in this disturbed state. She must dissuade him from taking too close a look at the cellar. Maybe she could rush him through the parlor and—

"Dear lady, I shall be watching you."

Unnerving how he seemed to read her mind. In an attempt to distract him, she summoned what feminine wiles she could muster in her disreputable state. "I hope so, sir."

A devastating smile heightened his powerful attraction. "How can I not?"

She pushed her advantage. "The evening is mild. Would you not prefer a stroll in the garden, inhaling the sweetness of lilac and peonies?"

He threw back his head and laughed, showing straight white teeth. "What a charmer you are. Yes, my fair Miss, I should prefer nothing more, but this is not a social call. Though I could wish it were."

Strangely, Claire found an irrational part of her wishing the same.

"And I sense a storm brewing," he added.

Didn't she know. And not only outdoors. A storm brewed within her as well. The sparks Captain Vaughan struck in Claire might consume her, like a glowing ember to dry tinder. Up she'd go in a flash. And what would follow then?

Chapter Three

Lord preserve him from temptation. The possibility of crossing paths with a captivating female today, or ever again, never occurred to Vaughan. But Claire Monroe roused him as if he were awakening from a deathlike slumber. Perhaps he was. He'd hardened his heart after Meriwether's rejection and slogged on, never expecting to encounter her equal.

Life was indeed strange, and at times, strangely wonderful. Claire's tantalizing suggestion of a stroll together through the scented garden was like stumbling into heaven from a smoky blood-soaked battlefield and finding an angel. A rebel angel. In a way, this only added to her fascination.

Concentrate, he chided himself.

He'd fail to get the promotion, yet again, if he didn't drag his distracted focus back to a thorough search of the house. He'd already dispatched McCray to ferret out anything suspicious on the grounds. The canny dragoon was nearly as adept at sniffing out hidden quarry as the best foxhound in Vaughan's pack in Devon. He'd rather both were at his service. There was nothing like a good dog.

And doctor. Glad the kindly man had come to tend to Percy, Vaughan more fully turned his attention to the house.

"This is the east parlor." Claire waved at the gray-streaked marble fireplace, its mantel festooned with dancing maidens and leafy vines.

Above the frieze, creamy peonies filled a green porcelain vase. A china Crown Derby shepherdess and her swain kept company with the blossoms. Cabinets built into niches on either side of the hearth held blue and white delftware.

"Exquisite." And he wasn't only referring to the room.

The war had taken a toll on the Monroes and countless other families, but they weren't impoverished when they built this home. Thornton Hall was superior to many he'd viewed in the colonies. The grandeur of Charleston exceeded anything he'd witnessed here, rivaled only by the grandest homes in New York where General Sir Henry Clinton, Commander-in-Chief of the British Forces in America, and his army were encamped.

That General Clinton would far rather return to England than remain in America was no secret. Given the chance, any sane officer would depart on the next ship sailing for home. And Vaughan's father desired him to return as soon as may be. But just now, his gaze straying to the woman at his side, he couldn't wish himself elsewhere. Not with such a rare jewel just a breath away.

"We have few guests these days," she continued, the tremor in her hands reflected in her voice. "I am unaccustomed to showing the house to anybody, let alone an officer of your illustrious heritage."

"You are a most charming hostess." One he wished he might kiss full on her tremulous mouth.

She pointed a tapered finger, directing his attention

to the china secured behind the glass. "This is my favorite figure."

"Ah. An English bulldog." He reflected on the miniature reproduction with a meld of affection and sadness. "Rather like my dog, Maximus."

A soulful wistfulness lessened the hesitancy in Claire's gaze. "Mine also. Do you miss him?"

"Every day. But I've been away so long he may have forgotten me."

"Dogs never forget and are absolutely devoted. Plato helped rear me."

"An admirable name. I'm sure he made a fine nursemaid."

"And a wise friend. How I wish him back."

Canine fervor seemed to overcome her reluctance at showing Vaughan the house, at least temporarily. He found himself wishing he could give her a bulldog puppy. Readily done if they were in England.

"Such constancy dogs have," she continued, breaking into his strange conjectures. "If only people were as true."

"Indeed." His gaze held her eyes, not easily done as they tended to slant away. "Some are."

Her brows arched. "Fewer and fewer," she lamented.

"I've never wavered in my loyalty."

"Yes, but 'tis to the—" She broke off.

"King?" he suggested.

She paled. "Forgive me. I forgot myself."

"Miss Monroe, I appreciate your devotion while disagreeing with your stand. But such speech is dangerous."

For a long moment, she stared into his eyes, her

own troubled, searching.

"You need fear no retribution from me."

A halting breath, and she conceded the truth he read in her face. "I know not what to anticipate from you, sir."

"Honorable behavior befitting a gentleman and officer of the Crown." Which ruled out taking her in his arms...

"Certainly," she allowed, but her manner didn't convey conviction. Quite the opposite.

He drew on the discipline relentlessly drilled into him both from his stern father and an unyielding army. "I give you my word."

A nod, and she tore her eyes from his.

Fluttering her fingers at the door, she beckoned him on. "Shall we continue our tour?"

Nothing in here aroused his suspicion. "After you."

Claire hastened out of the room and up the hall, her skirts brushing past a tall walnut case clock. The stately sentinel with its white moon face observed passersby while keeping the time. But she'd skirted a room.

Vaughan slowed her with a hand on her upper arm. Warding off the desire she provoked in him as he might the attack of charging soldiers, he focused on the quest. "Wait. What of the west parlor?"

Her shoulder tightened beneath his grasp. "Oh. 'Tis much like the other. Though not as elegant."

The tension in her bearing whet his interest. "Nonetheless, I should like to see it."

"As you wish." With the demeanor of a woman who'd far rather not comply, she turned and retraced her steps.

Surely, Stuart Monroe wasn't hidden behind the

couch or a cabinet? Puzzled by Claire's averseness, he followed her through the doorway ornamented with scrollwork.

Again, nothing appeared unusual. Trying to keep his gaze from her tempting curves, all too apparent in her state of undress, he skimmed his eyes over the marble mantel, not as ornate as the east parlor, but respectable. Was she ashamed?

Although accustomed to palatial ceilings at Hartford House, his family estate in Devon, the ceilings in Thornton Hall were light and airy. In the upper corners of this room, as in the other, plaster cornices designed with geometric motifs added embellishment. But the mood in here was different, more intimate.

The gracefully arched gold sofa, in frequent use judging from the indentations in the cushioning, shone in the buttery light flowing beneath the blue valance at the window. The glow burnished the yellow tabby curled on an embroidered pillow. Contented purrs rumbled from the dozing feline.

An open volume of Shakespeare's sonnets lay partly concealed beneath its tail. Leather-bound books, including Shakespeare's tragedies and another of his comedies, were stacked to overflowing on an end table beside a china cup, saucer, and plate dusted with crumbs. The remains of a hasty meal consumed while reading, perhaps. He suspected by whom.

Stretching out his hand, he stroked the tabby behind its ears. "You also dote on cats, I see."

Her expression warmed. "Yes. Aristotle keeps me company."

The vaulted names of her pets struck Vaughan. Despite her challenges, she was well-read, and not always without companionship. Two comfortable looking armchairs stood near the sofa, their floral seats worn. The center of the floor was open. The drop-leaf table at one side of the parlor waited to accommodate guests for a less formal meal than in the dining room.

Walnut, splat-back chairs were scattered about, scuffmarks on the floorboards indicative of their movement for seating at the table or nearer the hearth on a dreary day. It was here he imagined Claire and her older brother met, heads bent together over a private supper. With the exception of the sensible Mrs. Jenner, these two were the only sane members of this erratic household and would seek quiet times apart from the others. The east parlor was more sumptuous, but this room said *home*.

Unlike the gray wainscoting and wallpaper with nosegays of blue forget-me-nots and sweet peas in the east parlor, these walls were paneled and painted gray-blue. Paintings hung against this backdrop, landscapes mixed in with the portraits. One portrait above the hearth drew his eye. The girl, a younger Claire, her expression hopeful, posed beside a confident youth, likely Stuart Monroe.

What a comely pair. The devotion between brother and sister was evident. And with them sat the beloved bulldog.

Then and there, Vaughan determined to keep Lieutenant Monroe alive and unharmed if it were within his power. But he confined his remarks to the room. "Exquisite. Who did this portrait?"

"My father was an accomplished artist."

"The detail is remarkable. Do you also paint?"

"A little. He wanted me to receive further

instruction, but the war…" her voice trailed off.

"Yes." If these rebellious subjects had contained themselves, all might be well. But then, Vaughan would not be here with her. "What else did your father desire for you?"

"To be genteel and educated."

He gestured at the collection of books. "Yours?"

"And Stuart—Lieutenant Monroe's. Grandfather used to read heavily. No longer, and our younger brother takes scant notice."

"Young Master William is sorely in want of proper schooling and a firm hand."

"I can but apologize for his deplorable behavior. Nothing is as it should be, Captain. Father intended me to travel, gain further refinement, and—"

"Marry well," Vaughan finished for her.

The corners of her mouth puckered, then opened. Words tumbled out. "Whoever weds me must be prepared to undertake the care of this family."

"No small undertaking. Any proposals?"

She glanced away. "One."

"At a time, or total?"

"Total. But surely you jest?"

"In part. Though I can guess from whom the offer arose."

An affirming blush tinged her neck and spread over her cheeks. "The matter is under consideration."

"Then you have not yet accepted my cousin?"

She shook her head.

Relief welled in Vaughan. "I see."

In all practicality, the affairs of Claire Monroe should not concern him, but proprietary feelings for her dominated his thoughts, among other mounting sensations. No doubt the monetary benefits and household assistance from such a match weighed heavily in her contemplation of this *proposal*. He intended a word with his cousin.

A warning, more like.

"What of your brother? Is Lieutenant Monroe not to inherit Thornton Hall and manage the estate?"

"Yes. And he would do his duty by us, if…"

This damnable war ever ends. He sensed the unspoken thought between them. She must feel terribly alone with her burdens. Another reason to wed a man she did not love, and to confide in Vaughan when she let her guard down.

"How deeply does your regret run, Miss Monroe?"

"What do you mean?"

"Is your loyalty to this errant brother and revolution in conflict with your desire for order and a return to the life you once knew?"

"If such a life were possible after all the upheaval and loss." Her reply was barely audible. But he heard.

"Do you not see that accepting the sovereignty of Great Britain is the only way to achieve this end?"

Widened eyes reflected her shock. "And abandon the cause? My father would have died for nothing. And what of all the others who have fallen?"

"Only one can be the victor. Good men on either side of this excruciating struggle die every day and will continue to perish until the end. If they sacrifice their lives for the cause they deem just, they have not died in vain."

She lifted her chin, pride in her moist gaze. He'd seen this jutted determination many times before, and anticipated the equally repeated resolution.

"I cannot give up striving for independence," she declared, with a quaver in her voice.

"No more can I cease to be a king's man."

"Then we are irreconcilable, sir."

"I ascertained that the moment I saw you, and yet, it hasn't dampened my ardor any."

Her eyes flashed to his. "Ardor? For me?"

Never one to waver when boldness was required, he charged ahead. "My cousin is not the only Vaughan to find you appealing."

"You mean yourself?" she managed in a hushed whisper.

"Is that so unlikely?"

She eyed him wordlessly.

"I would take you under my protection, sweet lady."

The rose in her cheeks deepened. "Would you?"

"If permitted to do so. Are you not mightily in need?"

The barest nod. Then, as if anxious of being overheard, she swept her gaze over the room. Her focus halted on the inner wall. "Captain." Her voice dipped in the whispery tone she'd adopted earlier. "I thank you for your gracious offer. But fear we are at cross-purposes."

"Still, the offer stands."

The wonder in her gaze delighted him.

He slid a finger beneath the tender curve of her chin and tilted her face to meet his regard. Silken tendrils brushed his skin. A long silence passed between them, but it spoke more loudly than words. He sensed Claire's desire to voice her thoughts at odds with inherent wariness.

Dropping his hand from her face, he made a slight bow.

She inclined her head, and said nothing.

No utterance was needed. He easily read her fleeting and oh so revealing expressions, the purse of her pale pink lips, the crease at her smooth forehead. The almost continual scheming he perceived in her crumbled during those moments of candor when her true nature held sway. It was here he met the real Claire Monroe.

Though taken aback, she appeared to recollect herself. "Shall we hasten on, sir? Much yet remains to be seen."

"A moment." Leaving this sanctum meant rejoining the others, and Vaughan didn't want to do this just yet.

Plainly, she had no wish to linger. Come to think of it, she grew increasingly fidgety the longer they tarried, sidling in the low-heeled floral shoes peeping out from beneath her petticoat. Unless she was in want of the chamber pot, doubtful, he must conclude her agitation arose from another source. Uneasiness gripped her as surely as an unseen hand.

But why? He hadn't threatened her with ill-treatment, only expressed his esteem and desire to be of service. Granted, he'd caressed her cheek. Given half a chance, he'd caress a great deal more, but checked himself like a hound on the scent restrained by its master's command.

Had his intrusion into Claire's private hideaway magnified her distress, or was it something else? And why the sidelong glances at the inner wall? Was his preoccupied mind playing tricks on him or did she inadvertently focus on one spot in particular?

No. Her eyes bore holes into that side of the room.

As if suddenly conscious of his marked attention, she redirected her gaze to the window. "The trees are lovely this spring. So many shades of green. Do you not agree?"

"A veritable artist's palette." What in the name of Saint Peter was she concealing? Was she waiting for the wall to open up?

A staggering thought. In a way, she might very well be. Not only that, but he could just make out the barest outline of what appeared to be a doorway masked within the panels.

Was it still in use, and where did it lead?

If, as he suspected, Lieutenant Monroe was hidden somewhere in this house, it was entirely possible a secret passage existed. He was acquainted with concealed passages at Hartford, but the manor dated back to the Middle Ages when paranoia of enemy invasion ran rampant.

Why conceal a passage in Thornton Hall?

Terror over Indian attacks, perhaps. Any threat from pirates had passed by the time this home was built with its close proximity to a major shipping port on the Roanoke River, but warriors were another matter.

Apart from the hardiest frontiersmen and renegades who ran with war parties, most colonists had a horror of the red men. Vaughan wasn't eager to engage warriors in battle.

The Overmountain Men he'd fought in Backcountry wielded tomahawks and fired long rifles with deadly accuracy while unleashing the chilling war whoops they'd adopted from the Cherokee. The unearthly yowls made his blood run cold. McCray called them, *'those damn yelling boys.'* And forever would. They fit the description. Facing real braves would be even more daunting.

Yes. The more Vaughan considered, the more likely it seemed that a passage wound within Thornton as a result of fear over Indian reprisals, or perhaps her ancestor was simply eccentric, also a distinct possibility.

Given Claire's peculiar behavior, he imagined a hidden entryway existed in this very room. Possibly elsewhere as well. There might be several openings. She and her brother probably romped through these walls as children, playing hide and seek and other games. They knew the ins and outs of this house so well they could scamper it blindfolded.

Masking his suspicions from her, he took in the apprehension marking the young woman's face. Here was no consummate actress. She wasn't adept at guarding her emotions, and darted glances at him. Then an obviously forced smile transformed her.

What was she attempting now?

She took him by the arm. "Let us not loiter here, Captain. You did request a thorough tour of the house."

There could be no doubt, she was trying to lead him from this chamber and the secreted door.

He stayed her hand, his own tingling at the touch of her soft skin beneath his callused palm. "Not quite so hurriedly. Such a charming room begs me to dally awhile."

"B-but you've not yet seen the dining room, or upstairs, or kitchen. And we've a hall for dancing, should there ever be parties again."

"If there are, you will permit me to partner you?"

"As you wish."

A vision of him dancing with Claire, his arm encircling her waist, her hand in his, while fiddlers plied their bows and a musician plucked the harpsichord, swirled through his mind. "I should very much wish to do so. Without intruding on your admirer's preexisting claim, of course."

"No. Your invitation outweighs his."

"Oh good." He'd probably have returned to England by then, but what an inviting prospect.

Pushing aside the growing hunger to be with her, he returned his attention to the room.

She tugged at his coat sleeve. "I understood you to be in haste, sir."

He smiled. She really was most diverting and adorable. He hadn't enjoyed himself this much in ages. "Now that Doctor Philips has come to attend to Percy with the assistance of Ezekiel, my mind is more at ease. I am at my leisure."

"Truly?" If she'd added, *but don't you want to continue to search for my brother?*' he'd not be overly surprised.

"Oh, yes. I think, after a refreshing bath and change of linen, I should like nothing better than to sup with you in this very room."

Panic flitted across her gaze like one in the path of an oncoming rider. "But Lieutenant McCray and Ensign Anderson—"

"May dine elsewhere. I weary of their company."

"You do?"

"Exceedingly. While yours is incomparable."

She pinkened prettily at his compliment. "Surely

you object to the presence of the cat?"

"I adore the creatures."

"Really? Most men—"

He looked her straight in the eyes. "I am not most men."

"No." She gulped.

If she could, he expected she'd drive him through the door and lock it behind him. And if he could, he'd let the matter slide and throw himself into courting Claire, that traitorous brother and sought after letter be damned. But he must answer to higher authorities. And deserters were shot, generally at his own orders.

Keeping his tone nonchalant and his gaze locked on hers, he posed the foremost question. "Is there any particular feature you care to draw my attention to in this parlor?"

She squirmed. "Nothing of note. Why do you ask?"

Her failed attempt at casualness further tipped him off. If Lieutenant Monroe were within earshot, he must be having forty fits at her faltering. No doubt big brother could keep a straight face and lie expertly when required, not to mention his indignation if he'd spotted Vaughan's hand on her face, overheard his offer of protection.

"No particular reason, Miss Monroe. I look forward to supping with you in here this evening."

"How jolly."

He squelched a snort at her stunned expression, so at odds with her reply.

Breaking away from him, she bent to stroke the purring tabby. Then he saw it, a folded piece of parchment nestled in her bodice against rounded breasts. A letter. Not just any letter. The one he sought.

He'd stake his reputation on it.

Tearing his gaze from her enticing décolleté, he pretended unawareness when she glanced up, clearly ill-at-ease, but oblivious of his discovery.

He smiled reassuringly. "Please, do not let me detain you, dear lady. If you will direct me to my chamber and send a servant with water for bathing, and another with my portmanteau, I shall be most obliged to you."

"Our tour?"

"I have concluded you must be correct. Your brother cannot be here."

The furrows at her brow deepened. "Of course. Just as I said."

Was it possible this artless female knew how to decipher the missive? Stranger things had transpired with the clandestine goings on in this war. And women played their furtive part.

No. Not Claire Monroe. One glance in her perplexed eyes told him she was unfamiliar with the powers of deception.

Just because she appeared devoid of deviousness, didn't mean she wasn't clever, though. In fact, she struck Vaughan as remarkable, and Stuart Monroe could pressure her to do his bidding. Lord knows she was loyal to the cause. But she wasn't the one he'd anticipated apprehending at *Person's Ordinary*. His informant had led them to watch for an older man, perhaps a neighbor, to meet with Lieutenant Monroe.

Was he mistaken, or had he purposely mislead them? All hell would descend on the ne'er-do-well if he had.

What a mystery Claire and the letter combined to

make, not to mention the spy holed up somewhere in this house. If Vaughan kept close to her he'd have both the letter, possibly deciphered, and her brother in one. Doubtless, Stuart Monroe burned to know its contents, and Vaughan burned to be with Claire.

Part of him disliked having to deceive her in this matter, but how else was he to gain what he desired and been ordered to recover? His one concession, if he learned the contents of the letter, he might, in turn, feign ignorance of Lieutenant Monroe's stealthy presence and let the scalawag escape.

And he'd guard Claire with his life. That went without saying, and unsettled him most of all. Because he shouldn't. His first loyalty was to the Crown, or ought to be.

No longer. This enchanting woman had awakened an urge as primal as the ancient forests of this vast land and as strong as the natives who roamed them, to guard her from harm. There was no dishonor in her defense. Though it might cost him dearly.

Chapter Four

What in God's name was Captain Vaughan playing at?

Torn between demanding an answer—the height of idiocy—or bolting from the parlor, Claire hovered in an agony of uncertainty. Not that certainty would necessarily ease her mind. Lord knows it might well undo her even further. Still, she'd rather know his intent than wonder.

His abrupt alteration in plans rattled her like the parlor windows in the gusts of wind springing up beyond the panes of glass. Clouds eclipsed the late day sun. The sense of an impending storm bore down on her from within as well as without.

Did he honestly believe Stuart had gotten away and wasn't hidden within these walls, or had he tumbled to the truth? If he did suspect the existence of the secret passage, the fault lay with her. She'd allowed him to draw her out and peer into her soul.

What an unsettling man. Her legs threatened to buckle, and her heart raced beneath the constricting stays. In Minnie's haste to help her dress earlier, she'd tugged the laces too snugly, and there'd been no time to loosen them. The smothering sensation from the roped in corset coupled with volatile nerves left Claire in danger of toppling senseless onto the couch beside the cat. And that wouldn't advance her cause. He might even detect the letter.

God forbid. She instinctively clasped a protective hand to her bodice, as though he might tear it from her.

He arched an eyebrow at her. "Shall we proceed, Miss Monroe?"

Captain Vaughan's invitation intruded into her frantic deliberation. With a smile that shot to her shaky center, he proffered his arm, appearing every inch the lord he was destined to become. Maybe he already held some prestigious title. Claire wasn't well acquainted with the traditions regarding peerage, only that she was a commoner.

If her mother weren't dozy from cordials laden with poppy juice, the ambitious woman would consider him the catch of the century. Were he not a dragoon captain, of course, though the scheming matron might make an exception for a future earl.

Hardly trusting herself to speak, Claire accepted his genteel assistance. Dropping the hand from her chest, she gathered her skirts and walked beside this red-coated officer out the door and down the entrance hall. Tottered was a more apt description, given the wobble in her knees.

How strong his arm felt beneath hers in his scarlet sleeve, and right, as if it belonged there, which was madness. Utter madness, she sternly reminded herself.

She wasn't a turncoat, but at this moment, any onlooker might wonder if she'd changed horses in midstream and gone another route. Never. Hadn't she sworn undying faithfulness to the revolution on her father's grave?

The stairs rose before them. In an attempt to distract her escort from too close an examination of the entry hidden in the space beneath them, she pointed out its flaws. "See that crack in the ceiling? Thornton Hall will crumble about our ears. Hardly worthy of a tour for one of your exalted lineage. Your home must be magnificent."

"Do not belittle Thornton. Though, indeed, Hartford House is among the most impressive in Devon. However, the manor is lacking."

"In what possible way, sir?"

"Your presence, Miss Monroe."

Confounded by his assertion, she protested. "I am not so very fascinating."

"I beg to differ. You would grace any house in which you dwelt. I wish you might visit."

Did she actually detect a wistful note in his tone? Attempting a flippant reply, she brushed him off. "The next time I sail to England."

"Perhaps you might accompany me when I return."

She almost tripped over her feet. "Surely you jest, sir?"

"Not in the slightest."

Speechless, she made no reply.

Had he taken leave of his senses, or was he truly taken with her? His seeming interest might well stem from the desire to gain more information. His avowed attraction couldn't be genuine. Could it?

"Do not underestimate your appeal, Miss Monroe."

Dearest heaven above. He sounded sincere.

She wasn't *that* fetching, not such a beauty as to erase all thoughts of duty from his mind with hair chopped practically to her chin. Perhaps he was simply being courteous in that lofty manner the gentry sometimes adopted.

Beth Trissel

"Most gracious," she offered, her head spinning.

"Oh, I can be, but in this instance I assure you of my sincerity."

Maybe he really did find her alluring. She still had her face and figure, and hadn't she been praised for both? It wasn't out of the question for him to be smitten by her, she argued with the inner voice crying 'Nay!' Likely she'd have a great many more suitors if not for this endless war and her deranged relations.

One thing was certain, if she continued in this state of intolerable suspense, she'd be as unhinged as her mother and grandfather. And find herself dosed with elixirs for nervous hysteria, or committed to a lunatic asylum.

Hoping Captain Vaughan wasn't contemplating her, she glanced up at him. He was. Intently.

Her drumming heart caught in her throat. He was the most compelling man she'd ever seen. And those eyes. Her pulse ratcheted to an even greater height. If only she might read his mind as he seemed to delve into hers.

Not a chance. Especially with her giddy senses. His thoughts were well-guarded, fitting for a cagey dragoon captain. She was surprised he hadn't yet made colonel. But his wit went beyond mere rank to his very nature. She sensed secrecy inherent in him.

Hadn't Stuart warned her of this shrewd officer? She must tighten her defenses and remember who and what he was.

Protect the cypher. Stuart's decree, and she'd promised she would. Benedict Arnold must be held to account for his grievous sins.

Captain Vaughan hadn't come to Thornton Hall to

60

court her, Claire scolded herself, and he fought on the wrong side of the battle for America. If Great Britain did finally prevail in the end, then she supposed he'd ultimately be on the right side, but she couldn't ever forgive him.

Could she?

The ancestral portraits regarding them from the pale blue walls as they mounted the steps seemed even more disapproving than usual. Clearly, they thought not.

A wave of dizziness washed over her and she stumbled, secured by the captain's ready hand. "Steady, Miss Monroe. I fear events have distressed you."

Sympathy edged his voice, but how could she be certain his concern was genuine? Somehow, she must keep this all too charming and clever man from gaining another thing from her. And decipher that letter to make amends for her traitorous emotions.

If only her sharp-witted enemy weren't so damnably attractive. His courtliness undid her more than she'd ever have thought possible. He was easy to converse with and agreeable. More so than any of her acquaintances, even his esteemed cousin. But the discourse between her and Captain Vaughan was different. She'd never been caught up in an exchange with a gentleman while experiencing heart-pounding discomfort at what she might accidentally betray, like Stuart's whereabouts.

What a deplorable spy she'd make. Where trickery was wanted, she was heady. Even now, though anxious to escape his company, an obstinate part of her anticipated spending more time with him over supper.

Someone slap some sense into her! She'd

succumbed in the worst kind of way to this extraordinary man.

What would dear Papa say? And Stuart. So valiant. Sacrificing all. Had he heard, seen, her despairing efforts?

No. Well, maybe. She wasn't sure. He might have, depending on where he was in the house at any given moment.

Dear God. What was she to do?

Her head swirled and the stairs reeled. Without Captain Vaughan's support, Claire doubted she would have reached the landing.

Fighting for breath, she pointed down the long passageway, seeming longer now and the blasted thing wouldn't stay still. "Your chamber is there. Last door on the right." Each word was labored.

"And yours?"

Though wondering at the propriety of his query, she indicated the chamber situated diagonally across from his intended quarters.

"Miss Monroe, are you feeling quite well?"

A tingling in her fingers accompanied the revolving sensation in her head, and she could not get her breath. Her corset must be even tighter than she'd realized. "Captain—" Sucking in air like a drowning woman, she gasped. "Perhaps it might be best if you assist—"

Before she forced 'me' from her throat, she slumped against him and would have slid to the floor had he not prevented her. She was vaguely aware of his firm but gentle grasp as he caught her up in his arms.

"Easy. You will be all right."

Unconvinced, she gulped like a stranded fish, but

couldn't seem to fill her constricted lungs. "What's happening? Am I about to die?"

"No. I've witnessed this behavior before. 'Twill pass. Pinch your lips shut. Take slow breaths through your nose." The floor echoed beneath his boots as he strode down the passage. "Mrs. Jenner! Make haste!"

"What you want her for?" William shouted from the other side of his door.

"Your sister's in want of assistance."

"Let me out of my chamber and I'll fetch Jenner," the youth eagerly offered in his usual rude way of addressing their distant kin and housekeeper.

"Not yet, lad. Besides, I don't have the key."

The thump of a shoe hitting the wall, then a second shoe, bore witness to her brother's frustration. Grandfather must have nodded off or curses would fly. But Claire couldn't be bothered about them or anyone else just now. The all-consuming need for air occupied her hazy consciousness.

Terror coursed through her. "Captain—"

"Shhhh." Bearing her in his arms, he cupped one hand over her mouth. "Steady. Do not gasp. You will soon be well."

How sure he seemed. Though panicked, she tried to oblige. Her fight for breath eased slightly beneath his palm.

His long strides made short work of the passage. Was he bearing Claire to her chamber?

Yes. The knob turned. He flung open the door and carried her inside. He lowered her onto the four-poster bed, lifting his hand from her mouth. "Arms above your head."

Chest heaving, she did as he ordered.

He bent over her in a blur of red. "Have you suffered this malady before?"

Eyeing him dazedly, she shook her head.

"The vanity of women. Your stays are likely cutting you in half. I've observed this in my sisters."

But Claire wasn't vain. Well, not overly, or she'd weep shamelessly over the loss of her tresses. And she wasn't related to him in the slightest. Fresh alarm surged in her as he turned her, gasping protest, onto her side.

"On my honor, I am only lessening the pressure on your chest." Unimpeded by the gown or jacket she should have worn to complete her dress, he easily accessed the stays. His deft fingers soon freed her corset. Entirely. "There. That ought to ease your breathing a mite."

Terrified he'd spy the letter, and a great deal more, she clutched the flagging bodice as he rotated her onto her back. Whether the missive had worked its way up or down, she couldn't tell. But her stays were of scant use, and her loosened shift descended indecorously over her shoulders.

If the cypher were exposed, would he snatch it from her? Heaven forfend. She gulped even harder, and tried to gage his intent but his features grew hazier.

"Calm yourself. I will not harm you in any way. You should partly sit." After easing her into an upright posture against the pillows, he tugged the coverlet up around her. "Your modesty is preserved." Again, he cupped his palm over her mouth. "Breathe in through your nose and slowly exhale."

Her eyes locked on his, a lifeline in her battle for air. Ironic, considering he was the main cause of this struggle. His rock-solid gaze never wavered. Oddly, Claire found much reassurance in that. Here was a man capable of great devotion.

To the king! she reminded herself. But if she dwelled on the sin of gaining comfort from this enemy she'd—gasp.

"Easy," he soothed, as if sensing her turmoil. "Slow down."

She nodded, focusing only on taking one breath at a time. Under his calm encouragement, her inhalation grew more normal and the lightheadedness that had assailed her faded. Proper sensation returned to her hands. Unlike the storm brewing outside, her internal tempest dwindled.

"See. That's better." He withdrew his hand. "I should offer you some warm brandy, but my flask is empty. And your staff seem unduly preoccupied."

Was he suspicious? She envisioned all they had to attend to with their *guests*. And Stuart, if Mrs. Jenner thought to take him provision while the captain was otherwise involved and the other officers out of the house.

A smile flickered at his mouth. "I confess to having visited a ladies' boudoir before, though not for this purpose."

"No doubt."

"Rest assured, I'm no longer a wastrel. Though that is why my father bought me a commission in the army and sent me to America. To mend my wicked ways."

"And have you?"

"What do you think?"

Too unnerved even to blush, she gave a forthright reply. "You seem the perfect gentleman."

Beth Trissel

"Not entirely. I should very much like to steal a kiss."

She widened her eyes at him.

"Yet I will not." He flicked her a wink. "At least, not now."

The rogue. But Claire was equally brazen. She had no excuse for the anticipation welling inside her. Or the wish that he might tarry by her side.

He pressed his lips to her hand, clutching the coverlet nearly to her chin. "I leave you to recover yourself, sweet lady, and hope you are sufficiently restored to join me anon for a private supper."

"I also hope." Oh, what was to be done with her disloyal heart!

Rising to his feet, he gave a short bow and turned, as though adjourning to his study rather than tracking a spy. "I shall send Mrs. Jenner or one of the girls to wait on you. Pray do not bestir yourself until you are properly rested."

How was that remotely possible with him under the same roof. "Captain?"

Pivoting, he eyed her questioningly. "Yes?"

Something, anything, to soothe her troubled mind. "Might I ask your Christian name?"

"Jacob, but I do not go by this title. It's Vaughan, with or without *Captain*. Soon, it shall be *Major*."

"I am astonished you have not yet achieved that rank."

"Oh, I shall."

Another bold wink and he strode from the room, leaving her breathless from more than her recent episode.

Why, oh why, must he be a British officer, and

what on earth was Claire to do about him? Despite everything he stood for, and the considerable danger he presented to this household, it disconcerted her that she still wanted to do something *with him*.

Chapter Five

Vaughan departed Claire's bedchamber in a state of ecstatic bemusement. Despite the highly unusual circumstances between them, or perhaps because of their challenged situation, he hadn't ever felt quite that close to anyone. In the hall outside Claire's door, he encountered the tardy housekeeper. Over Mrs. Jenner's plump arm were clean towels, a fresh shirt, pleated and of quality linen, he assumed was meant for him. In her hands, she bore a tray with a mug of frothy ale, generous chunk of bread heavily buttered, and what appeared to be rhubarb tarts sprinkled with powdered sugar laid out on the best blue china. No effort spared. He was impressed.

"To assuage your hunger until supper, Captain."

"Most welcome, Mrs. Jenner."

Behind her trudged the two girls he'd heard referred to as Minnie and Maddie, the former still regarding him as if he might swallow her whole. The youth called Jim who'd gone for the doctor earlier accompanied his sisters. Each one lugged buckets of steaming water. "For your bath," the housekeeper added. "We trust you will find everything to your liking."

"I'm certain I shall." He already had. Visions of Claire danced through his head.

Mrs. Jenner waved the three toward his chamber.

"Empty those buckets into the tub. Don't go sloshing water on that floor, Minnie. Then step lively and see what your mama wants a hand with in the kitchen. Yer Aunt Beulah can't tend to it all, poor soul."

Vaughan stood beside her as the trio disappeared through the door. "Are they members of the same family?"

"Aye. Quite a brood, too. Been with the Monroes many a year. Beulah's a bit simple, but a help to Sally. The old gentleman sees they're treated well, or did before the madness came. Miss Claire and I look after the household now. Mister Monroe intends to free them upon his death."

"Does he, indeed?" That accounted for their loyalty. Slaves were streaming to the British side in droves after being offered their freedom in exchange for service to the Crown. "How will the Monroes manage if they take flight soon after his demise?"

"Oh, I dare say arrangements can be made to suit everybody. I gits paid for my pains, but it's piddling. No coins to be had these days, you see."

He was aware of the scarcity of money in the colonies, and the Continental currency was nearly worthless.

"Still, there's vittles enough," the housekeeper continued, "and a place to lay my head at night, a second best shawl and such, now and then. This lot won't be clamoring for more, and fortunate to git that. Mayhap a bit of earth to call their own, though the bulk of the land's rented out."

"To whom?"

"Mister Thomas Vaughan."

A new flash of resentment heated Vaughan. More

and more, he realized how entangled his cousin was with this family. The damnable reprobate. If they only knew—

"Course, he don't work the ground himself, being a gentleman," the outspoken woman wore on, breaking into his internal tirade. "Has field hands marched over under the overseer, and a nasty temper he's got too."

"My cousin, or the overseer?" Neither would surprise Vaughan, though Thomas maintained an irreproachable veneer.

Scarlet colored Mrs. Jenner's already florid face. "Pardon my foolish speech, Captain. I never meant a word against yer kin. A fine gentleman is Mister Vaughan."

"Apart from his overseer?"

"Aye. Well, a body can't be too choosy of his help with the war on."

"Clearly."

She flushed an even darker shade of red and Vaughan hastened to clarify his retort. "I was in no way referring to your faithful service, my good woman."

"Course not."

"Don't need no bit of earth," Jim muttered as the three trooped back out of Vaughan's quarters. He must have overheard her. "For my part, I want a pair of blue breeches with brass buttons and a black three cornered hat like Joe's got. Oh, and a new coat."

"Want, want. Enough of that talk. Yer brother's older and worked longer," Mrs. Jenner said tartly. "'Tis generous the Monroes have been as it is."

Vaughan held up a hand to break into the chatter. "One of you girls go fetch a drop of brandy and that salve for Miss Monroe. How many times must I remind you?"

The harried housekeeper rolled her eyes. "Clearly, once more. Now hop to and do as he says, Minnie, and be quick about it. Get on back to Sally and Beulah, the three of you. Jim carry up another bucket of warm water for the captain." Mrs. Jenner scurried into the room, speaking over her shoulder. "What ails Miss Claire, sir?"

"A bout of hysteria. I tended her, and she's quiet now. But the brandy wouldn't hurt to settle her nerves."

"No. Do her good. I'm right grateful to you. Poor lass. The weight laid on her shoulders is too much for most folks to bear up under, let alone one of her tender years. And she's not been out in the world."

"So I gathered." He smiled to himself at the image of Claire squirming as her shift slid down over those creamy shoulders. And she'd been terrified he'd spot the letter, naive girl, unaware he'd seen it earlier. She hadn't flinched when he'd kissed her hand, and blushed in expectation at the invitation in his wink. A thrill ran through him.

"Deserves all the help she can get, dear soul." Mrs. Jenner disrupted his reverie.

"Indeed. Miss Monroe can rely on my aid."

"Bless you, sir."

With a rustle of petticoats, the housekeeper set the tray on the small oval table beside the solid armchair upholstered in crimson and situated to one side of the hearth. Before the cheery blaze stood a brass tub misty with the freshly poured hot water. On a low stool beside the tub was a bar of white milled soap in a saucer.

Good heavens. Imported Castile soap. He was eager to strip from the confines of his uniform and descend into that inviting liquid for a good scrub, but the woman prattled on.

Laying the snowy linens over the stool, she angled her head at Vaughan. "Don't think Miss Claire faint of heart. No, sir. Got the heart of a lion, that girl."

"I witnessed her courage when she faced me and my men, then stood up to her grandfather, even pleaded for him."

"Aye. She has a generous nature. And so accomplished. Draws beautiful and can read anything you set before her."

Claire's mistress couldn't praise her enough, which suited Vaughan's inclination. "Does she write?"

"Letters and such? My yes. Always scribbling away. Never learnt myself, but she's able as any man. A proper scholar, her father said. Enjoys a good riddle, too. She and him used to make a game of it."

"How interesting." The loose-lipped female was a valuable source of information. Vaughan considered her with newfound appreciation. "What of Miss Monroe's brother?"

"Mister Stuart?" She shook her head. "Never took after his father in that regard. More the adventurous sort. Nor did young William, too full of mischief by half, but Miss Claire was a child after his own heart. How that man adored her. When her Papa set Miss Claire to work on a riddle, she was as happy as a pig in its muck." The color in her plump cheeks deepened at her phrasing. "Like a wee one with a new toy on Christmas day," she corrected.

Most enlightening.

"And she could puzzle out anything. Still can. She's a quick-witted young lady," the proud woman gushed.

Vaughan had every hope. "You speak so highly of her. It does you credit."

"Like a daughter she is to me, though I should have had my own." Somberness came over Mrs. Jenner like clouds blotting out the sun. "I could have done. Should have, if I'd not lost my husband, and unborn babe with him, from the shock of it all."

Uncertain how to reply to such a painful confession, he offered what he could. "Most unfortunate."

"Aye." She glanced around, her pale blue eyes guarded. Tapping a finger to the side of her nose, a sign for secrecy, she motioned him nearer.

Baffled by what else she might impart, he bent his head to oblige her. "Yes?"

"A word in your ear, Captain."

He thought she was already wearing it off.

Onions assaulted him and her tainted breath tickled his cheek as she explained in a conspiratorial whisper. "Voices can carry up through them chimneys."

To where, the attic? Did she fear someone was listening? He entertained the possibility.

"Come away from the hearth," she beckoned.

Although they were the only two in the chamber, he further indulged the furtive woman by huddling with her in a corner between the crimson sofa made up with bedding for his nightly repose and a chest of drawers. They were also out of sight from the windows, already darkened by gray clouds and a valance in a mahogany hue.

She'd taken every precaution. Against whom? Stuart Monroe?

73

Keeping his voice low, he pressed for revelation. "Mrs. Jenner, what is this about?"

"I'm gitting to that, Captain." In such muted tones he could scarcely hear her over the wind rattling the glass, she explained. "I'm not a devout Loyalist, but want you to know I have sympathies in that direction. Not that I'd ever betray this household. Been decent to me they have, but my Reuben served under you and that goes a long way with me."

A stroke of luck. Eyeing her sharply, he cast his mind back to the hot-headed Loyalist with the same last name. "You are Reuben Jenner's wife?"

Fierce pride welled in her moist gaze. "I am. You recall him?"

"I do. An able and devoted recruit."

Her eyes narrowed. "I was told he fell at Captain Jordan's plantation, in the house."

"Yes, in the dining room at Pleasant Grove. During the same fray in which I was shot. We both tumbled to the floor, though, sadly, your husband never got back up."

"I heard tell a turncoat fired on him in cold blood." Her dimpled fingers clenched at her sides. "The gutless traitor."

"Not a turncoat or gutless, Mrs. Jenner, but a conniving spy who passed himself off as a Loyalist."

"Shot you too, did he? An officer of the Crown. Took one hell of a nerve."

"Not him. Jordan's lady fired on me."

Her round face creased like a drawn apple and the corners of her eyes crimped. Pushing back an auburn tendril from her damp forehead, she gave a low whistle. "Well, I never. The rumors are true then. It was a woman. What of Captain Jordan?"

"Innocent on both counts *that* particular evening. I consider him a worthy adversary. One I despaired of catching, so left him to his cutthroat band and that Godforsaken Backcountry he rules like a king."

"And his woman?"

"Wife now. She resides at Pleasant Grove with their newborn son, in the care of his cousin, Rory Jordan. A Loyalist with divided sympathies. I expect the captain makes furtive visits home, but we do not exchange letters."

"No. Reckon you wouldn't."

Vaughan's wry humor was lost on Mrs. Jenner and he laid a sympathetic hand on her plump shoulder. "I am truly sorry for your loss. Mr. Jenner was a good man." He had the temper of a hungry bear emerging from hibernation ready to take the world by the throat, but was faithful to the Crown.

Apparently only fond memories of her deceased spouse swelled the generous bosom beneath the white apron. "Aye," she sighed. "I'll never find another to equal my Reuben. You see why I'm torn over taking sides in this everlasting war."

He strongly suspected she wasn't the only one with divergent emotions in this household.

"The Monroe's took me in soon after Reuben fell. I been with them ever since, and mean to go on here."

"As you should. Have no fear, Mrs. Jenner. Your confidence is safe with me. But how are they unaware of the circumstances surrounding your husband's death?"

"Knowing this was a Whig household, I said only Reuben was killed by a turncoat, not on which side.

You know what Backcountry is. A right mess. Who's fighting for who gets lost in the confusion, like too much seasoning in the stew."

"Aptly put. And wise of you to guard the truth in this instance."

"I thought it best and not an outright lie. I hate to be a deceiver. Mrs. Monroe's my fourth cousin or some such relation and right charitable to take me in when no one else would, or could."

"Seems to me they benefit greatly from a hard working woman of your diligence in this household."

"Most kind of you to say." A flush of gratification added a glow to her tearful gaze and she preened a moment, then cast a glance over her shoulder. "And now, I must go."

He stayed her with his hand. "Delay a moment longer." In lowest tones, he guarded his pointed query from the one he suspected had his ears perked. "Lieutenant Monroe is hidden within this house, is he not?"

Her reddish brows arched above stark eyes. "I can't speak to his whereabouts."

"Nor do I expect you to. Yet."

She caught her lower lip between her teeth and released it. "When?"

"Just see that he's tended to at present and leave matters to me. No one must know my suspicions."

A quiver ran through her tight mouth, then dissent tumbled forth. "I couldn't bear to see Miss Claire dismayed or Master Stuart come to harm."

"I intend no ill to come upon either one if it's in my power to prevent. You have my solemn word of honor. Far better I deal with this matter than have

Colonel Tarleton send another harsher officer. Captain Simmons loves to torch homes and estates." The jowls of the surly officer swam before his mind's eye and he grimaced. "I shudder to think of him coming here."

All color drained from Mrs. Jenner's face. "Heaven forbid."

"But I require your help to keep Simmons at bay."

Both chins wobbling, she gave a nod.

"If Lieutenant Monroe leaves this house, alert me at once."

She hung her head. A disconsolate sniff escaped her. "I'll do as you ask."

"There's no shame in this, my good woman, and simple enough service to render. It's what your husband would have wanted, God rest his soul."

That seemed to hearten the widow and she straightened her sagging shoulders. "True enough. He would. Might help put things right for Reuben."

Nothing could do that, but Vaughan welcomed the sentiment. He pressed the tips of his fingers to his forehead, aching now from fatigue. "Inform me of any visitors and Miss Monroe's whereabouts."

"Yes, sir."

"All others are to remain in their chambers unless I grant my consent for them to move about the house. See to it Mister Monroe receives his medicine regularly. Mrs. Monroe too, for that matter. None need be overly aware of the goings on and will suffer less agitation."

"I'll do my best, Captain. Young Master William will grow terribly fretful with the tedium, though."

"I may relent and assign him to the supervision of Ensign Anderson, if you think the lad would prefer the stables?"

She brightened. "Oh, aye. William loves horses. Spends many a happy hour out there."

"Good. I'll see you are rewarded for your faithfulness. One last query, have you any knowledge of the letter carried by Lieutenant Monroe?"

Her jaw dropped. "Nay. 'Tis news to me."

This rang true. As protective as Mrs. Jenner was of Claire, she must be in ignorance of the missive tucked in the young woman's bodice, possibly a riddle similar to the ones her father had set for her, fashioned by someone familiar with Captain Monroe, or perhaps, even the captain himself.

"Speak of my conjectures to no one," Vaughan ordered.

"No sir. Not a word."

Gripping the wooden arch of the upholstered couch, he struggled to think through the dull throb in his head. Captain Monroe may have relayed the cypher to a trusted friend, probably a fellow officer, possibly at the end as he lay gasping his last. Likely, the plot to exact revenge on Arnold was already underway and took a personal bent with Monroe's mortal injury, thus the allusions to the late captain that Claire might grasp and work out.

If this unlikely girl could solve the riddles the letter held, why deliver it to some mysterious man, unless involving her was considered too dangerous—which it was and annoyed Vaughan to contemplate. Besides, if the cypher were meant for Claire, why not stipulate Lieutenant Monroe carry it to her in the first place, instead of thrusting the parchment at her in the resulting chaos of his arrival.

Despite mind-fogging weariness, he strove to recall every detail his informant had conveyed about the intended recipient: an older man, possibly a neighbor, referred to as *The Patriarch* to protect his identity. Even Stuart Monroe didn't know who he was, and this Patriarch hadn't gone to meet him at *Person's Ordinary* as expected. Vaughan had inspected the premises. No one with that description was present.

Perhaps the man had been detained. Communications were unreliable at best these days, but surely whoever was meant to be on the receiving end of this letter would've been at the tavern if he could be. No one knew of Vaughan's advanced information. Stuart Monroe hadn't a clue. And his informant was well aware what fate would befall him if he betrayed his trust, such as it was, the self-serving scoundrel.

Still, needs must, and forced Vaughan to make do with whoever obtained valuable information for him. The noblest souls objected to spying on their fellowman, as would he. The pieces of this particular puzzle were taking shape, but how they all fit together hovered out of reach...like a butterfly fluttering just overhead.

Frustrated with the circles his aching mind traveled in, he conceded a temporary respite. The inviting tub, its brass burnished by the firelight, and refreshments awaited him. He gave Mrs. Jenner a nudge. "You have been most helpful. Return to your duties now before you arouse suspicion."

"Right away, sir." She fled in a flurry of striped petticoats. But the rotund figure halted before the door and turned. "I remember something."

He motioned to her, and she darted back over the

floorboards like a small terrier despite her girth. "You asked about a letter, sir."

Instantly alert, he perked up. "Yes?"

"I don't know as it means anything particular, but Mister Monroe received one by courier awhile back. He never let on what it said. Course, he don't know what day it is most of the time, poor man. But it might have mattered to the sender."

It might have indeed. A thought occurred to Vaughan. "How long has the old gentleman been ill?"

"Had spells on and off, but didn't truly go off his head until word reached us about Captain Monroe's death in April."

Was it possible the intended recipient was confined in his chamber due to madness? What irony. If so, Captain Monroe hadn't realized the extent of his father's decline. If one discounted insanity, Mister Monroe was the head of this family, thus the patriarch, and a diehard Patriot. And addled beyond his son's or anyone else's ability to foresee. The Monroes may have kept his deteriorating condition a secret, or as much of one as possible under the circumstances.

Another glimmer of insight struck Vaughan. "Did Mister Monroe enjoy a good riddle?"

The kindly woman smiled. "Nothing better. Though he's past all that now."

But Claire wasn't. Whoever penned the cypher knew its contents at that end, and this unwitting girl was the key to revealing them at the other. Once the puzzle was solved, the stash recovered, and the price on Arnold's head rendered useless, Vaughan would have fulfilled his mission. He might expect an increase in his rank.

"Thank you, Mistress. Most useful tidings."

She bobbed a curtsey. "If that's all ye require, Captain, I'll be on my way." Voice raised for their eavesdropper, she continued. "We'll see to your laundry, sir, and alert you when supper's served. Yes, we'll have new-made cornbread as you requested," she added, as though this was the extent of their conversation.

For a reluctant spy, she was a natural, and what a boon to gain an inside informant. This should speed the process. If only he didn't wish it would take at least a few precious days for Claire to decipher the message. Most disturbing how swiftly he was coming under her spell, and she didn't even realize she'd woven one.

Besting Claire at this game, if that's what it had become, held scant joy for him, though he admitted to being intrigued. He also enjoyed a good riddle, but doubted she'd be of a forgiving bent when she learned he'd deceived her. He must broach the matter delicately.

Failing in his mission wasn't an option Vaughan was willing to contemplate, but enticing her to fall in love with him? Now, that held sublime possibilities. And perhaps, ultimately, her heart.

A sobering thought. Apart from his adoring sisters, he'd never been entrusted with a woman's heart. And if he fell in battle, the girls would come to terms with his loss. But what of Claire, did he really want her to care for him?

He slid the buff-colored leather swordbelt from around his shoulder and laid it and his saber on the high-backed wooden settle positioned against one wall. His cross-belt of the same hue with the black cartridge box soon followed. The wallpaper behind the furniture was covered with roses streaked crimson and white, like the stain of blood in the snow. And he'd witnessed that.

His eye fell on the distinctive helmet laid on a corner table. Mrs. Jenner must have ordered it brought up here. How many battles had his faithful headgear seen him through?

Too many.

Unbuttoning his coat, he folded the red, white-faced uniform beside his blade and carefully weighed what he was undertaking. He unknotted the scarlet sash and removed his white waistcoat. He'd only just met Claire, and under the most unusual circumstances, but in war there wasn't the opportunity to linger over decisions. He untied the gorget at his throat, shining in the light, and added it to the growing pile.

How often he made life and death choices, sometimes on a daily, even hourly basis. In the blink of an eye. And not only for himself but those under his command. He'd learned to seize the moment, to trust his gut instinct.

Unbuckling his black neck stock, he tossed it aside and asked himself, did he want Claire? He'd already suffered acutely for the sake of one woman. Was he truly ready to undertake that risk for another?

He stripped off his shirt. Yes. When it came to Claire, the die was already cast.

****

After lathering every inch of his tired, aching body with the rich soap and savoring the suds, Vaughan settled back into the tub. A rap on the door announced Jim's return with another bucket of warm water. The youth upturned the warm liquid over Vaughan's head. What luxury after weeks, even months, of hardship. Years, if he allowed himself to venture that far back.

The young Negro set his portmanteau on the floor. "Mrs. Jenner says you'll be wanting this, Captain."

"Ah, yes. Good."

His shaving kit, a spare pair of buckskin breeches, clean shirt, stockings, and other personal effects were in the travel suitcase that rode behind his saddle on a pad. Anything more he'd had in several trunks with the baggage wagon in Cornwallis's army had been destroyed to lighten the load during that wretched, sometimes hellish race, through North Carolina Backcountry. His wallet, replenished by a doting mother and sisters on top of his pay, Vaughan kept close by. It took a bit more arm-twisting to get money from his father.

"Fetch me my waistcoat."

Jim retrieved the desired article and handed it to him. Fishing soapy fingers inside the pocket sewn into the lining, he extracted a shilling and tossed it to the astonished youth. Brown eyes alight, he clutched the coin, more money than he'd ever had, Vaughan didn't doubt.

"Under my orders, you are to escort Master William to the stables and tell Ensign Anderson I want him to take charge of the boy, then deliver word to Lieutenant McCray to come and see me." Vaughan debated how much to impart to his fellow officer and friend, and when, but he was determined the gamey Scotsman have a dunk in the water. "Then report back to me for further instruction."

"Right away, Captain." Shoulders squared, Jim

marched out the door, swinging the bucket.

It was a shame Vaughan couldn't take this willing lad with him when he left. He'd be a real asset. A sharp pain in his gut accompanied the awareness of his limited time here. But for now, he settled back and soaked in the blissful warmth. The ale and food in his stomach eased his aches, as did the water. His head nodded and he drowsed in contentment.

For the first time in ages, he could almost imagine himself home in his own chamber, back in civilization. What untold pleasures if Claire might be there too, in his arms...

How long he dozed, Vaughan couldn't be sure. Not too many minutes, or McCray would have awakened him. But he had the strangest sense of a figure, more of a shadow, really, hovering over him, before whoever it was slipped away.

A dream?

No. Nor the angel of death. This man—Vaughan sensed he was male—smelled of wood smoke from the chimney and horses.

Not Jim returned yet. He'd have knocked first and spoken to gain Vaughan's notice. Not one of his officers, either.

A thought occurred. Could it possibly be Lieutenant Monroe spying on him?

Of all the bloody nerve. Too damn bold. This brazen rebel needed sharp watching.

Even if Vaughan managed to hunt Monroe down in a house the spy could probably navigate blindfolded, and took him prisoner, Claire might be too besotted over his welfare to decipher the letter. Unless Vaughan threatened dire things against her sibling in return for that service, and then she'd surely hate him. And that, he could not abide.

Confound the fellow to perdition. And confound this blasted war. Vaughan was no coward. He'd fight a hundred battles and then some. But this clash with Stuart Monroe was one he had doubts of winning with Claire in the balance. Whether she realized it or not, she was caught in the middle. And he hated having to pressure the sweet lady, when he'd far rather make love to her.

Heaviness weighted him and he felt himself joining the ranks of those in this household conflicted in their loyalties. Not a sensation he savored. He was accustomed to knowing *exactly* where he stood. This was shifting ground, and he didn't like it. But he liked Claire. Far too much for his own good.

There must be a way to conquer both, to accomplish his mission and gain her love. Never one to concede defeat easily, if ever, he doubled his resolve. That cunning fox of a brother had met his match.

Chapter Six

A callused hand clamped over her mouth, jerking Claire from a late afternoon slumber in her bedchamber. Her heart beat so hard it drummed in her ears.

Had Captain Vaughan returned? Was she grossly mistaken in about his character? Did he intend to take indecent liberties?

Stealing a kiss was one thing, but lascivious assault didn't bear contemplating. Some of Tarleton's men were said to have ravished women, even *Bloody Ban* himself. Unarmed and at a great disadvantage, how would Claire stop Vaughan if he accosted her?

Fearsome conjectures tumbling through her mind, she snapped her eyes open. Rather than a smoldering blue gaze, to her amazement, the man assuring her silence was Stuart.

What on earth?

Blinking up at his shadowed face, partly revealed by firelight, she watched him withdraw his hand. He held one finger to his lips. "I must speak with you."

"Now?" She assumed they'd converse in the wee hours. It was all she could do not to slap him smartly across the cheek.

"Have you taken leave of your senses?" she hissed, as quietly as possible given her turbulent emotions.

"Have you?" he shot back in a fierce whisper.

She jerked as if he'd fired a musket ball through her. "What do you mean?"

Eyes the same hue as her greenish gaze held accusation in their ferny depths. "I'm watching and listening, Claire, and do not approve what I see taking place between you and Captain Vaughan."

So this was how it felt to be spied on. Molten lead sank in the pit of her stomach. But she was in no mood to tolerate his scolding when he'd nearly scared her to death.

"I don't approve your actions either." Thrusting her chin nearer his, she glared at him. "I live in an asylum as it is, and will thank you not to behave like a lunatic. What a risk you've taken coming in here."

He wore that stubborn glower. "Someone has to keep watch over you, carrying on shamelessly with our *enemy.*"

Guilt stung her, but the injustice of his rebuke hurt even more. Peering through chinks and keyholes, listening down chimneys and from behind walls didn't grant him access to the enormity of her internal struggles. Being too often away, he had no true grasp of the grief and loneliness she endured. He hadn't been subjected to the raving madness that accompanied her anxious days and tormented hours.

How could he begin to understand how she felt about the dashing captain, with his swordplay and courtly manners? A Knight of the Round Table hadn't ever darkened her door before, nor was it likely one would ever again, and she didn't know what to do with her near intoxicating attraction to him. Even so, for once in her life, Stuart should allow her to determine matters for herself.

Oh, who was she fooling? He'd always directed her actions. Normally she complied with the docility of an adoring lapdog, but resentment rushed her to a defensive posture. "I'm simply being a courteous hostess."

He gave her an arched look.

"Would you rather I defied the captain and endangered this entire household, or would you have me shoot him? Then Tarleton and his Legion will arrive on our doorstep."

She didn't add that she'd rather die than perform such an act. Instead she glared back at the brother she revered, now at odds with her in a most disagreeable manner.

Raking his fingers through light brown hair loosened from its queue and falling around his shoulders, Stuart appeared to be in a particularly ill humor. "Of course not. But must you be so familiar with this sly officer? He's taking advantage of his situation in this home and of your trusting nature."

"All he's done thus far is behave in a most gentlemanly fashion."

Mouth agape, Stuart thrust back. "The hell he has, touching your cheek. I thought he might even kiss you."

She'd wondered the same, and her chest pounded at the notion. But nothing would induce an admission from her, save torture. "I trust you will assure my honor, dear brother, acting as my unseen chaperone."

"You ought to have a visible one."

"Who? Our insane grandfather, stupefied mother, or unbridled younger brother? Mrs. Jenner has her duties to attend to. And if it's escaped your notice, Captain Vaughan has the family under house arrest."

Stuart loosed a growl of frustration. "I should get you away from here. From him."

"I am not disappearing into the walls with you. One of us must be present and see this predicament through. You brought these men to Thornton."

He threw his hands up. "What choice had I?"

"None, it would seem. We each have our part to play. I suggest you allow me to attend to mine."

"I don't like it, Claire."

"Captain Vaughan won't attack me, or sneak in here which is more than can be said for you. My heart could have stopped from fright."

Remorse crossed Stuart's gaze. "Forgive my thoughtlessness. I didn't dare risk you crying out."

"Which I most certainly would have done and—"

Both of them froze at the heavy tread of footfall beyond Claire's chamber door. Voices carried. "Did the captain say what he wants me for? I was favorably settled in the kitchen with a pint of ale and Cook passing me tasty morsels. Haven't had vittles like that in an age." The Scottish burr belonged to Lieutenant McCray.

"No sir." Jim replied evenly. "But I brung more water so you kin have a warm up in yer bath."

"If I fancied a dunking," McCray grumbled. "A man could catch his death. Where you fetching all this water from, anyway? Cook's not boiling it up in the kitchen. Fixing food, the woman is, sensible like."

"A fire's lit in the washhouse, sir. There's a big hearth out there. And kettles near as big as me."

"That's all right, then. Got no argument with doing laundry. Still, all this everlasting tearing around. Can't a man have a quiet sit down?"

"Yes, sir. All you like."

McCray snorted with the windiness of a bull. "Not 'til I'm back in my own bed or at rest in the grave. And now that turncoat Arnold expects the same respect I'd show Tarleton, or Cornwallis? Galloping around Virginia, belting out orders like a lord. A merchant's son? I don't bloody care if he has taken our side. Wouldn't trust the bastard as far as I could throw him."

"Yes, sir. I mean no," Jim hurriedly amended.

"You gonna agree with every word I utter, lad?"

"Yes, sir."

A low chuckle escaped the gruff officer. "You've been taught right."

"Uh huh."

"No use protesting my duty. I'm ordered to protect Arnold's worthless hide. You know where that Lieutenant Monroe's denned up? Save me a heap of bother if you'd just spit it out."

"No one done told me, sir."

"No. Reckon they wouldn't. More's the pity."

Claire resumed breathing as the exchange came from further away, likely Vaughan's chamber. "That was too close, Stuart."

"I would have rolled beneath your bed." He frowned at the door. "Why does the captain get a bath and not me?"

"Would you care to join him, along with the lieutenant?"

Sinking onto the blue floral armchair near her bed, he fumed. "All this fawning over him. Warm water isn't rushed to my chamber during my infrequent visits home."

"It could be, if you like. I'm turning into a duck, as

often as I take a dip in the tub."

"I saw one of my shirts waiting for him to use," Stuart muttered.

She absorbed the outrageous meaning of his words. "Good heavens above. You entered his room?"

He shrugged. "The captain wasn't aware of my presence, slumbering in his bath water."

"You might have roused him." She pushed back her shortened locks. "Insanity truly must run in this family."

A slightly rueful smile curved her brother's lips. "I pray not. Sorry about your hair, too. And that I wasn't able to prevent Grandfather from lighting into you."

"Thank God Captain Vaughan was. And so skilled with a sword. He's to be an earl upon his father's death. Think of it, Stuart. An earl."

He raised his eyebrows at her. "General *Lord* Cornwallis already holds that title, and I don't see you blathering like a ninny about him."

Letting the insult to her intelligence slide, she reasoned. "Cornwallis is pompous and middle aged. That's different."

"Both are our avowed enemy. It's evident you are far more impressed than you ought to be with this dragoon officer. Swooning over him. Practically at his feet."

"'Tisn't why I grew so breathless."

"What, then? It's not like you to be fainthearted."

"I can't explain."

"Never happened before his coming, did it?"

She made no denial.

"And the noble captain was only too happy to be of service."

Clutching the embroidered coverlet, she sat upright in bed. "Should he have left me on the stairs? He behaved admirably. What do you expect from me, Stuart? To bite the hand that offers assistance?"

"Cold aloofness. Treat him with the barest civility and see his *lordship* on his way."

"I have no control over when he departs."

Condemnation was written in every taut line of Stuart's face. "You're so inviting the captain will likely stay the week. It might behoove you to remember he's as ruthless as any of them when he has to be."

She stiffened. "No."

"You just don't want to believe it."

"Surely not as bad as Tarleton?"

"Not that harsh, but bad enough. And dragoons will be swarming Halifax by now." Stuart waved at her shuttered windows, closed against the world. "You have no idea what it's like out there, beyond Thornton Hall. Lord knows I've tried to protect you." He groaned, pressing his forehead against his palm. "And failed."

"Not yet." Her already tormented stomach churned even more. "But you must have more care. If you're taken, what will become of the rest of us? You ought not creep about before all are sound asleep. Perhaps not even then."

"At least I'm in uniform. Not like André."

Only last autumn, the attractive British Major John André, much liked by all, was regretfully hanged by General Washington, though it should have been Arnold who swung in his stead as André was apprehended while assisting that traitor in his black hearted schemes. Washington offered to release André in exchange for Arnold, but Arnold didn't come forward and André perished.

A soldier caught spying while in civilian dress was executed. No exceptions on either side. The British hanged poor Nathan Hale without even the comfort of a Bible and clergyman beforehand.

"Even so. Dear God, Stuart. Being in uniform isn't assurance enough for your safety."

He relaxed his stern aspect. "Don't look so alarmed. I have no intention of being taken."

"Alive, or at all?" Surely, he wouldn't risk death to avoid capture.

"At all. I know every inch of this house as well if not better than you. I'll keep out of sight."

"Unless the captain knocks on my door this instant."

Disapproval returned to Stuart's narrowed eyes. "And why should he do that?"

"We are to dine together this evening."

"Are you, indeed? And when do you plan to study the cypher?"

"Later. Unless you prefer I do it over supper. Maybe the captain would be of use. He's quite clever. You said so yourself."

Stuart bristled like an offended dog. "Just keep that letter well hidden. Where is it now?"

"Here." She withdrew the parchment from beneath her pillow and handed it to him. "Hide it under the loose board."

He got to his feet, crept across the chamber, and knelt at the far right corner between a tall chest of drawers and her dressing table. No one could tell at a glance this portion of the floor had a space beneath it for just such a purpose. She and Stuart had stowed their treasures here as children…brightly colored bird feathers, special stones, pilfered sweets, the collar of their beloved bulldog. Memories of them at play rushed back.

"Stuart, we're on the same side," she reminded him, in a hushed voice.

"Don't forget."

"As if for a single second I could." But wistfulness to neglect all else and think only of a certain captain assailed her. She envisioned those compelling blue eyes.

Surely he wasn't as vile as Stuart said. Besides, this was war and men on both sides behaved in a violent manner. It was the nature of conflict. Captain Vaughan had been all graciousness to her. Still, he was a British officer and she must remain aware of their pronounced differences. If only…

Stuart blew out his breath in a whistling sigh.

She glanced around to find him shaking his head at her. "God in heaven, girl. 'Tis plain you're mightily taken with the fellow. I thought you had more sense. Besides, don't you have an understanding with Thomas Vaughan?"

"Not a formal agreement."

"Informal?"

"Not on my part."

"Thomas is rather a dandy, I admit. But amiable enough and certainly the gentleman."

"I require more persuasion than good manners and a fashionable wardrobe to entice me into marriage."

"You mean *now* that you've met the captain," Stuart added. "Unwelcome tidings for your admirer.

Not to mention our mother when she rouses from her stupor. She's set her cap at the wealthy merchant for you both."

"But you don't know all. There's more." Claire bent toward her annoyed brother. "The two men are related, and Vaughan has little praise for his American cousin."

"Vaughan?"

Ooops.

Stuart fixed her with the stern expression he kept in his arsenal, though never for her. "What happened to *Captain*?"

Claire launched into whispered justification. "A mere slip of the tongue. The important thing is that Thomas Vaughan may be a turncoat."

"As many suspect. Need I remind you this British *Vaughan*, as you so familiarly referred to him, is most definitely not on our side?"

"At least he's true."

Head in his hands, Stuart groaned. "To the bloody king."

"I know." It was burnt into her soul.

Stuart eyed her from between his fingers. "Bear that in mind while you dine. And as you're so eager for this tête-à-tête, see if you can discover what he knows of the Patriarch."

"Shall I ask him outright?"

"I hoped you might contrive something more subtle."

"I'll try."

His voice took on a familiar intensity. "It's important Claire."

"It always is. First with Grandfather, then Father,

and now you. The first is afflicted, the second dead, and you are in grave danger. And we're no nearer to winning this war. I vow I shall perish an old maid."

"You are only two and twenty."

"Only? Our mother was a bride by seventeen. I'm a spinster by comparison."

"A youthful one."

"The years are mounting, Stuart."

Earnestness charged his demeanor. "Do not despair. I know you suffer and are deprived of the life a young lady should enjoy."

She waved aside his attempt at sympathy. Her woes went far deeper.

"And the husband and family you desire," he amended. "But in time the right of our cause will prevail. We shall triumph. And you will better understand."

Oddly, Vaughan had uttered something similar to her, though from an entirely different doctrine. She better believed Stuart, but wanted the captain.

Stuart rose and cuffed her affectionately under the chin. "Wear the green gown and your best silk shawl. Your spirits lift when you don that attire." He studied her thoughtfully. "Now I consider the matter, we may be further ahead if our lauded guest does regard you favorably."

"You think he will surrender?"

The corners of Stuart's mouth dipped. "Not burn the home to the ground, at least, and see to it you are safe."

Urgency welled in her to gain the slightest nod from her brother, something to justify her interactions with Captain Vaughan. "He has offered his protection."

"As long as that is the extent of his offerings."

Stuart sidled toward the door.

"Where are you going?"

"It's gone quiet. Maybe they both nodded off."

"Not in the tub together."

"There's a couch and cushioned armchairs in that chamber. I'll slip away while they are enjoying our hospitality."

She strained to hear the slightest tread of feet. "Take care."

He smiled. "I'm the legendary ghost of Thornton Hall."

"Just don't become a real one."

"Take heart," he encouraged.

She suspected a certain captain had already snared hers.

Chapter Seven

Oh, Claire. She swished through the door in a rustle of taffeta. Vaughan caught his breath as he beheld the vision joining him for supper in the room normally reserved for family and close friends.

In a single beat of his pounding heart, the formerly dreary parlor was transformed into a realm of cozy intimacy. The lashing rain and distant booms of thunder no longer dispirited him, and he'd spent gloomy minutes staring out the streaked glass at a black sky. It was all Claire. Without her this room held no charm, only bleak emptiness.

Smiling his approval, he offered a short bow. "Miss Monroe. How splendid you look."

A becoming flush pinkened her cheeks and she curtsied. "Thank you, sir."

"I feared you might not come."

"Forgive my tardiness. I was overlong in dressing."

Something, or someone, else had delayed her as well, he'd wager. "No matter. The effect is stunning, and all is righted now you are here."

He strode to her and took her hands in his, a bold move, but he didn't hesitate. A faint heart never won a lady or a battle. Nor did she pull away, but dropped her eyes demurely. He couldn't have asked for a more receptive response.

Big brother must be grinding his teeth if he looked

on; no doubt, he did, the elusive, yet highly present chaperone. What a peculiar state for Vaughan to find himself in, but he didn't protest the conditions of this most unlikely dinner party. Simply to be near Claire was enough.

He lingered a moment, savoring the softness of her skin in his coarse grasp and inhaling her rose perfume. "Your scent is divine. French?"

She raised her gaze to his. "Yes. A gift from my father."

"A fragrance fit for the gods, like some rare nectar, for a lovely lady."

Her creamy neck flushed. "You are too kind."

"Rarely."

How refreshing she was. The green ribbon encircling her shortened hair enhanced the color of her eyes. He found the unpretentious style far preferable to a high, powdered wig, although she would also wear that well. The green-gold gown flattered her elegant figure, as did the flowered silk shawl loosely covering her shoulders. Iridescent pearl drops shone at her perfect ears and emeralds entwined with garnets sparkled in the brooch pinned to the lace at her bodice. She hadn't held back in her adornment for the occasion. All she lacked was an elegant comb for her hair and plumy feathers.

If he'd had the opportunity, he would have turned out in full regimental regalia. As it was, he was sadly underdressed by comparison. At least he'd bathed and wore fresh linen and breeches. His ivory waistcoat was tolerable, though a trifle shabby, and his coat was being cleaned, leaving him only in shirtsleeves. Hardly resplendent attire. He doubted she minded, though, given the way she gazed at him. His heart drummed a rhythm akin to the pounding hooves of a runaway steed. Again, he reined himself in.

Releasing her fingers, he gestured at the table draped in spotless linen and laden with food. "Shall we proceed?"

"Gladly, sir."

"The pleasure is mine."

He linked his arm though hers and escorted her across the parlor, wishing the room were larger so he might remain by her side for a greater distance. Better still, partner her in a dance, many dances, the night long.

Sweeping his free hand at the table situated near the hearth, he invited. "Pray be seated."

In a whisper of skirts, she settled in the chair he drew back for her. He assisted in adjusting her seat, then lowered himself into the one across from hers. The high ceilinged room had chilled with the descending storm and the low blaze crackling in the fireplace lent cheer. Fire and candles cast honeyed light over her expressive face.

Before them were place settings of blue and white patterned china, crystal goblets, silver tankards, knives, spoons, and forks. Mouthwatering aromas escaped the gleaming silver serving dishes. Savory squares of the new-made cornbread Mrs. Jenner had spoken of upstairs were heaped on a floral platter. A decorative, fluted pastry gave out meaty whiffs, rabbit pie, he'd been told. Assorted cheeses, tender salad leaves, pickles, beetroot, and a spicy bread pudding dotted with currents vied for space on the table.

No stinting here. Mrs. Jenner had taken pains to lay

out the best she and her help could muster for this impromptu supper. That it wasn't served in a dozen courses by footmen with polished manners mattered not a whit to him. "A welcome repast, Miss Monroe. With such civility and exquisite company, I am transported to Hartford House."

Pleasure warmed Claire's eyes. "Hardly that, given the opulence you must know there, but I am gratified you find our small efforts agreeable."

"Inestimably."

Mrs. Jenner sailed in bearing a tray of tarts. The kitchen must be hopping with all the preparations they'd undertaken for the evening. The workers here might not compare in size to the numerous staff at his home in Devon, but they were eager to please.

"Everything to yer liking, is it, Captain?"

He detected a twinge of anxiety in her tone, and she'd attended to them herself rather than sending one of the girls. Doing right by him meant a great deal to this hardworking woman and he hastened to reassure her.

"Excellent. Thank you. Particularly with Miss Monroe's enchanting presence to share this meal."

A broad smile creased the housekeeper's reddened face. "Has the looks of a proper duchess, that one."

"Finer than any noblewomen of my acquaintance."

"Surely not," Claire protested. "You flatter me, sir."

"And how many noblewomen are you familiar with?"

She stared mutely at him.

He simply smiled.

The chiding in Mrs. Jenner's eyes took voice in her

speech. "When a gentleman of Captain Vaughan's standing pays you a compliment, Miss Claire, you ought to accept it. Far too hard on yourself, you are. But there, it's not my place to speak out of turn."

He imagined Mrs. Jenner speaking her mind was a common, probably daily, occurrence.

Claire brushed aside her last statement. "Your opinions are valued, Mrs. Jenner. We are, after all, blood kin."

The bustling female beamed. "That's all right, then." She laid the tray on the crowded table and lifted a bottle of wine. "Shall I pour, or would you prefer the ale, Captain?"

"The wine first."

A red stream gushed forth and she filled the goblets nearly to the brim, then gestured at the blue jug. "There's the ale whenever you like, sir." She indicated the small brass bell polished until it gleamed. "Or you might ring."

"No need. We are amply provided for. Please, attend to your other duties."

"I'll leave you to your meal, shall I? You have all you need?"

He gazed across at Claire. "Everything I could possibly desire."

She colored responsively, and he smiled to himself.

Nodding her satisfaction, the housekeeper turned with the dexterity he'd observed before, despite her bulk, and skirted across the parlor in the accompanying flurry of petticoats. She paused at the door. "Sally's preparing trifle for desert. I'll bring it along directly." With that promise, she embarked up the hall like a frigate in full sail.

"A most diligent woman," he remarked.

Claire sighed. "And a good body to the core, despite her ready tongue. I do not know how we should manage without her."

"You also are blessed with an able cook, I see."

"Sally is the very best and her daughters at her elbow learning. Six children she has now. Two sets of twins."

Scuffling sounded in the hall, and Minnie scuttled past the door like the mouse she resembled. With her, trailed two wide-eyed little girls in long white shifts and blue jackets. Neat caps covered their dark, tousled heads.

"So I see. Quite a brood. They seem content."

"For the most part." Claire waved away the curious pair. "Those two should be abed," she added in an elevated voice. "Go on now, darling. You too, precious."

Vaughan eyed her quizzically.

"Precious and Darling are their names," Claire explained. "Sally let her Aunt Beulah choose this time, and she's a bit odd."

"Quite." The imps darted off, and he returned his gaze to the vision seated opposite him. "Is the healer, Ezekiel, any relation to this lot?"

"He's Sally's father and Beulah's brother."

"Does Sally claim any man as husband?"

Sadness creased Claire's brow. "A kindly soul. He died of fever. Ezekiel couldn't save him. Two of her brothers, one partly crippled, remain with us. Grandfather will free them all at his death."

This much Vaughan already knew from Mrs. Jenner, but his aim lay in encouraging Claire to speak.

"Most generous. I trust his will was drawn before the madness settled in?"

"Well before."

"You must find some means to induce Sally and her family to stay on, or you shall be hard-pressed for help."

"That is also my hope. We are shorthanded now."

"A toast, I think." Closing his fingers around the reddened goblet, he raised it in tribute, his ring sparking in the light. "To Thornton Hall and all who reside within its sheltering walls this wet eve."

Claire lifted her glass. "May these blessed walls stand for years to come." She sipped and swallowed. An air of solemnity came over her, like a weighty blanket. "I wish you might ensure our safety from the advancing army, Captain."

"So, you know Lord Cornwallis is en route and Tarleton's Legion out in front?"

She shifted uneasily in her chair. "I heard talk."

From her brother, he'd bet. "Did you also know Tarleton is angered by the loss of three dragoons and several horses in a skirmish with the local militia?"

She paled and shook her head.

Which meant Stuart Monroe was also in ignorance. Vaughan elevated his voice for appreciative ears. "The Patriots retreated across the Roanoke River to a redoubt. From there, they may continue resistance. Tarleton will come down hard on the town of Halifax if they do."

A shudder ran through her. "Do you think they will?"

"Rebels, as you're aware, are a tenacious lot."

"Extraordinarily so. Is Thornton Hall in danger,

sir?"

Vaughan met the apprehension in her eyes. "I give you my word to do all within my power to protect this household."

The tension in her face eased a little. "I wish you were a general."

An unexpected sentiment, and he chuckled. "Then I would not be here with you, dear lady."

"But you would outrank Tarleton," she said under her breath.

"If it is of comfort, my standing in the Legion holds more weight than my rank alone signifies."

"Why is this?"

He took a long sip of wine before answering. "My father. There are those among the senior officers who wish Lord Vaughan no offense."

"Yet you are competent in your own right."

Basking in her assertion, he gave a nod. "Absolutely. I must earn my merits, but the weight of a powerful father and the future title I will one day hold is a legacy I carry with me for better or ill in America as well as England. Some men allot me added honor, while others resent my perceived privilege." One brusque officer came to mind.

Claire was thoughtful as she weighed his explanation. "I see. What of your mother? Is she also titled?"

"For centuries, and with valuable ties to prominent families." He tapped the onyx ring on his middle finger. "She gave me this band on my sixteenth birthday. She's a Parker from Devon. The stag is on their coat of arms."

"A most impressive ring and lineage."

"Granted, but—" He paused, deliberating whether

or not to continue. The earnestness in her gaze entreated him and he succumbed. "Mama is overly fond of laudanum and often confined to her chamber."

Claire's telltale eyes widened, then washed with empathy. "So, you do know what it is."

"All too well."

"Is your mother also of a delicate constitution?"

He shrugged. "Browbeaten by her surly husband, but Lord Vaughan grows more pliant in his old age at the tender hands of my sisters."

A soft light suffused her eyes. "I always longed for a sister."

"You are most welcome to share mine."

Her brow arched, and he laughed softly. "You do not believe my sincerity?"

Making no reply, she scrutinized him doubtfully.

"Trust me."

"Are we not on opposing sides of the conflict embroiling this land, sir?"

"You and I need not be at odds, Miss." Reaching across the table, he lightly pressed her hand. "Let us not dwell on the state of our two nations. We are simply a gentleman and fair lady dining together. We have food aplenty, and the joys of the evening stretch before us."

She inclined her head, the caramel streaks in her light brown hair shining in the radiance of many candles. Wistfulness glistened in her gaze, like the dewy promise of a new day. "A lovely sentiment."

"Indeed. Let us eat, drink, and be merry." He didn't add, 'for tomorrow we die.' Rather, he was determined they should both live. And together. He did not yet know when or how, only that he was resolved to make her his wife, if she were agreeable.

There was one way to discover, but it was too soon. This wasn't the hour to press the matter, rather a time to savor the moment. Lord only knew when it might come again, if ever. After harsh months in Backcountry, he was famished in more ways than one. And hadn't even fully realized how difficult his life had been until now.

For a while they ate in silence, the gentle clink of cutlery, the drumming rain, and crackle of wood in the hearth the only sounds. Noises from the kitchen didn't carry to the parlor. No wailing emanated from overhead. The troubled members of the family must have succumbed to their medicines. That young reprobate, Master William, was lodged in the stable under the eye of Ensign Anderson with plenty of victuals to sustain them both. And Vaughan was satisfied as to Percy's condition and care.

After a blustery protest, Lieutenant McCray had his obligatory bath. The ornery officer even allowed the water 'weren't too bad' and fell asleep in the tub. He slumbered upstairs now, bedded down before the hearth in the chamber allotted to Vaughan. McCray's fortuitous absence left this room free for Vaughan's private supper with Claire.

Momentarily relieved of his burdens, he soaked in the blissful quiet and her bewitching company. What heaven on earth to dine with Claire in this fashion. Even though few words were exchanged as they ate, an unspoken language passed between them, more compelling than mere speech alone could possibly convey.

Now and then, he caught her eye on him. Once, he even smiled, smiling again at how he'd disconcerted her. What wouldn't he give to linger in this inviting spot with this fascinating woman indefinitely? But it wasn't lost on Vaughan that they were never truly alone. He'd bet his life, Stuart Monroe was lodged beyond the wall, peering through the chink he'd spied in the panel. The sneaky devil had a peephole.

So much for privacy. Claire must also be aware. Her eyes fluttered to that side of the room like a moth to a flame.

Damnable spy. This particular thorn in Vaughan's side reminded him he mustn't neglect the business that brought him to her door in the first place. If he did, even his father's influence couldn't win him the coveted promotion. He'd fought hard to prove himself and not depend on his vaulted name and fortune to further his career. He mustn't let up now. No matter how tantalizing the company.

Well, maybe just for a little while. And he'd enjoy taunting that brother of hers a bit, might even irk their resident spy into showing himself.

A triumphant Mrs. Jenner reappeared bearing the promised trifle, bread layered with custard and strawberries oozing rich red syrup. Vaughan applauded as she set it on the groaning table. "Perhaps a portion after we have proper time to digest our meal."

"As you like, sir. I shall return with the Madeira."

He raised his hand. "Truly. We have sufficient."

"Yes. Thank you." Claire motioned her on. "Please see to the others, Mrs. Jenner."

"I can see to all. But, as you're satisfied." Appearing slightly disgruntled, she turned and swept out the door.

Vaughan laid down his fork and lightly blotted his

mouth with a pristine napkin. More food remained on the table than they'd consumed, but Mrs. Jenner had fed him earlier and he wasn't in the habit of gorging himself. Claire nibbled with the daintiness of a debutante and regarded the newest acquisition to the supper fare in distaste, as if she'd been served uncooked meat rather than rich dessert. Plainly, her nerves were on edge and she had no appetite.

"Shall we adjourn to the couch, Miss Monroe? We can hardly take a turn in the garden with this deluge, and I am not prepared to be deprived of your charming company so soon." Not only for the sheer pleasure of her presence, though that was uppermost in his mind, but he might gain more information.

He almost added, *You needn't worry over the lack of a chaperone, with your brother keeping watch*, but thought better of it. The ever-present awareness of Stuart Monroe accounted for the pistol he'd stuck in his boot and the saber hung around his shoulder. The cartridge belt he'd left behind. A single shot would serve if need be. McCray had better be dozing with one eye open.

Claire's gaze flitted from Vaughan to the wall and back again. Then she smiled a little uncertainly. "I should enjoy reclining on the couch. If you like, I might read aloud?"

What he'd like had nothing to do with books, although he'd welcome a reading of that furtive letter. "Simply conversing with you would bring me much gratification, Miss Monroe. I am too much in the company of boorish men."

"As you like, sir."

"There is nothing I should like more." At least,

nothing he dared voice aloud.

Claire's heart raced beneath her lacy bodice like a frightened hare's, only she didn't fear the fox seated by her side on the couch as she ought, nor did she attempt to escape him. Quite the reverse. What a traitor she was. In defiance of her staunch resolve and deepest loyalties.

Lost in the swell of sensations, she coveted every heady moment with this would be predator, the enemy she'd dreaded ever coming to Thornton Hall. But he would help keep *the Butcher Tarleton* from their door, she silently argued, in justification of each shivery touch he elicited. His hand sent exquisite tingles pulsing through her.

Those penetrating glances spoke to the nameless yearning she hadn't realized she had, until now. And more, to the knowledge that in Vaughan she'd found the one she sought, and he did, indeed, have a name. But this inherent intimacy didn't stem from a meeting of minds, for they were not in accord. She vehemently disagreed with his stand in this war and decried the king whose empire he battled to secure. But she didn't—couldn't—decry him.

While she glimpsed the man beyond the uniform, Stuart perceived only the British captain. And her brother looked on, of that she was certain. If only she and Vaughan might have two minutes alone. She could hardly invite him to adjourn to the east parlor without arousing undue suspicion.

Mrs. Jenner breezed back in with a tray and two glasses. "A drop of whiskey for the captain. As rare a brew as is to be found in the whole of North Carolina, sir."

"Quite a declaration, Mrs. Jenner."

"One I stand behind."

And her bulk was not to be shifted. This particular whiskey, of which she was inordinately proud, was distilled from a family recipe she'd brought with her belonging to her late husband and could peel the shell off an egg.

Vaughan graciously accepted the crystal filled with amber colored fluid she pushed into his hand. And to his credit, he didn't grimace at the swallow he undertook.

Claire accepted the glass offered to her. Objection was futile with Mrs. Jenner bent on hospitality. She obliged the zealous woman with a sip of the fiery liquid, though she failed to stifle a cough.

"There now. Miss Claire's not one for strong drink, Captain, but you, being a proper gentleman, will have a liking for sound whiskey."

"Indubitably." He imbibed a second swallow and a third, though Claire noted his eyes water a little.

Some partakers of the potent brew choked up and thumped their chests with strangled exclamations. Not Vaughan, but why was Mrs. Jenner offering it to him now? They had plenty to drink. And why did she continually reappear?

Did she think to appease any remaining wrath she feared he might have with the household? He didn't seem the least bit vengeful and had given assurance of his protection. Was she smitten at having gentry under the roof? Claire had mentioned his illustrious birthright when Mrs. Jenner came to her bedchamber to assist her in dressing for this occasion. If he drank everything the housekeeper offered him, he'd surely be as drunk as a lord.

Another thought occurred. Maybe Stuart had sent Mrs. Jenner to spy for him. A distinct possibility. Whatever her reasoning, she seemed bent on emptying the cellar.

"You needn't worry for your faithful guide who saved your life from that dreadful blast of the pistol," Mrs. Jenner assured their prestigious guest. "Ezekiel's tending Percy with all the care of a mother to her newborn babe. Got him well dosed with his best potion and a healing poultice on the stitched wound. The fellow's resting as comfortable as a body can who suffered lead shot dug out of his side."

"Welcome tidings. Percy seemed in able hands when I looked in on him. Alert me if there's any change in his condition, or if he's moved to a *new location* in the house."

A nod of her cap. "So I will, sir."

Had Claire's giddy rush over the striking captain made her imagination run wild, or did the avid woman angle her head at the opposite wall where Stuart, doubtless, lurked?

No. Impossible. It must be a fancy of her addled senses.

"If that will be all, Captain?" Mrs. Jenner inquired.

"For now. Attend to your other duties."

With a quick curtsy, she scuttled from the parlor.

A smile playing at his lips, Vaughan turned to Claire. "Now she's gone, I believe we may dispose of these." Taking her glass and his in hand, he rose and walked to the window, opened it, and tossed the contents to the wind-swept rain. What remained of Claire's shorn hair tossed in the damp breeze he let into the room and brushed her cheek.

Muffling laughter, she applauded his action. "You are a man of decision."

"Always." He closed the window and returned to her.

Setting the glasses on the end table beside her sprawl of books, he lowered himself onto the couch. The humor in his expression faded, replaced by gravity. "I must be decisive. Delay can be costly."

The intensity of his gaze sped the pounding in Claire's heart. For a long moment, no words passed between them. She scarcely breathed. Those eyes, a truer blue she'd never seen, or a more perceptive gaze.

Slightly winded, she forced out a query. "What are you pondering now, sir?"

Lifting a hand to her cheek, he lightly cupped her face. "You, Miss Monroe." He covered her lips with his seeking mouth.

The world fell away, and with it all the cares weighing so heavily on Claire's shoulders, as she gave herself to this utterly absorbing and earthshaking pressure on her mouth. The discreet pecks offered by his cousin, Thomas, paled to nothingness in comparison to Vaughan's tender, yet compelling lips. This is how a kiss, in its purest, most romantic form, was meant to be, and she never wanted to be kissed any other way, by any other man. Ever again.

Desire surged in her to close her arms around his neck and be enfolded in return. But he slowly pulled back, and smoothed a tendril curling at her temple.

"You are perfection," he said softly.

As was he, apart from his scarlet uniform, the cause he fought for, his reason for coming to Thornton

Hall and—

Dear God in heaven. To her horror, from the corner of her eye, she saw Stuart's scowl dangerously visible in the cracked door in the panel.

Was he totally insane? Did she detect the glint of a pistol in his hand?

He wouldn't dare shoot the captain. Would he?

Surely not. He couldn't possibly fire without the risk of striking her. Stuart would never take that chance.

Gulping in shock, she fixed her eyes on Vaughan, praying she held his gaze and he didn't glance across the room and spot what she had.

His brow arched and he lowered his hand from her face. "Why Miss Monroe, you've gone quite pale, as though you've seen a ghost."

She nodded. "The resident spirit of Thornton Hall. He comes and *goes*," she emphasized.

"Indeed? I heard no talk of such an apparition from Mrs. Jenner, even with her wagging tongue."

"A family *secret*." One Claire was doing her best to guard.

"He must be terribly frightful to cause such alarm in your lovely face."

"Ghastly," she agreed.

"And exceedingly possessive of you to appear at this instant."

"He can be. But really ought to *depart*."

"Then you forgive me for taking liberties?"

Not daring to look, and praying Stuart had the sense to retreat before Vaughan detected him, she shook her head. Then caught herself. "I mean yes. I forgive you, and fear I'm too disturbed to know what I speak."

"Poor lady. It must be an intolerable strain not knowing when or at what hour this vagrant spirit may appear. Is it not, Lieutenant Monroe?"

In the blink of an eye, the captain pulled a pistol from his boot and aimed it at the doorway.

The standoff between the two men held her in terrible suspense. She feared the worst, and thought she might erupt in hysterics or collapse in a heap on the floor. After tense moments, that seemed far longer, the door shut behind Stuart's retreating back and he was gone. She stared in horror. What would Vaughan do?

Rather than attempt to pursue Stuart through the hidden pathways in the house, he lowered the pistol. "I believe you and I have much to discuss, Miss Monroe. But first, let me assure you I relished every moment your lips touched mine."

So had Claire, but a deepening suspicion took root that he'd used her to lure Stuart nearer. What a fool she'd been. If only she didn't want Vaughan to kiss her again.

"Perhaps we ought to consider what's to be done about this *spirit*," he suggested.

But it was more than a suggestion.

Wishing for the whiskey he'd tipped out the window, she gripped the couch as if it might run away with her. "What can one do?"

"Tell me all you know of him, unless you would prefer to discuss a particular letter I am instructed to find."

He knew about that, too? Her heart nearly stopped. And the breathing difficulty she'd experienced earlier today threatened to reassert itself. She found herself shaking.

Vaughan reached out and gently gathered her against him with strong arms. She sagged in his support. Her cheek fit in the hollow of his shoulder, his chest solid, warm. He spoke quietly. "My assurance stands. I mean you and your family no ill. But I require your assistance."

A dogged tenacity beat in this man. "I foolishly thought you cared for me, sir."

"I do." And in the faintest whisper… "Claire."

Chapter Eight

"Shhhh…" Vaughan soothed, cradling the badly shaken young woman in his arms.

Consoling Claire held undeniable appeal and he couldn't protest the intoxicating scent of her rose perfume in his nose, or her softness pressed against him, but he had no desire to achieve this level of intimacy under these circumstances.

Blast that Rebel brother of hers, and this confounded mission, forcing him to cause Claire such distress. Lieutenant Monroe might be willing to suffer martyrdom for the cause, but must he drag his sweet sister down with him?

"What will become of Stuart?" Her voice quavered and she choked out the words.

"Do not fear so." If Vaughan failed to calm her down, her breathing could grow so labored she'd fight for each inhalation of air, as she'd done earlier today.

"But you know what he is—why he's at Thornton."

"From the beginning. Yet, here we sit."

Her breath warm on his chest, she sucked in a tremulous gasp. "Too many have perished. I could not bear to lose him."

"This I am also mindful of."

"He's wearing his Regimentals," she panted, as if that made all the difference in the world.

"Duly noted."

"He wouldn't have fired at you," she hastened to assure him.

"Not with you seated so near, but that's another matter. I have a proposal to put to you. A highly unorthodox one."

Lifting her face, she scrutinized him through the glaze of tears. "You speak of the letter?"

He kept his voice low. "I do. This message is of importance to Tarleton and, consequently, to me."

She further paled at the mention of the infamous officer in charge of British intelligence. "What of Stuart?"

"He's also of value to us. However, the most significant aim of my assignment here is the recovery of the message carried by Lieutenant Monroe."

Reluctance was heavy in eyes sparkling with tears. "And if I give it to you?"

It would require a sacrifice on his part, and cost him, but for her sake, Vaughan conceded. "You may convey word to your errant brother that if he remains in this home hidden from view, I shall consider him under house arrest and will neglect any mention of his whereabouts to my men, or in my report. As far as I'm concerned, he escaped. After our departure from Halifax, he may safely leave Thornton Hall, though I advise him to keep out of mischief."

A shuddering sigh, and she nodded. "I will tell him."

"Excellent. And stress the immediate annulment of this agreement should I again discover him in my bedchamber."

Her gaze widened. "You knew he entered there?"

"As did you, it would seem."

Shortened tresses flew with the adamant shaking of her head. "Only afterward. When he confided in me."

"I see." So, Vaughan had been correct. The troublemaker was responsible for her delay in joining him at supper. What a thorn in his side this Rebel was, and yet, how dear to Claire. "It is greatly to Lieutenant Monroe's advantage to remain undetected in this house. Now, regarding the letter."

She stilled, shaking, in his hold. "Yes?"

"Not only do I require this message from you, but also that you decipher it."

"I do not know if I'm able to do so. Truly. I am not the intended recipient."

"Yet your brother entrusted it to you for a reason."

A heavy exhalation of breath escaped her. "He thinks I may be able to fathom the meaning as the cypher has to do with our father. But I do not share Stuart's confidence."

Vaughan met the insistence in her face. "Have you examined the letter?"

"Not yet. 'Tis hidden at present."

"But you are aware of its location."

"I am," she conceded, in a small voice.

"Pray do not be coy with me, dear lady. Where, precisely, is it concealed?"

"Tucked beneath the floorboards of my bedchamber." She spoke with the aversion of one ascending the gallows.

"And you understand the purpose of the clues it holds? The site of the wealth collected for a price on General Arnold's head."

Disdain in her eyes, she gave an unwilling nod. "You know what a fiend he is?"

"I do. And I abhor him."

Her brows arched like twin birds in flight.

"He betrayed General Washington who considered Arnold his right arm. No British officer fully trusts his allegiance to the Crown will endure. But my orders do not include second-guessing his loyalty, or allow for my opinion of him."

"So you will protect such a despicable scoundrel?"

Vaughan lifted a shoulder and let it drop. "General Arnold's wellbeing is not entrusted to me. I am to deliver a deciphered letter that leads to the goods or coins taken, I assume, from Loyalists."

"I cannot say."

He spoke sternly. "Doubtless, you are in ignorance. But by enlisting your aid in this effort, your brother has involved you in a willful act of sedition."

Alarm in her eyes, she lifted her hands palms up. "I never intended to take part."

"Yet you have." Vaughan gentled his tone. "A dangerous charge, indeed. One that must remain our secret."

Breath whooshed from her as if she'd been holding it a long time. "And in return?"

"You will endeavor to solve the riddle of this undoubtedly cryptic message."

"May God be with me," she said softly.

A dark weight settled over Vaughan. "With us both, if my complicity in this matter is discovered."

Fresh dismay furrowed her smooth forehead. "Might it be?"

Her seemingly genuine concern touched him. "Not if we have care. None but the three of us know. Can we trust Lieutenant Monroe to hold his tongue?"

"I believe so, when he realizes the full extent of the danger to me."

"With that I must be satisfied." This rogue brother wouldn't care a whit if it earned Vaughan a court-martial.

She cupped a trembling hand at his cheek. "Thank you, Captain. Such forbearance I should never have expected."

"Or received, were I not so taken with you. I am not known for my mild manner." He caught her fingers in his and pressed them lightly. "But I will do my all to shield you from harm. I swear it." Even if he must be the shield.

For a moment filled only by the steady drum of rain, no words passed between them, then he continued. "I'm aware of how little you wish to show me this missive, let alone truthfully decipher it. But I shall be watching you."

A bob of her head. "What do you know of a man called *The Patriarch*?" she asked, in barely detectable tones.

"He resides in this house."

Vaughan hadn't ever seen anyone quite so dumbfounded; Claire stared at him much as she had at the appearance of the resident ghost, with the addition of utter bewilderment. Then protest replaced the incredulity in her face.

Drawing back from him, she sat bolt upright on the couch. "No. It cannot be Grandfather. Mister Monroe does not possess the wits to compose cyphers or decipher messages."

"Not now. Before the madness," Vaughan reasoned.

"I dwell in this house and knew nothing of such actions on his part. Surely, I am more perceptive than the cat."

The tabby contemplated them with the inscrutable green gaze of felines, as Vaughan contested the point. "Master spies are experts at deception."

"I realize this," she whispered heatedly. "But even Stuart has no idea who the Patriarch is."

"Your father must have, if he composed the letter."

"My brother believes it to be the work of a fellow officer of Captain Monroe's, familiar with his thoughts."

"Possibly dictated by Captain Monroe himself at the last and intended for your grandfather, also well-versed with your father."

"If this were so, why did neither of them ever tell us?"

"The fewer acquainted with Mister Monroe's true identity, the better. Stuart was meant to learn at *Person's Ordinary* today when he waited to hand off the letter. Your grandfather received correspondence a while ago, likely penned in code, alerting him to the rendezvous. But he no longer possessed the mental capability to grasp its meaning."

She regarded Vaughan in confusion. "How do you know this?"

"I have my informants."

"I should very much like their names."

He smiled faintly. "Spoken like a true Rebel."

"So, you believe the Patriarch wasn't at the Ordinary because he's here, confined to his bedchamber most of the day?" She shook her head. "This makes no sense."

"Are you certain? Consider carefully."

"I can scarcely do otherwise, sir, as you are so decided."

"Not unalterably, yet I am strongly inclined to this conclusion."

"Very well, Captain. I shall endeavor to push through my cluttered thoughts."

"Venture back to the early days, before the war."

"A great distance, indeed. I was scarcely more than a child."

"Yet, you do remember."

At Vaughan's persistence, Claire pressed fingertips to her now aching forehead and snatched at memories. Glimpses of Grandfather and Papa conversing together at the table and by the fireside came to her. Though deeply religious, her grandfather hadn't been rabid then. The fanaticism came with the affliction. And he was a learned scholar, her father much like him. She recalled the exchange of wit between the two men, the word games they enjoyed devising. True, her father had put many of these puzzles to her to solve, but only in play. Perhaps, without her knowing, the sport had taken a dangerous bent.

More and more, she was forced to acknowledge the possible connection between her now-afflicted relation and the craft of spying. Wind whistled beyond the walls and the parlor door slammed shut, propelled by the bluster, as the golden knight at her side awaited a reply.

With the utmost disinclination, she allowed an admission. "There may be something to what you say."

Satisfaction glinted in those blue eyes. "For months, a master spy has eluded us. I suspect Mister Monroe to be that man. Your father also knew."

The likelihood of Vaughan's claim sank in. She remembered her grandfather's frequent absences from home, presumably on business, and those long stretches of time when he holed up in his chamber composing what she assumed were letters to friends, family, or conducting yet more business correspondence.

She slumped back against the couch. "Dear God."

"Precisely. Your grandfather was deeply engaged in what the French call *espionnage*. And your father became involved."

"Now Papa is dead and Grandfather's stricken."

"Leaving you, their granddaughter and daughter, in possession of the last exchange between them."

"If that is, indeed, what it was."

"I've no doubt, and you are gifted with an equally clever mind."

"I'm but a babe-in-arms by comparison, scarcely deserving of such a pronouncement. Everything in me speaks of my unworthiness."

He twirled a tendril at her cheek around one finger. "Then allow me to speak of your worth."

Chills prickled through her. "'Tis a weighty confidence, sir."

"And well-placed. I have an inherent sense of a man or woman that guides me."

"And you know of me?"

"Enough to trust what I perceive. And much depends upon this missive. Shall we adjourn to your chamber and examine the letter, or would you prefer to bring it to mine?"

"Both are highly improper rooms for me to undertake this study in."

"I would indulge you in all civility, were I able.

Yet, propriety holds scant importance in such matters. We must have no interruptions. No one else can learn of this communication until the message is deciphered and I proclaim my mission accomplished. Lieutenant McCray is trustworthy unless he imbibes too much ale, then his tongue loosens. He slumbers soundly, but may awake."

"My chamber, then. Though Stuart would be loath to allow such effrontery, apart from his objection to the hated task you've set before me."

"If Lieutenant Monroe wishes to remain at large, he must tolerate my presence in this house and permit you to proceed."

"But in my bedchamber?"

"Would you prefer a dark, windswept corner on the grounds, or the smokehouse? I give you my word to behave as a gentleman, Officer of the Crown, and future lord."

"It's that bit about Officer of the Crown I find particularly troublesome. *Future lord* also goads me." The door in the wall opened again and, unbelievably, Stuart stepped out, bristling resentment. Though thankfully the pistol was at his side, not directed at the captain.

Claire was too shocked by his effrontery to notice when Vaughan reclaimed his weapon, only that he aimed the barrel at her brazen brother. Clapping her palm to her mouth, she gasped. "Stuart."

"Lieutenant Monroe, have you a death wish?" Vaughan coolly inquired.

Stuart studied him through narrowed eyes. "No."

"Then perhaps I was correct when I inquired of Miss Monroe if *all* her relations were quite mad?"

"I haven't taken leave of my senses, Captain, but will see to the honor of my sister."

"Admirable, I grant you. And I intend her no dishonor."

"Indeed?" Stuart bit back.

"My intentions toward Miss Monroe are the very best, and shall be made clear at my first opportunity."

"What?" Stuart appeared thunderstruck.

His demeanor mirrored Claire's astonishment.

"Hear me out, sir," Vaughan said firmly.

Though momentarily rendered speechless, Stuart's eyes fired daggers at the captain as he continued. "You are a hunted spy who coerced your sister into concealing a treasonable document. Your actions endanger the lady. Not mine."

A red flush heightened the color in Stuart's face.

Vaughan's sharp gaze never left his slitted regard. "There is but one course open to you, Lieutenant, if you do, indeed, wish to avoid imprisonment and the gallows. Become the ghost your sister proclaimed you to be. Disappear back into those walls and leave the letter to us."

Refusal glittered in Stuart's eyes.

His gall in confronting the captain and Vaughan's bargain took Claire completely by surprise—and what did he mean by his intentions would be made clear? She'd rather expected him to shoot her audacious sibling on sight, not this astounding revelation.

Thoroughly rattled, she opened quivering lips. "Please, Stuart. Our family is in grave danger."

That mulish expression was entrenched in his face. "Many have sacrificed for the sake of that cypher."

"Do not add your sweet sister to the toll. If you

force the matter, I shall be hard-pressed to prevent her being implicated," Vaughan warned. "I may even have to whisk her away to some place of safety."

Out thrust Stuart's chin. "You are not whisking her anywhere. It's me you seek, Captain. Arrest me. I assume full responsibility for my actions."

"Bravely spoken for one never actually incarcerated in a black hole or faced with the noose."

Claire's heart beat wildly. "Stuart, for God's sake. Do not bring more evil on us. Do you not realize who *the Patriarch* is?"

He swung his head at her, eyeing her blankly.

"Perhaps your ear was not at the wall during that exchange of conversation," Vaughan remarked.

"Would you have our grandfather carted away, too?" she demanded.

Stuart looked as if she'd struck him, and Claire was tempted to beat some sense into his thick skull.

"No." He shook his head. "Not Grandfather."

"Yes. The more I ponder, the more I see," she reasoned. "Also how close is the walk between ingenious wit and madness."

Stuart stood staring at her.

In that stunned moment, Vaughan took command. "Lay your pistol down, Lieutenant, and kick it across the floor to me."

Even more extraordinary, Stuart numbly did as he ordered, and Vaughan snatched it up.

Claire chose that instant to rush at her brother in a swirl of green skirts. Shoving against his bulk, she furiously insisted on compliance. "Retreat behind those walls and do not exit again until I give the signal. Or you shall have our entire family borne away and that will rest on your head."

Thrown off balance, he attempted to reason. "Claire—"

"No." She gave him a shove. "All of us are guilty, from our younger brother to Grandfather. Our shattered mother will be left alone. You must trust me in this."

"'Tisn't you I'm wary of."

"Be thankful Captain Vaughan has allowed you this opportunity. Now go. Leave me to cope with the cypher. As you did your favorite colt, Balthazar, when you went to war."

He stood stock-still and shot her a speculative glance. Then with a face like the black, rain-lashed sky, he fired a parting threat at the captain. "Do not deprive my sister of more than her knowledge of the cypher alone."

Vaughan inclined his head and lowered his pistol as, once again, her brother disappeared through the door and beyond the walls. The faint tread of feet indicated he was climbing to a higher recess, likely the attic. Shaken from her action, Claire inhaled deeply to steady herself.

Admiration in his gaze, the captain gave a low whistle. "If ever I'm in want of an ally, I pray you will come to my aid. I should not wish to skirmish with such a woman."

"If ever you're in such want, I swear by all that's sacred you shall have my aid."

He assessed her with an expression of bemusement. "War makes for unlikely alliances."

"The most improbable in the world."

Tucking a pistol in the top of each boot, he swept her a bow. "Lead on, dear lady. I am eager to see this cypher."

"I pray my cunning is equal to the task, sir," and that the distraction of such a blindingly handsome man wouldn't render her witless.

Incredulity swirled in the jumble of sensations coursing through her. She could scarcely believe Vaughan's tenderness to her, nor could she comprehend his generous offer regarding Stuart, given the grievous circumstances and her brother's brash behavior. Still, she sought some means to safeguard the most pertinent detail hidden in the message—assuming she was able to discern it—a way to reveal its contents to Vaughan's satisfaction, while concealing the crux of the missive. Rather like removing one's garments while desiring to remain hidden from view. Impossible. Unless one were in the dark.

Vaughan was far too cagey not to notice the wool being pulled over his eyes. But Claire wasn't a simpleton, herself. Stuart never had a colt named Balthazar. It was a signal between them that meant, somehow, she would get word to him.

Chapter Nine

Seated at her desk, Vaughan poised behind her, Claire studied the folded parchment by candlelight. Fresh grief at the loss of her father, and a sense of awe that she grasped the final communication from him, overcame her. She barely trusting her quavery voice. "'Tis stained."

"Very. Given the smudges on the outside, we can but hope the inside is legible. Are those Captain Monroe's initials?"

She fingered the red seal securing the missive. The letters J. M. impressed in the wax were still detectable. "Yes. John Monroe. From Papa's ring. Yet Stuart says it was written by a fellow officer. Dictating this letter must have been his last act." Her voice caught. "Done with his dying breath, and his ring used to seal it."

Vaughan clasped her shoulder. "Captain Monroe sounds an admirable officer, despite his siding against the king."

"The finest. And regarding his stance in this war, I admire him all the more for his courage."

"I should expect no less of you. That he dictated this message indicates there's at least one other who knows its meaning."

Bitterness edged her reply. "Unless that man has also fallen."

"I cannot pretend otherwise. Pray open the

message and satisfy my curiosity. Yours, too, I'll wager."

She couldn't argue a consuming inquisitiveness. Still, she hesitated to trespass on script akin to Holy Writ. The letter hadn't been meant for her eyes.

"You are the only one who can interpret this."

At Vaughan's gentle prodding, she broke the seal. Shaky with emotion, she spread the folded parchment open on the wooden surface where she'd composed many letters, the last one to the father who'd perished in this endless conflict.

She scanned the page. Although smudged, the text was discernible, and familiar. "As Stuart thought, this wasn't penned by our father. The writing isn't his hand. But the quote is very like him."

Battling to keep the tremor from her voice, like one fighting a strong current, she quietly read. "'Mine honour lives when his dishonour dies, Or my shamed life in his dishonour lies: Thou kill'st me in his life; giving him breath, The traitor lives, the true man's put to death.'"

Deeply pensive, she let the words sink in for a moment. "'Tis from Shakespeare's tragedy, *Richard II*. A favorite of Papa's."

"Yes. Act Five. The Duke of York is speaking."

She angled her head at Vaughan, considering him through the glistening sheen in her eyes. "Captain, you impress me."

A wry smile touched his lips. "That I am able to read, or remember Shakespeare?"

"I hadn't thought one so consumed by warfare had thought for gentler pursuits."

"I have many such thoughts, sweet lady." He bent

low, smoothing her tears with his fingers. Taking a clean handkerchief from his waistcoat pocket, he pressed it into her hand. "From Mrs. Jenner. I think you have the greater need."

"Thank you." Touched by his tenderness, she clutched the linen and returned her attention to the letter. Not trusting herself to speak, she whisper-read. "'Where the corbie flies and the fallen lie, there I am.'" Puzzled, she turned again to Vaughan. "'Tisn't a quote from any author or poet I know."

"Nor I."

"Papa must have contrived this himself." Her voice caught again. "Forgive me."

"Pray do not apologize. I realize this is terribly difficult for you."

She blotted her face and cleared her throat. "Have you any thoughts on the significance of *corbie*?"

His gaze was thoughtful. "It's the old Scottish word for raven."

"I recall that now. Ravens are an ill-omen, a harbinger of death."

"Not always. Apart from its dark associations, the bird is also known as a trickster. Which lore would most impress your father?"

"Both. Death is a key symbol in the Shakespeare quote, and Papa was most definitely a trickster."

"Also profound, it would seem."

"Yes." She reread the last line of the quote. "'The traitor lives, the true man's put to death.' How much nearer the mark could this be? Clearly, he speaks of Arnold."

Directing her blurry gaze at Vaughan, she targeted him with reproach. "How can you in any way support that vile man?"

"I don't on a personal level. Do you stand behind every Rebel act? Are you aware of the harsh treatment Patriots dealt to a Loyalist woman accused of spying?"

"No," and Claire sensed she'd rather not know.

"I will not offend your delicate sensibilities by relaying the sordid details. Suffice it to say, atrocities have occurred on both sides of this drawn out conflict."

"Surely, Crown forces are worse?"

He shrugged. "War is rarely conducted with civility. The harshness it inflicts vary with the people embroiled at any given time or place. Carolina Backcountry was hell for all—the gathering of the clans in all their fury."

"Tarleton enraged the Patriots by giving no quarter at the Battle of Waxhaws and butchering many of Colonel Buford's men. Were you present?"

"No. I was on a separate campaign but found reports of the affair distasteful. However, I must remind you, the Patriots gave no quarter at Kings Mountain. I shouldn't be alive today had I fought in that battle."

She stilled at the validity of his charge. Many Loyalists attempting to surrender were cut down or later hanged.

He continued. "There need be no British reprisals at all, if the authority of His Majesty King George is recognized and this rebellion at an end."

"'Twill never happen."

"Do not be so certain. The people weary of war. Are you not sick to death of it?"

"Unspeakably. And I do not approve every bloody act my fellow Patriots undertake, but I support the struggle for freedom."

"So you've emphatically stated, and been duly cautioned."

At his rebuke, she pursed her lips and dropped her gaze to the parchment, seemingly empty of further communication. But with cyphers one could never be sure. And a great deal of the paper remained empty.

Vaughan held out his hand. "Give me the letter. Warmth is needed to expose what's hidden from view."

Heaviness weighing her spirit, she surrendered the precious parchment to him. Fearful he might consume it in the flames, she watched him carefully pass the paper back and forth over the flickering candle in the brass stand on her desk. His actions made weird shadows on the wall. One line slowly appeared on the bottom of the page as the heat brought the sentence to light.

He peered at the script. "'Beside my brother now I rest.' Is your father buried next to his brother?"

"No. He has none."

"Are you quite certain?"

"Of his grave, or the lack of a brother? Of course. I was present at his burial and saw the casket lowered into the cold ground."

"What of Captain Monroe? Did you actually see his body?"

"No. But—" A horrific thought. She swiveled toward Vaughan. The handkerchief at her mouth muffled her gasp. "Dear God. You cannot seriously contemplate defiling his grave. I would never ever speak to you again."

His expression reflected the seriousness of the matter under discussion. "What do you suggest I do? For, by heaven, you know more than you say."

She did. And if it kept him from opening her

father's grave, she'd better confide her discovery. She lowered the cloth from her lips. "Look again at the letter."

"Where, exactly?"

"In the bottom right hand corner is a mottled spot, like a faded stain. But I think something else, words or symbols, are hid beneath this blot."

"Ah. I see now. What substance will reveal it?"

"That we have yet to discover." She debated whether or not to divulge any further details. Though eager to learn the message her father had bequeathed them, she didn't want to share this information with a Legion officer, no matter how devastatingly attractive and seemingly sympathetic.

"Perhaps vinegar or lemon juice might expose the hidden writing?" she suggested.

Vaughan wasn't so readily fooled and shook his head. "The former invisible ink was writ in that and already revealed. More of the same will not achieve results for the remainder of the missive."

As she well knew. "Grape juice, or some other compound, is wanted," she allowed. "Perhaps a journey to the cellar?"

"Wait." Holding up a hand, he glanced around her chamber.

"What do you seek in here?"

"I shall know when I find it."

She followed his gaze to the fireplace. The opening was small, but surrounded by black marble and Greek Key molding embellished with carvings of children at play with forest creatures. The fire burning in the hearth lent cheer to her chamber and dappled the green damask chair tucked before it.

His eyes swept past the figurines on the mantel to the high chest of drawers and chest on chest for her clothes standing against one cornflower blue wall. He skimmed over these furnishings to her bed. A glowing candle on the bedside stand illuminated the blue damask bed hangings. The rich cloth matched her curtains, closed against the night. Though sorely neglected now, she'd been indulged as a child and her chamber reflected familial devotion.

Not that spot either, it seemed. He looked away. His gaze came to rest on her dressing table.

"Let's try a drop of that intoxicating scent your father gave you."

Her jaw dropped. "Why would my perfume be effective?"

"Because, the more I ponder, the more I believe Captain Monroe intended you to play a part in this. That you, like your brother, were also to be introduced to the Patriarch. He never foresaw the madness that would overcome the man he trusted to guide his children."

Floored by the possibility, Claire sat motionless in her chair. Vaughan's assertion rang out like a clarion bell, one she didn't want to heed, but couldn't deny.

Parchment in hand, he walked to her dressing table situated near the tall chest of drawers. Sprigged porcelain boxes of powder and ointment, her silver-handled brush and comb, scarcely needed now, and a carved mahogany box with her few remaining pieces of jewelry were reflected in the mirror above the table.

He lifted the stopper of the delicate perfume bottle and lightly stroked the fragrant liquid over the bottom of the paper. Then returned to her and held it above the flame.

The sweetness of roses charged the air as a row of numbers gradually appeared. He whistled with satisfaction. "As I thought."

Claire was almost too flabbergasted to speak. "How on earth were we to know to use my perfume?"

"I suspect the reference was in that correspondence to your grandfather."

She ran her eyes over the numbers:

19/24/10/4/6
1/22/17/10/6/3
1/6/13/6/2/19/7
6/2/8/11/6/18
24/10/13/8/20

"Separated into groups of five, likely a sentence," Vaughan said. "And below this, a shorter line of two words. Perhaps a location." He traced a finger over the next set.

19/16/13/17/22/1
10/20/7/15/2/17

"What's this?" He tapped two final numbers in the lower right hand corner of the letter.

19. 21.

"Initials again, maybe. The answer lies here, unless it only furthers the mystery."

"I expect it will." Indeed, this was her hope.

He dipped his eyes to hers. "Quite possibly. For now, I leave you to rest and recover yourself. But the cypher remains in my care for safekeeping."

"Upon my word, I would not destroy it."

"I dare say you wouldn't, until you grasp the meaning. But will you share that with me?"

She met the question in his perceptive gaze. How

could she defend her seditious brother and family and yet guard this near sacred message from Vaughan when the bargain she'd struck required her compliance? Nor did she wish him to suffer from failure to produce what his superiors demanded. Especially when one of those senior officers was the infamous Tarleton.

Truly, she was in a bind. And, truth be told, she knew how to go about solving the cypher, though she needed time.

The expression in Vaughan's eyes told her he saw right through her. He slipped the parchment into his waistcoat pocket. "Consider carefully, Claire."

She rose shakily from the chair. "I am."

"Weigh everything." Cupping her face in his hands, he looked long into her eyes, then covered her lips in a soft, slow kiss.

She closed her arms around his neck and returned his seductive tenderness. Circling strong arms around her, he caught her to him, kissing her harder. The flame pulsing through her chest jolted her beyond anything she'd ever experienced, alarming in its intensity.

Her traitorous heart beating wildly, she broke away from him. "I can't—you shouldn't."

He seemed to be exerting a powerful effort not to reclaim her mouth. "Forgive me. I promised your brother not to take liberties." He slid his fingers over her cheek in a parting caress. "Sleep well. We will speak again in the morning."

Exactly what she feared. And then what? How could she possibly fulfill everyone's expectation of her?

Restful slumber would surely elude her tonight, unless she succumbed to the oblivion of the utterly exhausted, or took a potion. But what herbal concoction could mend her torn heart, or ease a mind as troubled as hers? It would take more than a spoonful or two of Ezekiel's sovereign remedy; if she downed the whole bottle she wouldn't awaken for days, possibly ever. And despite everything, she couldn't bear not to see Vaughan again.

His quiet tread and the click of the door behind her indicated he'd gone from her chamber. She sank into her favorite chair before the hearth to consider what was to be done, and pray Stuart didn't appear like an avenging spirit dispensing yet more recrimination. Lord grant her wisdom and courage. She sensed she'd need a powerful measure of both.

Chapter Ten

Sunrise brought Mrs. Jenner to Vaughan's chamber with a tray of provisions, clucking around him like the chickens scrabbling out in the yard beyond his window. She even overrode the boisterous cockerel crowing to greet the day. Only a pack of baying hounds could rival her in full flow.

An early riser, he'd dressed, but lingered in the armchair before the crackling hearth. The tangy wood smoke, pleasant scent of the soap he'd used to shave, and beeswax candles mingled with his thoughts as he pondered his fate and that of a certain young lady.

Although appreciative of quiet, he didn't really mind Mrs. Jenner's chatter. Her homey warmth lapped over him, a refreshing change from the salty language that normally peppered the start to his day in camp. The genial woman reminded him of an impoverished cousin of whom he was fond who acted as companion to his mother. And the dramatic embellishments Mrs. Jenner added to her mostly one-sided conversation were amusing, rather like watching a play.

"What an uproar." She raised both hands heavenward. "Thank the Lord that fearsome storm breaking in the night didn't take us with it."

He'd slept through the worst of the blow, but Mrs. Jenner was in her element and he didn't disrupt her.

Down came her arms. "I feared the house would

crash around our ears in a mighty roar, leaving us in a splintering heap."

Grabbing the poker, she vigorously stirred up the fire in the hearth, then waved it with dramatic flair. "A maple tree's lying on its side like a slain giant, big old root ball sticking up. We could all be dead. Smited in our beds when it toppled, but praise be the trunk didn't strike nothing or nobody. That bluster surely left a chill in its wake. Sometimes happens in the sheep rain."

"The what?" he interjected.

"Hard rain that comes in spring, 'bout the time sheep are sheared. 'Tis bone cold thereafter."

She set the poker aside and rubbed her fingers together before the blaze. "This fire feels right good."

"Indeed." After months spent out of doors, the warmth was doubly welcome. Although he preferred cool air to the sultry heat smothering him like a wet blanket last summer. A man could warm up with a good fire, but cooling down in an interminable Carolina summer was another matter.

"Jim's a hard worker." The youth who'd impressed Vaughan yesterday had arrived in the predawn light, wiry arms stacked with kindling, then made another trip with a bucket of fresh water for his morning ablutions.

"Aye. All Sally's children are good workers. Bless 'em. And the wee ones will learn." Mrs. Jenner rolled her eyes. "Though that Minnie's as scattered as a headless hen."

He smiled faintly at the apt comparison. The comforts Thornton Hall provided, once as second nature to him as his own name, were now prized. Particularly sleeping on the couch instead of the hard ground. McCray had slumbered on the bed made-up on the floor. The thought of sharing a real bed with Claire was a dizzying prospect Vaughan scarcely dared to contemplate, and distracting to the extreme. To think, this time yesterday, he hadn't even laid eyes on her—

"Look there." He glanced around at Mrs. Jenner's summons to see her staring out the window. "Lieutenant McCray's at the stables. Fine strapping man," she added under her breath.

Did she fancy the burly lieutenant?

She spun back toward Vaughan. "Oh, I nearly forgot to tell you, Percy's tolerable this morning. Not like he's got one foot in the grave. I left him sipping a little broth."

"Good. I'll look in on him." Then Vaughan asked about the woman who consumed his thoughts. "How fares Miss Monroe?"

Mrs. Jenner leveled knowing eyes at him. "Awake and brooding afore her hearth, same as you, sir."

For all her running on at the mouth, little escaped Mrs. Jenner's notice. Vaughan didn't deny her allegation or rebuke her. Sipping the sweetened herbal brew that passed for tea in the colonies these days, 'with a dollop of *good whiskey*', she'd assured him, and munching the cornbread smeared with molasses she'd brought, 'lest he grow faint afore breakfast', he brooded, as she'd termed it, before the toasty fire.

Everything had changed since he first charged into the cobbled yard on his mare. Nothing, not even dreams of his coveted promotion, diverted him from the woman who'd laid siege to his heart. If Rebels had laid a trap for him, they couldn't have devised a more effective snare than Claire Monroe. Like a sailor finding his bearings guided by the North Star, his mind was fixed on her, and that wouldn't change whether she deciphered the mysterious letter, or not. Doubtless, she wanted to honor the agreement they'd forged last evening, but was rent in half. This also weighed on him.

How he wished he could just let sleeping dogs lie, but they very well might awake and bite him if he let the cypher go. Truly, he was caught between duty and fast-growing ardor. A most uncomfortable situation to find himself in and he'd occupied some mighty disagreeable spots in his time, and no doubt would again in the days ahead. Possibly this very one.

Taking care to guard his voice from eavesdroppers, he posed a question. "Tell me, Mrs. Jenner, what is a man ensnared by a beautiful lady on the wrong side of this war to do?"

Despite her own candor, his frank query took her aback and she paused to deliberate—an unlikely judge in the case. If she'd donned a long wig and black robe, she couldn't have appeared more earnest. Passing a hand over her flushed forehead, she tucked in reddish curls escaping her cap and bent toward him.

"Well, sir. These are troublesome times, no mistake. And it might be foolish, but I always believe love finds a way."

"Not foolish, though it's a lofty and romantic sentiment. I agree, love may triumph, but only if both parties are willing to sacrifice."

She blew out her breath in a whistling sigh. "A truer word was never spoke. I couldn't say what lengths Miss Claire is willing to go, only that she fancies you, right enough. A heap more'n yer cousin. Not that I mean Mister Vaughan any disrespect."

Vaughan waved aside her apology. "I know what

he is, and will give you a piece of advice. Never trust Thomas Vaughan with anything of importance. And if Miss Monroe will heed you, advise her accordingly."

For once, Mrs. Jenner simply nodded.

Conferring with the housekeeper, or anyone else for that matter, wasn't Vaughan's usual means of gaining direction in matters of the heart, but if anyone knew Claire, apart from her irksome brother, it was Mrs. Jenner. From what he'd seen, Claire regarded her as she might a surrogate mother, which had forged a unique bond between the two women.

Unable to still her tongue for another second, Mrs. Jenner continued, though she observed caution by tickling his ear with her confidence. "Miss Claire is as fine a young lady as you'd ever care to meet and deserves a far better lot than she's been dealt here."

"Unquestionably. And I will champion her."

Agog at his revelation, the good woman paused before pressing him. "In what manner, sir?"

"As her guardian or intended, if she will allow me that privilege."

The pale blue eyes exploring him widened. "Would you, indeed? Upon my word. And you to be a lord." Fanning herself with her apron, she sank onto a stool near the hearth. "My, oh my." She gaped at him. "Our Claire would be a duchess?"

"Countess, actually, as the wife of an earl. Someday, God willing."

"Heavens above." An anxious glance at the chimney she feared might carry their conversation to listening ears halted her briefly. "What of the Monroe family?"

"As Lieutenant Monroe is unable to do his duty by

144

them, and seems hell-bent on getting himself killed or captured, I would take Master William in hand. But the Legion travels light and rides hard. If you can contain the unruly lad until autumn, I might take young William and Miss Monroe with me."

"Why then?"

"I've arrived at a decision to sail home before winter squalls make travel perilous."

If he'd declared his intent to venture to India, Mrs. Jenner couldn't have appeared more unprepared. Her mouth opening and closing like a fish, it took her a moment to recover herself. "Have ye, now?"

"Lord Vaughan desires I return as soon as I may honorably conclude my already extended service in America and assume my rightful place in the family. As to the Monroes, the mother who suffers with her nerves is better here under your tender care, as is the afflicted senior Monroe. However, I can provide some money for their support before I go."

She eyed him as if he were a saint. Not the usual regard he received from colonials. "'Twould be a blessing, sir."

"One that may not be welcome."

"Surely, Miss Claire wouldn't say no."

"She very well may. By accepting my aid, she risks incurring accusations of being in the pay of the Crown. An unpopular position with Patriot neighbors."

Tapping a finger to the side of her nose, Mrs. Jenner considered. "Then we say nothing to no one. Or tell 'em her father give her the money afore he died."

Vaughan dropped his voice even lower. "In these turbulent times, say whatever is wanted to protect yourselves. I will entrust the coins to you. Advise Miss

Monroe of their readiness whenever you deem suitable."

Mrs. Jenner goggled her eyes at him. "Me, sir?"

"Your late husband served me faithfully. I trust you to do the same. Use the money wisely for the family and keep it well hidden."

Dabbing at tears with the hem of her checked apron, she breathed out an assent. "Aye, sir. Upon my life. Mr. Jenner would be right proud of the honor ye do us. Bless ye, sir. How long will you tarry at Thornton Hall?"

"Not long. Now that Lieutenant Monroe has escaped—" Here he paused for the surprise he anticipated.

She arched reddish brows. "Has he, now?"

"Unless I am proven otherwise."

"Ah. I see." She gave a perceptive nod.

"Miss Monroe and I have business to attend to, and Percy needs several days to mend before we move him."

"Mayhap even longer than that. He's as weak as a kitten."

"If he cannot mount a horse, he must be transported in a wagon. I will not leave Percy behind. He may be returned to slavery."

Fierce pride in her eyes, Mrs. Jenner thrust out an ample bosom. "Not if he remains here. Miss Claire will assure his safety."

"But who can assure hers? This is a defenseless household headed by a deranged old man, Mrs. Jenner."

Her swelled chest deflated a little. "True enough."

"Has Miss Monroe any friends or family who might come to her aid?"

"Friends are few, given the state of Mister Monroe and us trying to keep his madness a secret. But a widowed aunt, Mrs. Peyton, Mrs. Monroe's sister, lives in Williamsburg. She might send her ward, Miss Smith. The young woman is plain in appearance, I'm told, and penniless, but has a cheerful disposition and can turn her hand to anything."

A nugget Vaughan tucked away. Miss Smith sounded just the sort of useful female to settle at Thornton indefinitely. "Excellent. Perhaps Mrs. Peyton might spare her most able ward to journey here and lend her assistance."

She raised one rounded shoulder and let it fall. "Mayhap."

"Meanwhile," he continued. "Miss Monroe relies on your sound head, my good woman. Conditions in the countryside will worsen before they improve. Alert your staff and take every precaution with the foodstuff. Conceal provisions from marauders, Rebel and Loyalist alike. I must warn you, a sizable British force will soon overrun Halifax. No one wants an army on their doorstep."

She clutched at his sleeve. "They'll pick us clean, like a pack of crows. Can you keep soldiers from the house?"

He patted her plump fingers. "I will do my utmost to preserve Thornton Hall."

"What of the livestock?"

"The animals, too, if it's in any way within my power. Meanwhile, take heed."

Her expression was grave. "So we shall. This very day."

"Before you attend to these pressing duties, if you

would provide me with paper. I spotted an inkwell and quill on the desk."

Her glum countenance brightened, and she nodded at the table in the corner. "There's sheets of paper in the drawer. You writing a letter?"

"To Lord Vaughan. Will you see it's posted?"

"Aye, sir. As soon as the ink's dry."

If Vaughan were serious about his desire to wed Claire, and he fervently was, he must alert his curmudgeonly father. If fortune didn't smile on him and he fell in battle before he returned with her to England, assuming she'd consent to a betrothal—better still, a wedding—he wanted his father to provide for her. Given Lord Vaughan's declining health, those instructions had best be in writing, and the sooner, the better. Whether or not the earl approved of Vaughan's union with an untitled, not particularly wealthy, American mattered not a jot. He was eager to have his son come home and beget heirs. He'd come on his own terms and Claire was one of them.

He signaled Mrs. Jenner. "One more thing. Pray give Miss Monroe word to dress for an outing."

"At once, Captain. You can rely on me."

"I have every confidence."

"Thank ye, sir. I best be off. So much to see to." Aflutter from all these tidings, she rose, bobbed a curtsy, and flew from the room like a fluffed up hen.

How events would unfold and affairs play out, Vaughan had no idea, but Mrs. Jenner was a solid ally and in possession of the knowledge he wished her to be. What to do about the treasonous letter in his possession left him in a quandary. Claire could decipher it if she chose. The expression in her face after the numbers were revealed had given her away.

If he allowed her access to the cypher, would she reveal her findings? He'd readily detect any lies she attempted, but could hardly coerce the truth from the woman he was tumbling in love with. And he'd hit the ground hard if she betrayed him. Any threats he'd thought to hold over her also paled.

Tarleton would be none too pleased if Vaughan failed to produce either the spy or the deciphered letter. He'd hoped to cover himself in glory before retiring from his regiment and return home a hero, not with a dark cloud of disgrace hanging over his head.

This bloody war. What a harsh taskmaster. Granted, the embittered conflict had brought him to Claire and for that he was thankful, but it could just as easily tear them apart.

Like a potion working its magic, her allure had seeped through his very marrow. How much would she care if, after he left, they never laid eyes on each other again?

Everything hinged on Claire's regard for him. Without the will to fight for a future together, the battle was already lost.

****

"You want to wed me?" Claire's cloak, the shade of summer leaves, shielded her from the cool breeze and a bonnet of the same hue enhanced those lovely, now reproachful, eyes.

Good old Mrs. Jenner. She'd distracted Claire from obsessing over the cypher and provoked her into contemplating a betrothal. She was completely caught off guard and that suited Vaughan's strategy.

"Walk with me. I will explain."

Stiff with reproof, she gave a short nod. "Very well."

Taking her by the arm, he ushered her across the yard, skirting the great stone. Overhead, new green leaves rippled in the stiff breeze. The uprooted maple, whose fall Mrs. Jenner had proclaimed, lay at the backside of the massive rock where it toppled from the small copse of trees.

Apart from the felled giant, fragrant peonies blushed pink in the sunlight, and purple lilacs nodded in the wind. A pleasing prospect, but he and Claire were readily visible from the second story and attic windows. And he had that skin crawling sensation of being observed.

Behind the house, the weave of green, rose, and silvery hues in the kitchen garden held promise. The sharp mint of pennyroyal charged the air as they trod on the tiny ground plant where it crept over the path. Chamomile lent a pleasant apple scent. The whiskery faces of blue and yellow violas spangled the muted herb border, but he had to get Claire farther away from her spying brother.

Ahead of them, the split rail fence outlined a wide swathe of meadow. Grazing cattle lifted their heads and idly considered the approaching couple as they rhythmically worked their jaws. Picking his way between cow pies with Claire wasn't what he'd envisioned doing together. Not that he had a great many options out of doors on this brisk May morning. A pity the grounds didn't have a sheltering maze of clipped boxwood where he and she might lose themselves for happy hours as they could at Hartford House in Devon.

"There." Beside the fence grew an ancient, many

branched, mulberry tree that must suffice.

Vaughan ducked with her behind the gnarled trunk, beyond listening ears and shielded from views angled out the second story windows or the attic. Even if Stuart had a spyglass, which Vaughan wouldn't doubt, the fellow couldn't possibly survey them back here, and must be pacing like a caged cat.

Claire appeared similarly perturbed. Once in their nook, he bent nearer to assure her. "I intended to consult you myself, as soon as possible."

She drew herself up, her chin level with his shoulder. "I should hope so, sir, if you are, indeed, proposing marriage."

"Indeed I am, Miss. Now you have two Vaughan's to choose between."

"Mrs. Jenner is strongly in your favor."

He'd rather assumed she would be. "What of you?"

Her mouth opened in dissent. "How can I love a man whom my family, apart from Mrs. Jenner, will scorn, and who is opposed to the cause we hold sacred?"

Clasping her shoulders, he looked down into Claire's upturned face. Pain and yearning mingled in her accusing gaze. "I expect you already do."

She blinked furiously. "I thought you wished to discuss the letter, not our possible engagement."

"So, now it's *possible*? A moment ago you declared a betrothal between us unthinkable."

"It is—completely out of the question."

The hitch in her voice gave him hope. "I will not press you for an answer now. You have a day or two before I leave."

A wince crossed her face. "Leave?"

"Did you think I could remain here, indefinitely?"

"Of course not. I never meant anything of the sort. What utter nonsense." Tears, like dewdrops, sparkled in her eyes.

"Utter," he echoed gruffly.

"Where will you go?"

"Virginia."

"I have an aunt in Williamsburg."

"Perhaps, you might undertake a visit to her? Our paths might cross."

For a moment she seemed to consider, then waved her hands as if to ward off such a disloyal suggestion. "You are a dragoon captain."

"I fear the uniform betrays me," he quipped.

A faint smile hovered at her quivering mouth, then she glanced down. "How could I introduce you to my aunt, a staunch Patriot?"

"You might mention that I will not always be in uniform."

Jerking up her head, she countered. "You will still be British."

"Is that so very objectionable?"

"Yes."

"Your *Mother* country?" he stressed. "Will you heap contempt on everything English?"

Doubt crossed her eyes. "No. But my family—"

"What of you?" he broke in.

She looked away once more. "They will feel betrayed."

"Are you saying you have no real objection to me, apart from the opinion of others?"

Again, she raised her head, confusion and protest in her face. "No—I—well, not as much. But the cause.

Papa. Stuart. My poor deranged grandfather. So many have fought for years."

"And doubtless will battle on without you, and when my term is done, without me. Enough, Claire. Say it's enough."

She stilled at his intimate use of her name.

"Say we might have a chance to make a new life together in England," he softly pleaded.

Wistfulness tinged her glittering gaze. "Not here?"

"My birthright does not lie in America."

"Mine does."

"Thornton Hall belongs to your elder brother. If he claims it. You are free to make your own choice."

"Free?" The word tore from her. "I feel anything but."

The despair in her face was piteous. "You have more cares on your slender shoulders than the slaves. At least Sally and her family anticipate freedom upon your grandfather's death. Is there to be no release for you, ever?"

"No." She stabbed a finger at the house. "I am a prisoner in there. Stuart comes and goes as he pleases. But not me—" Her voice cracked and she broke down.

Vaughan circled his arms around Claire and enfolded her. Clouds scudded in the blue sky and the breeze tossed her cloak as she shuddered against him. He suspected this release was a long time coming and would not soon depart.

After some minutes had passed—he didn't know how many, lost as he was in this closeness with Claire—her shaking eased and sobs slowed to sniffles. "You have my handkerchief," he reminded her.

A muffled "Oh" and she fished in her cloak,

pulling out the linen square.

"Here." He took the cloth, gently mopped her face, and cupped her chilled cheeks in his hands. "Can you love the man, apart from his uniform?"

She gazed at him through reddened eyes. "'Tis difficult to see beyond it."

"In the not too distant future, Lord willing, I will wear a gentleman's coat, not an officer's. And it shan't be scarlet."

A pensive expression displaced the hurt in her gaze. "What color do you fancy?"

Envisioning Claire at his side comparing bolts of cloth and a tailor busy at his measurements, Vaughan answered half in earnest, half in jest. "Blue or golden brown. Perhaps a deep velvety charcoal."

She considered. "Becoming hues. And what shall you do in this new attire?"

"Ride over my estate and count sheep."

A smile tugged at the corners of her mouth. "Truly?"

"Or cows. I have no notion yet the responsibilities of the lord of the manor. I have been in uniform since I was eighteen. My elder brother, Edward, was to assume the mantle."

"Why is he not?"

The usual blackness came over Vaughan, and he dropped his hands from her face. "A riding accident."

"How tragic."

"Yes." He well remembered the scrawled letter from his oldest sister, the ink blotted with tears. In those few jottings, he lost a much admired sibling and his future changed.

"Is this why your mother takes laudanum?"

"Mama had already begun, but her habit worsened, as did my father's disposition, evidenced by his letters."

"I see."

"Not entirely."

"Tell me."

Feigning nonchalance, he embarked on the tale he'd kept from all. "The willful son sent to America to mend his wicked ways was never meant to be the future lord. I was to pursue an illustrious career in the law. I squandered that opportunity so was packed off to war. Then my noble brother fell. A trio of devoted sisters will not serve the purpose, even if they marry well. And the eldest, Mary, is betrothed to a duke. But a son is needed to carry on the Vaughan name and lineage. Our mother is beyond childbearing and our father's health declines. Lord Vaughan writes to say he requires my presence at home."

She jerked up her head. "But your duties?"

"I will honorably discharge them and have requested leave by autumn, which Cornwallis has granted. He and my father are fellow peers. I've already put Lord Vaughan off for a year and cannot delay my departure much longer. Still, many skirmishes may lie between here and my sailing from these shores."

Her eyes dimmed. "A long summer filled with potential battles."

"I think my father would have preferred it was me who died. He may yet get his wish."

With a vehement shake of her head, she chided him. "Do not speak so."

Rancor edged Vaughan's heart. "What is one more fallen dragoon to you?"

She stopped him with a hand on his arm. "This

particular one is fast-gaining my affection."

For a timeless moment he looked into her eyes. Then traced a finger over her cheek. "Is he, indeed?"

A nod accompanied the faint blush coloring her face.

He scarcely dared to exhale for fear she'd turn and hightail away like a bounding deer. Badly wanting to kiss her again, he eyed her beguiling lips. That dratted brother of hers couldn't see them here—

"You still haven't mentioned the letter, sir."

Her abrupt query intruded. For a blissful second, he'd forgotten that blasted missive. Was she testing him?

"No. I've not said a word. Yet you have. Twice now."

The flush in her cheeks heightened. "I must know. What are your intentions regarding the cypher?"

"Either both must be in possession of its meaning, or none. And it will remain forever guarded."

"You will not force me to decipher it?"

"No. Those are my terms."

"What will happen to Stuart?"

"Nothing. If he has the sense to keep out of sight."

A sigh of relief escaped her, then fresh alarm flitted across her gaze. "What of you, if I refuse?"

"Good of you to spare me a thought."

"I do. What will follow?"

"I will not be promoted for my failure to produce either the spy or the translated message, nor do I anticipate Tarleton's displeasure with any joy."

She grimaced at his mention of the infamous officer. "How will you approach him?"

"With care. I will attempt to assuage his anger and

pray my excuses are accepted."

"Or?" she asked.

Vaughan was grim. "He may send another in my stead. Captain Simmons would be the worst. The bullying lout."

All color drained from her face. "Dear Lord."

"Yes. In this event, petitioning the Almighty is advisable."

Chapter Eleven

"Found his horse hidden behind a false wall, Captain."

Oh no. Claire stopped in the yard beside Vaughan and swiveled toward the stable to see Lieutenant McCray lead a familiar mount from the stone and timber building. Shod hooves clip clopped on the cobbles as the well-trained gelding walked behind the dragoon.

Her heart sank. She supposed they couldn't hope to keep Bryan concealed for much longer. It was only supposed to be a matter of minutes, hours at most, that he remained secreted. Stuart had never intended to delay this long.

What would Vaughan do?

Lifting her face to his, she observed him intently. They were just on route to the parlor to discreetly examine that vexing letter and she already on the verge of another emotional collapse. Now this.

He spoke in measured tones. "That's Monroe's bay, right enough. Admirable beast. See he's well-tended, Lieutenant."

"Oh, he has been and no mistake. Fed, watered, rubbed down." McCray thumbed a thick finger at the house. "Someone's helping cover for the fellow, or he snuck out here himself and tended the gelding."

"I wouldn't put it past him. Either Monroe's legged

it away or he's still nearby."

"Doubt he'd go on foot and leave such a good horse behind," Lieutenant McCray pointed out.

"Perhaps a fresh search of the grounds. He might be hidden under our noses," Vaughan suggested.

"Not sure we gave the house a thorough going over, Captain."

"See to it, then. I have other matters to tend to."

A smirk played at the lieutenant's mouth. "You and Miss Monroe?"

The narrow glance Vaughan shot him stifled the hint of insolence. "Yes. Important business. I do not wish to be disturbed—"

Cries of outrage broke into Vaughan's reprimand and William tore from the stable. Head down, he ran at the beefy lieutenant. "Leave Bryan be!"

Puny fists flying, Claire's firebrand of a brother lit into the dragoon, beating his thighs and whatever else he could reach. The big man tried to shake him off as he might an enraged terrier attached at the ankle.

"Git off, ye little hellion!"

"William! No!" Jerking up her skirts, she dashed to the boy.

Vaughan was there before her. He wrapped his arms around the skinny youth, effectively restraining the kicking fury, and hauled him back. "Stop this at once. No one will injure the horse, lad."

Red-faced, teary, William reared his curly head around at the captain. "But he's Stuart's!"

"Plainly."

Before Claire could think what to say or do under the incriminating circumstances, Ensign Anderson pounded from the stable. The young Loyalist arrived bare-headed, his dark hair dripping. He must've been sluicing himself in a bucket of water when William took off. His uniform awry, he'd hastily pulled on the green jacket of Tarleton's Legion. Vaughan and McCray wore the red coats of the distinguished Seventeenth Light Dragoons, but they all served under *Bloody Ban.*

As if she needed reminding.

"Sorry, Captain—Lieutenant—" Anderson panted. "The boy got away from me."

"Keep closer watch, or Master William is going back in his chamber." Vaughan fixed her brother with a stern eye. "And I'm locking the door, lad. Do you hear me?"

A sullen nod was the nearest he'd get to cooperation from William. "What will you do with Bryan?" the boy asked.

"Make a present of him to your sister. What do you think?"

Claire was speechless.

William eyed the captain with newfound appreciation. "Claire would like that."

"Yes. I believe she would."

The junior officers exchanged glances, but Vaughan ignored them. He released his hold on William. "Put the horse in a loose box, McCray. Anderson, take the boy and see if Cook has any tidbits. You could both do with feeding up."

Clearly, this suited the Ensign, and William brightened. Anderson didn't look any older than nineteen, if that much, and the gangly officer was all arms and legs. He and William headed toward the kitchen at a brisk clip.

Lieutenant McCray grunted his assent. "Believe I'll have a look around."

"Do that and leave me in peace unless you find the elusive Monroe or something momentous occurs," Vaughan directed. "And take heart, Lieutenant. Be glad you're here seeking a spy and not camped out cheek by jowl with a quarrelsome company of soldiers. Makes a welcome change."

"Aye. Might stop by the kitchen for a bite myself. Feeling a bit peckish," McCray said gruffly.

A nod from Vaughan, and McCray turned toward the stable with Bryan.

Vaughan reclaimed Claire's arm. "That many men together reek worse than a badger's armpit."

"I can well imagine," she managed shakily, even smiling a little at his comparison.

"It's all right. Crisis averted," he soothed, under his breath.

"On this occasion." She trusted Stuart to keep out of sight, and Lieutenant McCray didn't appear eager for extra work. Nor did she know how much he'd press for action if Vaughan gave no encouragement. The two seemed to have an inherent understanding between them, and words were not always needed.

"One calamity at a time, sweet lady." Vaughan escorted her across the cobbles and up the brick steps.

And now, for the letter. She couldn't stall any longer. If only she dared allow herself the pleasure of just being in the company of this amazing man. All too soon, he'd be gone.

****

Fortified with swigs of ale, Vaughan sat on the couch beside Claire, keeping one eye on his fair companion and the other on the door concealed in the wall. He'd given Stuart Monroe every chance. If the willful officer made another rash appearance, he was arresting the rapscallion and the consequences be damned, confound him. Vaughan had already strained every ounce of patience he possessed, not to mention broken orders and risked court-martial by ignoring the spy's furtive presence in the house. All for Claire.

Was she worth it?

Utterly. He ran his gaze across her contemplative face as she studied the letter in her hand. Downcast lashes swept over intelligent eyes, the hue of water lilies, and cast shadows against a cheek as soft as a kitten's paw. Tiny furrows lined her smooth brow and she absently twirled a light brown tendril in one finger, a tendency he found endearing.

Letting his gaze wander lower, he followed the green jacket laced up over her alluringly curved, floral bodice. She tapped a toe, drawing his attention to nut-brown shoes with brass buckles peeking out beneath her chestnut skirts, and, as she shifted impatiently, a well-shaped ankle.

This exquisite woman mesmerized him. Visions of her seated by his side, better still, lying beside him in bed at Hartford House, flitted enticingly through his mind. Beset by distractions, he had difficulty keeping his focus on the paper. Like turning the key in an intriguing door and entering a new room, his all-consuming passion had gone from 'catch the spy, decipher the letter, and gain a promotion' to wanting Claire. And only her.

Attend! he ordered himself. He was as bad as a green boy and needed a punch to the jaw. He pictured the line of men who would gladly oblige him. Duty mustn't be abandoned because something, or someone, had besotted his every sense.

But Lord help him, Claire had.

She lifted her eyes to his, reluctance in their depths. "This will require some labor to work out."

"I thought it might. What are your initial impressions? *Truthfully*, mind."

"As you insist." She pointed at the numbers in the first set. "When Papa and I used to play our word games he said nineteen always stood for the letter T. That was a constant. Though how he arranged the other letters varied."

"Such as?" Vaughan prompted.

"In one of his favorite sequences, he reversed the alphabet so that two stood for A, rather than B, and it followed in that order."

"So, if he used that arrangement now, C would be four?"

"Yes. In this collection of numbers there are two T's." Dipping the quill into the inkpot on the stand beside the couch, she wrote a T beneath each nineteen.

Vaughan pondered the seemingly random arrangement. "Proceed with the order you suspect Captain Monroe used."

Slowly, heaviness in her every move, she inked in letters beneath the first sequence of numbers until 'Twice' appeared. An actual word. She was on the right path.

Bringing his hands together, he applauded. "Bravo, clever girl. You found the way."

A hint of triumph lit her eyes, followed by uncertainty.

"Is not your interest piqued? You must admit to curiosity as to the remainder of the message," he coaxed.

"I did always love to solve Papa's riddles."

"This is your final opportunity."

"But in doing so, I am betraying him."

"Perhaps not. By applying your wits to cooperate with me, and consequently Tarleton, you are protecting your family from retribution. Surely, a cause also dear to your father's heart. And who can say what will ultimately come of this discovery?"

Light and shadows passed over her eyes, like ferny pools beneath wind driven clouds. "I hadn't thought of it that way."

"Do," he urged.

With a new purpose, she bent to her work. He was equally entranced watching her lips move as she silently sounded out the letters, as he was in observing her progression. Given her divulgement of the method used, he could have figured the code out himself, but wouldn't deprive either of them of this rapt experience for all the world.

A fly buzzed in the window, kindling settled in the hearth, shooting up orange sparks, and the clatter of people working in various parts of the house resonated in the background while she labored at her task. Fortunately, the more unstable members of the family were unusually silent. Mrs. Jenner must have seen to their medicines, or they'd escaped and made for the hills. He hoped not.

Claire seemed to have no such concern and was engrossed in the letter. Gradually, she inked more words beneath the numbers until the phrase took shape.

'Twice buried beneath eagle's wings.'

"It makes no sense." She seemed oddly disappointed for one so bent on concealing the meaning of this cypher.

"Not in itself. More yet remains," he encouraged.

With a nod, she returned to her task and arrived at the disjointed scramble: 'TONRUB ISHPAR.'

"Gibberish," she concluded. At least, aloud.

Wondering if she truly didn't see what he did, Vaughan pointed. "Look closely. It's a word scramble."

"So it is. Bruton Parish, the church in Williamsburg," she said, projecting her voice a bit more than necessary.

"If you're trying to alert your brother, you are likely to cause him more harm than help." Vaughan nodded at the remaining numbers. "Nor is the puzzle yet solved."

"True." The letters T. V. took form, set apart by periods. "What on earth?" She eyed Vaughan questioningly.

"Whom do you know with these initials?"

She covered her mouth, releasing her lips to argue. "It couldn't be Thomas Vaughan. Could it?"

"Who else?"

Her eyes grew enormous, and conjecture tumbled from her. "Was Grandfather to deliver the message to him? It only stands to reason he was supposed to entrust this to someone."

"No," he said flatly.

"But an old man couldn't see to it that Arnold was betrayed. Perhaps Thomas was meant to know of the hidden bounty. He might be the very man Papa intended to carry word and see the mission through to the end."

"Do not hasten to conclusions."

It seemed far more likely to Vaughan the initials were intended as a warning that Thomas Vaughan was the British informant who'd given away this letter in the first place. If not for his conniving cousin, he wouldn't have known about the proposed rendezvous at *Person's Ordinary*. But he couldn't confide this information to Claire without betraying a valuable resource. Though it goaded him beyond bearing to have her think that snake in the grass was a hero chosen by her adored father.

He spoke sternly. "Hear me well. We are *not* entrusting this missive to Thomas Vaughan. Or anything else. He's not deserving of confidence."

The grit in Vaughan's voice and sting in his eyes stopped Claire in her headlong rush. She drew up, as if reining in a runaway horse. "Your opinion of your cousin is exceedingly low, sir."

"So might yours be, Miss, were you privy to my knowledge, but I am not at liberty to share it."

"Just because he's a Patriot—"

She startled as Vaughan gripped her by the shoulders. "He's no Patriot."

"What are you saying?"

He clamped his lips together, then parted them. "Only that."

"Why do you resent him so? It goes beyond politics."

"Well beyond, though that is reason enough. But bear this in mind. If I fall before returning to England, who stands to inherit upon my father's death?"

Realization seized her. "Dear God."

Lowering his hands, he folded them across his chest. "Exactly. After me, Lord Vaughan's closest living male relative is his nephew, Thomas Vaughan."

She swallowed hard. "Does Thomas wish you ill?"

"He doesn't wish me well, I assure you, and is eaten up with jealously over his lot in comparison to mine."

"Why is he here and not in England?"

"A falling out occurred between both our fathers over a woman. About which I shall say no more."

"Then I'll not pry. But if Thomas isn't a Patriot, as you hinted, then he must be a Loyalist. And the initials in the letter, a warning."

"I cannot speak to the inclusion of his initials. Only this. Whatever his position, Thomas Vaughan is out for his own gain. And beware, he is not an enemy you wish to make."

"But he appears so amiable."

"Until crossed. Do not speak of this exchange between us or there will be the devil to pay on more than one front."

At his somber warning, she gave a nod, while trying to envision the affable gentleman she knew as a potential threat. If this were true, and not simply bitterness between two rivals over such a vast inheritance, then Thomas wore quite a mask. One she'd never peeked behind.

Vaughan raked fingers through blond hair, partly loosened from his queue. "You must pardon me. I never intended to divulge this much to you. But how could I know Thomas had so entwined himself with your family, so wormed his way into your affections?"

"He has not succeeded so well as you fear."

The ghost of a smile, and Vaughan gave a nod. "That's a mercy." He groaned under his breath. "We still have not deciphered this message to my satisfaction."

"No. We haven't," she agreed, more shaken than she cared to admit.

With apparent effort at control, he opened and closed his fists. "What, exactly, does it impart?"

"Shall I read all, slowly, aloud?"

Clearly vexed with himself, as well as his cousin, he gave an impatient wave. "Only the last part, and we shall carefully consider."

She firmed the tremor in her voice and repeated the final line from the Shakespeare quote. "'The traitor lives, the true man's put to death.' And then it goes on. 'Where the corbie flies and the fallen lie, there I am. Twice hidden beneath eagle's wings.'"

"Everything points to death. What of the eagle's wings?" he asked, as if musing aloud.

An idea occurred, but she remained silent, startling as he drove a finger onto the parchment.

With a keen light in his eyes, he raised both hands in victory. "An eagle perches atop the Monroe family crest. I saw it etched into Mister Monroe's sword hilt."

"Yes. It is," she conceded.

"You are a most reluctant assistant, Miss. But I have what I need now."

"What, pray, is that, sir?"

"Your father is buried twice."

"But that's not possible."

"No. We must assume one of the graves contains a stash of goods rather than a body."

She sucked in her breath. "Bruton Parish."

"Where else? And such an ingenious location. Arnold is skulking around Eastern Virginia even as we speak."

"So close." There must be a Loyalist who might betray him for the wealth hidden in the casket. Was that man, perhaps, Thomas Vaughan? Was this the reason his initials were included in the cypher, because he could be bought?

Vaughan gave her a sharp look. "Whatever you're contemplating, do not act rashly."

But she must do something. And she wondered, how much had Stuart overheard?

"Claire, I cannot tell you what my cousin is, only that he is not to be trusted. What more caution do you need?"

"Warning directly from my father wouldn't come amiss."

A hard line tightened Vaughan's sensuous lips. Then he parted them. "You just received one, if you will heed it." The letter in his hand, he rose abruptly.

She scrambled to her feet. "Where will you go?"

"I must report to Tarleton. Likely, to be found at *Person's Ordinary*. He enjoys a good tavern."

"May I go with you?"

He turned disbelieving eyes on her. "You wish to accompany me into the lion's den?"

"I wish not to be left behind."

Admiration glinted back at her. "Well then, my bold Miss, have you a carriage we might take, or shall we ride?"

"Ride."

He smiled slightly. "On Balthazar?"

"Balthazar no longer lives." She barely kept the

stammer from her voice.

"According to Mrs. Jenner he never did."

That's what Claire got for having such a chatty housekeeper. "If he did, I might ride him to Williamsburg."

"I trust you would go by coach. And if Lieutenant Monroe thinks to ride to Williamsburg, he will find himself in a swell of British soldiers. Highly inadvisable."

She could make no argument.

If anyone were to go after Arnold and claim the reward it must be Thomas. And soon. Being a civilian, he could blend in. But could she trust him? Vaughan had given her sound reason to pause. Perhaps her father, as well. If only she could be sure what those initials in the cypher meant.

A firm hand on her shoulder broke into her scheming. "Claire."

At Vaughan's low summons, she glanced up into those dizzying blue eyes. "Have you visited the cemetery at Bruton Parish?"

"Once or twice as a child. It's rather a blur. Why?"

"Unless your father's name is engraved on a headstone, there may be more than one with the symbol of an eagle."

"Not newly dug."

"Sadly, in wartime, there are many fresh graves."

"I suppose so. I hadn't thought."

"No. You've been spared from the worst of it. And another thing, the letter refers to him being buried at his brother's side."

"So it did. But he doesn't have one."

"A fallen comrade, perhaps. Do you not see that

finding the exact grave may not be as simple as you think?"

She sighed. "Nothing and no one is as simple as I might think. Certainly not you, sir."

He dropped his voice so low she could scarcely hear. "Might you call me Vaughan, when we're alone?"

Whispering his name filled her with sweet warmth, heightened by his seductive smile. Then—and she couldn't think why with the possibility of Stuart looking on—except that she badly wanted to, she arched up on her toes and pressed her lips to Vaughan's cool mouth. His lips heated as he caught her to him and kissed her back long and hard. She circled her arms around his neck, as she'd been tempted to do before, and clung to him in turn.

Desire pulsed in her, and flashed back at her tenfold from him. As fire from a hearth when kindling is added to the flames. They may only have known each other for short time, but it made no difference. The attraction between them was instantaneous and growing like flames in a high wind, both thrilling and terrifying in its intensity. But Claire didn't pull back. She should, heaven knows. She was behaving shamelessly.

Likely Stuart would burst through the wall to tear them apart. Even so, she couldn't resist the strong arms enfolding her, the exhilarating crush of Vaughan's heated lips, his well-muscled chest. He circled with her in the room, never releasing her mouth, holding her so closely they were locked together except for the layers of clothing between them, and stopped before the door hidden in the wall, blocking it. Stuart couldn't get in if he tried.

Clever. She almost giggled.

Her heart pounded so hard, Vaughan must feel the drumming, hear it over their panted breathes. If he carried her up to her chamber right now, she'd not protest. Surely, the madness in this house had caught hold of her, like a contagious fever. His unique scent, mingled with the soap, made her heady and drew her like a fox on the prowl. Or maybe he was the fox. More apt. No matter. She'd never tire of this man and wanted only more.

Then he slid his lips to her ear. "Are you ready to go for a ride?"

Heavens above. The double meaning in his hushed query made her gasp.

He laughed softly, tickling her ear. "That, too, but I was referring to our horses."

Claire was too breathless to have the last word, to speak at all. Winded, she leaned against him as they walked from the parlor to face Lord only knows what.

Chapter Twelve

Stamping hooves, tossing manes, low nickers, high-pitched whinnies, and the earthy aroma of horses filled the stable and spilled out into the yard at *Person's Ordinary*. Dragoons normally tended the mounts themselves, as did Vaughan, but harried grooms rushed between their charges with added feed and water. Staying at a tavern with sleeping accommodations wasn't the dragoons usual lodging. This was a rare respite from the day-to-day slog of camp. And not all could stay the night, only the afternoon and evening, before reporting back.

Vaughan glanced around the tree-lined yard. At the rear of the property, a leafy grove spread into the countryside. Branches bent and green boughs tossed in the wind. Trunks splintered from last night's storm slumped drunkenly among their fellows. Shingles torn from the slanted eves of the two story reddish-brown structure littered the ground. Cleanup and repairs were in order, but the building had weathered the storm. The lingering bluster would soon die down.

Smoke curled from the prominent stone chimney in the main building and the hearth in the log and stone kitchen behind it. The tang of hickory scented the air, the best wood for flavorful cooking. Male voices carried from inside the sturdy walls and resounded above the breeze. The establishment bustled with activity. Likely the owner, his family, and help were busier than they'd ever been in their lives, rushing back and forth with food and drink.

Swinging a leg over the saddle, Vaughan sprang to the ground. La Belle waited calmly while he turned and reached up for Claire. "Let's have you down."

Uncertainty was written in every taut line of her face. Her cheeks were flushed and she was wonderfully blowsy from cantering much of the way, but the sparkle had gone from her eyes. The bold demeanor he'd witnessed in her on the ride, and the unbelievably rousing kiss she'd thrilled him with earlier at Thornton Hall, belonged to the unabashed woman who'd faded when they trotted into the yard.

The wary look she cast over the premises reminded him of one anticipating an ambush, a foreboding he knew all too well, as though he forever marched to the beat of drums announcing an impending battle.

Did she sense something he didn't? "What troubles you?"

"I've never seen the Ordinary so congested. Not that I've been here often, and never unescorted."

"It's not a terribly large tavern. All this upheaval further dwarves it. Nor are you unattended, Miss. I shan't allow you out of my sight."

Savoring the slide of feminine softness into his arms, he helped Claire dismount, and held her a moment longer than needed before standing her on the rain-slicked cobbles. Petticoats whipping around her ankles, she sidled from foot to foot like one of the unsettled mounts. How difficult it must have been for her to accompany him here in the first place. She had a vibrant spirit, but hesitation stifled her daring.

Possibly for the best. A little caution never came amiss. Winding the reins of both horses in his hand, he made efforts to reassure her. "You'll be quite safe in my care," he said, not entirely certain she would be otherwise.

Some of the Legion were less than chivalrous, to put it mildly. Not any of his disciplined regiment, of course. But others in the ranks. Loyalists on a vendetta were the worst offenders. And Tarleton did little to check the men, unless they crossed him. Whether the colonials realized it or not, this revolt against the king had become a vicious civil war with brother pitted against brother and neighbor against neighbor.

Frantic clucking disrupted Vaughan's thoughts. Two bronze hens flapped past, squawking, feathers flying. A skinny mulatto boy rounded the corner of the tavern and pelted after the escapees. Behind him, a buxom Negro woman in striped aprons grasping a hatchet covered ground with surprising speed.

Fortunately, neither Vaughan nor Claire's mounts were spooked by the commotion. He smiled. "Appears chicken is on the menu."

"If those two catch the runaways. The hens have a head start."

"They may have to chase the birds into town. I'll see to the horses."

"Lad!" He beckoned to a stable boy who responded promptly to the summons. "Relocate two of the mounts out front and tether ours in their place. See they are watered and rubbed down. Take this for your trouble." He tossed the youth a shilling.

Clutching the coin, he grinned his willingness to oblige and scurried off to tether two horses among the trees, then raced back to take the reins from Vaughan. Off he went to the hitching posts with La Belle and Bryan.

In answer to the bewilderment in Claire's expression, Vaughan offered his father's adage. "Always turn the horses for home."

"Even here? Isn't the Ordinary filled with dragoons—yours?"

"Mostly. And I'm not anticipating trouble, but it's best to be prepared for a hasty departure anywhere. Your brother was. That's how he beat us back to Thornton Hall. That and the secret entrance." Vaughan rubbed his chin. "Where, exactly, does the outside opening to the tunnel lie?"

Misgiving shadowed her eyes beneath the brim of her green bonnet.

"In the event I need to know. I will not share this confidence with anyone. I swear it."

She spoke so softly, he strained to hear. "By the great stone."

"And?"

"It leads through a door hidden in the cellar wall."

"Ah. Is there a furtive route to the house other than the road we took?"

"A narrow path cuts off from the main road and leads through the trees in behind Thornton. You have to jump the fences at either end of our meadow, but it shaves precious minutes off the route. When we were younger, Stuart and I sometimes went this way for sport. But Grandpa insisted we only go by that path in an emergency."

"Wise. A route too often traveled is a dead giveaway. We have something similar in place at

Hartford House. Only there, you must leap stone walls."

"Both our ancestors must have been quite fearful of attack. Or mad."

"I prefer to describe them as diligent. Possibly mad, too." He peeled off his gloves, freshly cleaned by Mrs. Jenner, and slipped them into his coat pockets. Then removed his helmet and tucked it under his left arm. Crooking his right arm, he extended it to Claire. "Shall we proceed inside?"

She appeared as though she'd far rather not. "Gird your loins," he quipped.

"Girding." She retained her gloves, clearly ready to remount in an instant, and held the crop in one hand. Gripping his arm with the other, skirts blowing, she mounted the wooden steps at the entrance by his side. The doorway wasn't particularly spacious and she lagged a pace or two behind him as they walked into the Ordinary.

A small chamber serving as a foyer buffered them from the garrulous crowd in the central room. Vaughan nearly collided with a flustered servant girl whisking past him with an empty tray. She successfully dodged Claire, still blocked by him, and hastened out the door for more refreshments. Normally servants used the back entry, nearest the kitchen housed separately from the main building, but the establishment was in a state of semi-chaos. Bedlam might erupt any moment.

He paused before the archway to the larger room. "Stay where you are while I take a look around."

"As if I would push past you."

With Claire at his back, he paused just inside the door. She peered around his side as he surveyed the boisterous assembly. A smattering of dragoons in redcoats from the distinguished Seventeenth were splotches of color among the ubiquitous green of the broader company. Apart from the handful of men from his regiment, this gathering was a mix of Loyalist troops serving in the Legion and a few civilians, and possibly the ever-present spies. Like a plague of locusts, they were everywhere. But a necessary evil, unless they were on the other side.

Tables surrounded by chairs slammed with men jostled for the limited floor space. The oak sideboard, a steaming soup tureen and foamy jugs of ale on top, had men crammed so closely beside it only a narrow path remained for the servants to navigate. All told, there weren't more than several dozen soldiers here, but it seemed more. The way Claire shrank at his elbow, she must fear the entire Legion were within.

The rowdy assembly spilled over into the back room. Bed chambers were upstairs. Not enough for this swell. Overnight visitors would be crammed mighty close, even if half the number returned to camp for the night. The rest of the Legion, called *Tarleton's Raiders* by locals, must be in and around the town of Halifax, a goodly jaunt up the road. Here, men carried on animated conversations while shoveling stew into their mouths and swigging ale as if they were at their leisure.

Was the Halifax area secured? What about the militia forted up across the river? Vaughan needed additional information to better gauge the situation. More pressing, where was Tarleton?

He scanned the room. At the far end of the chamber, a cheery fire crackled in the hearth, its simple blue mantel framed by white plaster walls. Normally,

Tarleton would have the best seat in the house and should be located right about there. But the senior officer he sought wasn't present.

Then—*Damn it all*. By the light of the flames, he spotted his conniving cousin tucked into a cozy corner.

Thomas's back was to them, but the thick dark hair smoothed in a queue and tied with a black ribbon, the ruffled lace at his throat, and elegant figure in an immaculate and expertly tailored mauve coat was unmistakable. Always the dandy. Thomas's late mother had been a French beauty besotted with fashion, a trait she'd passed on to her only child. Then she'd died of fever before age had a chance to spoil her looks and would forever be remembered as flawless.

Although Thomas was hardier than his mother, he wasn't what Vaughan would term *robust*. The walking stick he was never without, ribbons knotted at the end, was used to support the limp a riding accident had inflicted upon him. Or so he'd claimed, an assertion that coincided conveniently with the war. Granted, Vaughan shuddered to think of Thomas on the battlefield. He belonged in an opulent English drawing room, and likely that's what his untrustworthy relation was conspiring to acquire.

If his cousin's sly presence weren't bad enough, seated across from him was the one man Vaughan disliked even more. Massive shoulders stretched the seams of the forest green coat, a hue Vaughan was coming to loathe. When he chose a new wardrobe, that color would fall out of favor.

"Claire." He bent his head, inhaling the pleasurable scent of her perfume. "Tarleton's nowhere to be seen." She relaxed visibly, until he gestured at the shadows.

"Guess who is."

"What's Thomas doing here?" she hissed.

"Likely plotting my demise."

She glanced up, brows arched in a questioning V. "Truly?"

"Forget what you know, or think you know, and study his companion. I should have guessed the pair of them would brew something up together."

She swiveled her head at Thomas. Unaware of her gaze boring into him, he was engaged in an earnest exchange with the corpulent officer, though the content of their conversation was lost in the surrounding cacophony.

Her eyes flashed back to Vaughan's. "Who is that?"

"My nemesis. Captain Simmons."

"The villainous officer you mentioned?"

"The same."

She wrinkled her nose. "I thought you both fought for the Crown?"

"We do. But there are battles within battles when dealing with ambitious and unworthy men. Not all warfare occurs between contending sides. I suspect there's more to this tête-à-tête than the present state of the revolution."

What are you not telling me about Thomas?" she demanded, keeping her voice low.

"Can you not guess? Your father spelled it out. Would you further imperil me by insisting I do the same?"

She paled, and the disdain in her eyes said it all.

With an expression of extreme distaste, as though she'd smelled something bad, and given the pungent musk in this den of males, probably had, she scrutinized Simmons.

"Why are you and he at odds?"

"He's a Loyalist from New York who resents my vaulted birth. He can only rise so high in the British Army."

"While you keep soaring."

"If my wings aren't clipped. He'd love to do the honors."

The potential threat hanging over Vaughan seemed to embolden her. "Maybe someone will clip his first."

"Maybe. He's landed on the wrong side of Lord Cornwallis more than once."

Chin raised, she smiled. "Good. 'Tis shortsighted to soar too near the sun when your wings are made of wax."

Despite Vaughan's annoyance and suspicion with the pair, he chuckled at her analogy.

She appraised the duo speculatively. "Do you really think they may be conspiring against you?"

"I do now."

Alarm crossed her gaze. "What do you fear they'll do?"

"Thomas might enlist Simmons to clear the way for him to inherit. *Accidental fire* during a skirmish, or some such *misfortune* that cannot be proven to be intentional. Simmons is rid of me and gains whatever reward he's promised.

"Dear God. No."

The clamor around them muffled her strident objection, but Vaughan heard, and the strength of her concern touched him. Then she narrowed her eyes and shifted her focus between Thomas, still blithely unaware of her presence, to the vindictive Captain Simmons, and back to Vaughan.

Scheming in those green depths, she gestured at his cousin. "We may have to get Thomas first."

"*We*?" He almost lurched forward. "Be careful, Claire. You mustn't go off half-cocked."

"Oh, I shall be fully charged and fire true. Never fear. Do not forget, sir, this is war."

"So I've observed." He gave a low whistle. "I am grateful not to battle you, Miss."

She raised reluctant eyes. "You may yet."

Mindful of curious onlookers they were beginning to draw, he lightly stroked her cheek. "I pray not, dear lady."

A tremor passed through her. "As do I."

He dropped his voice to a husky whisper. "Let us make a pact. Come what may, we shall remain allies."

"For my part, I would agree."

"Will you give me your word?"

"I will." She clasped his fingers in her gloved hand, and his heart doubled its beat.

"Then we have an accord. One I dearly wish I might seal with a kiss."

"Here? Now?" She pinkened delightfully.

He battled a near overpowering desire to do just that. But it would be to her detriment to behave brazenly before their mounting audience. "Consider my earlier proposal, one I pray you might also accept. I will drop on bended knee and repeat it if such a gesture will hasten your acceptance."

The tenderness in her gaze promised the consideration he wished. "No need for an unseemly display in this public house. I shall contemplate your proposal in the recesses of my very soul. For now, our mutual enemy is clear."

"Enemies," Vaughan amended, dragging his attention back to that worm of a cousin. "Well, then. Shall we greet Thomas and his contemptible comrade?"

A dangerous smile at her lips, she nodded.

Now *this* was the Claire he'd come to know. The shrinking woman who'd entered the Ordinary with him had been replaced by a fighter. She had the best of her grandfather, father, and brother combined in her. This Claire was a force to be reckoned with.

He almost pitied Thomas. Almost. And gestured her ahead with a flourish. "After you."

An already complex situation just ratcheted up to further heights. One hand upheld to acknowledge his fellows and the other fingering his sword, mindful of the pistol stuck in the top of his boot, he strode behind her, a no-nonsense presence. Not Claire. She was all charm. Honey colored tendrils curled around her sweet face beneath the bonnet, the embodiment of innocence, but she might as well have a dagger hidden in that cloak. Hell, maybe she did. Vaughan was prepared for anything.

Heads turned. He and Claire, especially her, and Vaughan only because of her, became the objects of scrutiny. Chairs scraped as the gentlemanly males got to their feet. The most mannered among them offered her a bow, others a nod. She returned the civility with a brief curtsy or nod, ignoring the rude men who ogled her.

These vulgar sorts, Vaughan quelled with a stern glance. He really wasn't interested in how long some of them had gone without a woman; he'd endured months of deprivation himself. They would behave with decency toward Claire or he was fully willing to issue a reprimand. Better still, a swift fist to the jaw and lashes laid on. He outranked all present except Simmons and commanded greater respect. Still, he was keenly aware of her appeal and the magic she unintentionally wove.

Even partly hidden beneath the cloak and bonnet, her beauty attracted attention. He'd known it would. But when she asserted her wish to ride with him, he found her request impossible to resist, much as he found her entwining throughout his every sense like a seductive vine.

No man called to her in friendly banter or uttered a coarse remark. Only an occasional "Miss" or "Ma'am" passed their lips in common courtesy. Vaughan's presence stilled their tongues from any further indulgence, but long glances sought her every move and eager eyes followed her across the room. Except for two. She swished up to the corner table where Thomas and Simmons were seated, so engrossed in each other they failed to notice her arrival until she was upon them.

That in itself struck Vaughan as significant. Neither man would seriously prefer the other's company, and Simmons normally kept closer watch on his surroundings. The convivial gathering in the tavern must've lulled him into complacency, and he'd upended generous tankards of ale—made his way through a cask by the looks of him. Never wise. Nor had he expected Vaughan to turn up this afternoon with the word out he was off chasing a spy. If Simmons had known his rival was on route, the braggart would have been more alert so as to not be caught with his guard down.

Vaughan shot him an 'I caught you' look, and Simmons glowered uncomfortably.

Thomas chose that instant to glance around. The astonishment in his face when he saw Claire was comical. Vaughan choked back a chuckle at the dropped jaw and staring eyes. It was as if a spirit had materialized before him, and this most definitely was not the hour he would have appointed for her visitation.

This cousin who prided himself on proper deportment, goggled at her in a most ungentlemanly manner. Not a sound escaped his slack jaws. She must be the last person on earth he'd thought to encounter here. Vaughan doubted he'd be more astounded if a bolt of lightning sizzled across the room and struck him.

Simmons, on the other hand, surveyed Claire with a critical light in his reddened eyes, like slits in the puffy flesh. How he'd acquired double chins on their rations, Vaughan didn't know, except the greedy officer raided the countryside at every opportunity and wasn't always mindful of whom the Loyalists were among the inhabitants—an irritant to Lord Cornwallis who preferred not to leave a trail of antagonism in their wake.

What a contrast the two men made, the striking young gentleman and 'the Codfish' as the soldiers referred to Simmons behind his back. No one had dared say it to his face. At least, not yet.

Vaughan gave a short bow. "Why, Cousin. Fancy meeting you here." Allowing no time for a stammered reply, he swept his hand toward Claire. "Miss Monroe, I believe you are acquainted with Mister Thomas Vaughan." He indicated the bloated officer. "And this is Captain Simmons."

Coolly surveying her admirer, she inclined her head. "Mister Vaughan."

"Good day, Miss Monroe." Thomas nearly upset the table in his haste to scramble to his feet in lilac shoes adorned with shiny buckles.

How on earth had he ridden here in those? He should have arrived by carriage, but Vaughan saw none in the yard. Was Thomas in such a tearing hurry to meet Simmons, he couldn't wait for the carriage to be prepared?

Claire may have wondered the same. Her chilly stare slid to Simmons. "Good day to you, sir. I trust you are finding Halifax to your liking."

The downturned mouth and grunt he offered by way of reply did not bode well. Trouble must be brewing in the town.

Reeking of drink, Simmons rose with deliberation. His bleary focus was on Claire, but not, Vaughan suspected, for the normal reasons. "Ma'am."

Thomas managed a bow, though lacking in his usual assurance. Not because he was intoxicated, just badly rattled. "How delightful to see you, and unexpected."

Vaughan nearly guffawed at the understatement.

To give Thomas his due, he collected himself enough to shut his slack jaw and curve his lips in the semblance of a smile. He extended his hand to Claire. "Always a pleasure."

If he thought to take her gloved fingers in his, he was sorely disappointed. She ignored the hopeful gesture and stared though him, increasing the discomfort he made obvious efforts to mask. "Indeed, sir. Nor did I anticipate *your* presence."

"No. I, ummm, thought it best to strive for harmony with the new arrivals." He drew back his hand and slanted glances at Vaughan in another attempt to disguise his shock. "How is it you are accompanied by my cousin?"

Waving the crop, she replied. "Have you not heard? Thornton Hall is hosting Captain Vaughan, Lieutenant McCray, and Lieutenant Anderson for the duration of their stay. An unfortunate accident left their guide wounded, but his injury is being carefully tended. The Monroe family are doing their duty to the Crown."

"Certainly," Thomas murmured politely. Clearly, this wasn't his view of the rabidly rebellious Monroe clan.

Simmons swung his head at Vaughan, suspicion swimming in his watery eyes. "What of the spy you went in pursuit of? Wasn't he a Lieutenant Monroe?"

"Yes. Now you mention it. Stuart Monroe. Miss Monroe's elder brother."

She directed a winsome smile at Simmons. "I fear there has been a misunderstanding. Stuart's no spy."

Her allure was lost on him. She might as well bestow it on the chimney. "We have information to the contrary, Miss."

"Is that so?" She fixed her gaze on Thomas.

Her would be suitor squirmed mutely while Simmons wore on. "What's more, we are in want of the letter Lieutenant Monroe carried. Any word on its whereabouts, *Captain*?"

His emphasis on their equal rank irked Vaughan. This pitiful excuse of an officer shouldn't have made sergeant, let alone captain. And the gall behind his implication that the whole matter would be laid at

Vaughan's door if any part failed to suit Simmons set his teeth on edge. It was all he could do not to drive his balled up fingers into that arrogant mouth.

Restraining himself, just, he ground out. "I've a great deal to report. To *Tarleton*. Where is he?"

Jowls quivering with indignation, Simmons lashed back. "The *Lieutenant Colonel* is off with a company seeing how much force is wanted to rebuff the rebels holed up across the water. Damn devils are sniping at us again. On top of the men we already lost." He leveled those accusing slits that passed for eyes at Claire as if she were personally responsible for the local resistance. "Now, about your traitorous brother—"

Vaughan cut him off. "Lieutenant Monroe is at large, but we continue to search for him."

"I should bloody well hope so. I'd have the bastard strung up by now while you're mincing about."

A gasp escaped Claire, and her face creased in a wince beneath the palm she'd clasped to her mouth.

Vaughan pinned Simmons with a glare. "Then you would be hard-pressed to gain information. And I will thank you to refrain from using foul language in Miss Monroe's presence and frightening her unduly. She's proving most amenable."

Thomas jerked to life. "What do you mean by that, sir?"

"The lady is assisting me."

"In what way?" Thomas pressed, with Simmons drinking in every word.

"That is between Tarleton and me. I will divulge no more to the present company. Suffice it to say, I am well pleased with her cooperation."

Blotches mottled Thomas's pale complexion and

his brown eyes glinted. He thrust his face near Vaughan's. "You do realize Miss Monroe and I have an understanding between us?"

The cloying scent of his cousin's pomade irritated Vaughan, in addition to his sheer cheek. Before he yanked Thomas up by the ruffle at his neck and further entertained onlookers by throwing him against the wall, Claire spoke out.

"Pardon me, Mister Vaughan. We have no such agreement to my certain knowledge."

He gaped at her. "But you said you would consider it."

"I am."

The intensity in his gaze lessened slightly. "So, you are not averse to my proposal?"

Claire appeared nearer to slapping the scoundrel than wedding him. She indicated their intent onlookers with her crop. "I am averse to finding you here in company with dragoons, rather than in attendance upon me and my family."

Neglecting his cane, Thomas lifted both hands in supplication. "I never intended to neglect you, my dearest. Truly."

A spasm, akin to toothache, crossed her face at the endearment. And Vaughan nearly took Thomas by the throat.

Claire chastised him first. "We are under house arrest, Mister Vaughan. Were you aware of this, or are you too much in your cups?"

"No. I've scarcely had a drop." He rounded on Vaughan. "What is the meaning of this treatment, Cousin?"

"Containing the Monroe household was a

necessary measure."

Simmons grunted his approval.

"Poor Mama is prostrate with her nerves, and my grandfather most disturbed. And I discover you here carousing," she reproached Thomas, heaping coals of guilt on him.

"Hardly that—"

She tossed her head. "No matter. Do not trouble yourself over my welfare, sir. I find I no longer mind so very much." With that parting shot across the bow, she circled her arm through Vaughan's. "Your English cousin is most charming."

Together, they turned away from the disbelief in Thomas's face. "Fare thee well, sir." Giving a wave, Vaughan strode with her toward the door.

"What of that spy Monroe?" Simmons hurled after them.

"The matter is in hand," Vaughan bit out.

"Tarleton will demand a report!"

"He shall have one."

"And the letter!"

"Deciphered," Vaughan assured him, if such assurances were to be accepted.

"Tarleton said for me to tend to the matter in his absence."

Vaughan doubted the accuracy of that claim. "We shall see, sir."

"We bloody well shall!"

He pivoted toward Simmons. "Do you really wish to test your popularity with Tarleton? With Lord Cornwallis?" They both knew Vaughan's noble father and Lord Cornwallis were on friendly terms. If push came to shove, which it might, the general would side with Vaughan, and Cornwallis had the final word. But his Lordship hadn't yet arrived.

Simmons eyed him like a baited bull targeting his next attack. His neck was thick enough for the beast. "Tarleton will hear me."

"When you're sober, perhaps, and have a sensible word to utter. You have taken too much drink."

He stabbed a thick finger at Vaughan. "Not too much to see an officer neglecting his duties for a fetching woman."

"How dare you—" Before Vaughan rebuffed Simmons, or attacked him, Thomas burst out.

"Enough of this spat, gentlemen! There is more pressing business. Miss Monroe! Allow me to make amends. I beg you." He hastened after her, his beribboned walking stick tapping the floorboards. "I beseech your forbearance, dear lady."

This was better than a play. With the heated skirmish breaking out between Vaughan and Simmons, and Thomas acting the lovesick swain, every man looked on.

Blotting his forehead with a scented handkerchief, Thomas pleaded with her. "Do not think ill of me, Miss Monroe. I shall make amends and call upon you anon. We, too, will visit more at length, Cousin."

In the face of her chilly silence, Vaughan replied. "I can scarcely contain my joy, and think it fair to say I speak for us both." He turned and swept her through the door, leaving Thomas to fume amid amusement and ribald comments. And Simmons to smolder alongside him.

Once down the steps and out of earshot, he could speak more freely. "Claire, I think you should know the woman our fathers fought over was Thomas's mother."

"I take it his father won?"

"And mine never forgave him. Family history repeats itself."

"This rivalry between you could get ugly."

"It already is. I cannot countenance the way my father cut off my uncle, but he can be brusque when crossed."

"How will Lord Vaughan react if you bring home an American bride with no title or wealth to increase the family coffers?"

He cupped her face in his hands. "You have everything I desire, and as I'm the only remaining son my father will be forced to accept my choice. Unless Thomas and Simmons render that option null and void."

"Another way of saying, if they kill you first? I wish you could sail for England. Now. Ride to the coast and take the first ship out of port."

"I wish we both could. If it were possible, would you come with me?"

The wistfulness he'd glimpsed before filled her eyes. She pressed those pretty lips together, then parted them. "I might, sir."

Hope swelled in him. "Vaughan," he gently coaxed.

"I might, Vaughan," she whispered.

Halleluiah. He wanted to shout huzzah and kiss her all in one. But raised voices carried from inside.

He distinctly detected his name in a slurred cry, followed by Monroe—an ominous blend, in this instance.

Plainly, she'd also heard.

He pulled on his gloves. "Good thing I bribed the stable boy to reposition our mounts. We're riding out of here now."

She gulped. "Lord only knows what Thomas is inciting."

"In a crowd of drunken men, spurred on by Simmons. Anything. I'll wager Simmons is putting it about my partiality for you has rendered me unfit to track this particular spy."

Admittedly, it had, but Vaughan could produce the coveted letter and Lieutenant Monroe wasn't going anywhere just now, so the rebel was adequately contained. Not a situation he cared to elaborate on, or one that would advance his cause with this intoxicated crowd.

There was nothing for it other than to defend Claire and her home to the best of his ability, and hold out for Tarleton or Cornwallis. At this point, he had more hope in the latter. Sounded like Tarleton was in one of his black moods. Sometimes he wished he served under George Washington. That general better kept his temper

Banishing the disloyal thought from his mind, Vaughan fixed the plumed helmet onto his head and hastened with Claire toward their horses. He untied La Belle while she freed Bryan. Placing one gloved hand on the pommel, clutching the crop, she gathered her skirts and prepared to mount. It was a lady's sidesaddle and tricky to manage without a block.

"Let me give you a boost. Wait—someone's come."

A lone rider clattered into the yard and reined in his winded mount before them. In an olive green coat, the newcomer appeared to be a Loyalist, but might simply be cautious, or neutral. Whatever he was, worry lined his weathered face and shaggy gray eyebrows drew together under the black tricorn. He embodied urgency.

"Mister Ellis!" She hailed the mature gentleman. "It's Claire Monroe. What has happened, sir?"

He panted from his hasty ride. "Soldiers are sacking Halifax!"

She threw one hand up. "Whatever for?"

"Tarleton's angry with the militia's resistance and refuses to interfere. Is there nothing to be done, Captain?"

"Go home and bolt your doors. Warn your neighbors to do the same. The men in the tavern are drunk and growing dangerous. I cannot control the Legion if Tarleton won't. But assure you, Lord Cornwallis will be furious when he arrives."

"When will that be?" the newcomer asked.

"A few days, possibly. The Legion are out ahead of the rest of the army."

"What damage will they have inflicted by then?" With a despairing shake of his head, the man cantered his horse back the way he'd come.

Claire's face was white in the late afternoon light. "Vaughan, please. Mister Ellis is a kind neighbor. Can you do nothing to protect him or Halifax?"

"Men of my regiment will heed me. The sober ones, at least. But our numbers are diminished in the ranks, and I do not know who is where in the disorder descending on Halifax. Do you want me to strive for the town's protection, or Thornton's? Your family may be in danger. I cannot defend both."

Her eyes spoke for her.

"As I thought. Lead the way. Let's go by that furtive route."

Chapter Thirteen

A cool dusk was descending. The wind diminished with its coming. Sounds reached Claire from farther away in the gathering twilight. From her rolling seat atop Bryan, she strained to detect the distant drum of hooves.

Her stomach sank. "Vaughan! I hear them."

He and his mare streaked behind her. "They'll be upon us before you know it." His tone was grim and matter-of-fact.

What had he endured to be so hardened? Claire was quite the opposite. "No they won't. Let them catch this."

Desperate to reach Thornton Hall ahead of their pursuers, she galloped Bryan over the dirt road through ankle deep puddles. She made no effort to go around them as she'd done before. Muddy water splashed in an arch, wetting her skirts. Repeatedly. If her bonnet weren't tied tightly to her head, it would've flown off. And it was new. Odd to think of bonnets at a time like this. But anything new was rare these days.

Thank heavens Bryan had quickly adapted to the sidesaddle and readily took instruction from her. He wasn't trained for a lady's saddle. Truly, he was proving a most superior horse and faster than the mare she'd left in the stable at Thornton.

Vaughan's hunter, La Belle, was bred from

champion lines and likely worth a small fortune. No doubt, horse and rider could thunder past her and Bryan, but only she knew the way. And must keep watch. They were almost to the hidden track.

She signaled to him. "Here!"

Slowing the gelding, she turned his head to the left. A light tap of the crop and nudge of her heel guided him off the main road. Bryan pushed through damp evergreen boughs, showering her with droplets, and veered onto the path concealed among the close stand of trees.

Vaughan followed. "Clever. I never noticed this route."

"'Tis seldom used, to guard it."

"Good. The more riders shoulder through the trees, the more evident the path becomes. Your secret is safe with me."

She prayed so. How ironic to look to a British dragoon captain for protection, but she trusted he would defend her, her family, and her home. It was also the height of irony to be out ahead of such an expert equestrian. She drew on all her riding skills, summoning even more from deep inside.

The aromatic scent of pine hung on the crisp evening air and the thick carpet of needles muffled the rapid fall of hooves. On either side of the path, white dogwood blossoms glowed like pearls in the lessening light. Overhead, nighthawks sounded their peculiar cry. The first owl hooted.

Both horses made short work of the grove. They sped through the trees, leaving the last of the trunks. With Vaughan right behind her, she dipped into the rain-washed gully running along the field, and then emerged back onto the secret route.

"There!" The outline of the split rail fence enclosing their meadow rose before her. "Dodge to the right!"

Claire didn't hesitate. Bryan's long legs reached out and he sailed over it. She lurched in the saddle, but kept her seat. Just. Thank God. Jumping wasn't something she'd done a lot of, especially lately.

Of course, Vaughan landed smoothly. They tore through the grass on a furtive maneuver toward the backside of Thornton Hall and unsuspecting folk who had no notion what was coming at them. Rather like a storm barreling their way.

Faster! They couldn't get there soon enough to suit Claire.

Turf flew up under Bryan's hooves. Pale buttercups dotting the meadow went by in a rush, trampled in the charge. Grazing cattle bolted aside. Calves kicked up their heels and sprang in play. Everything was a game to the very young.

Not her. Claire was in dead earnest. Her thoughts churned with the knot in her gut. She might lead the way now, but her ultimate challenge was how to follow the man she was fast falling in love with and remain true to the cause. Her world, as she knew it, had turned on its head. Come to think of it, Vaughan's had too. This mission couldn't possibly be one he'd ever contemplated undertaking.

What riled her the most to consider, apart from the damnable rogues who pursued them, was how closely she'd come to accepting Thomas's offer of marriage. If Vaughan hadn't arrived, she might, even now, be mouthing words of agreement and acquiescing to

Thomas's proposal. That conniving toad must've used his connection with her family as a means of spying on them.

How long had this been taking place? Had he ever truly cared for her at all? She'd fancied he adored her. Even if she were less than ardent in return, she'd thought to rely on his fervor to sustain them. How gullible she'd been. The man possessed no regard for anyone other than himself.

Benedict Arnold wasn't the only traitor. Claire would see to it Thomas reaped what he'd sown. Stuart must learn of his treachery.

For now, she swept home faster than she'd ever flown on any horse in her life. One more fence to jump, then on to the house. An added quality she valued about Vaughan, he never cautioned her to slow down. Stuart would have. Everyone else would have. But Vaughan seemed confident of her ability to ride, and it wasn't misplaced.

If this were an all-out race between the two of them, she wondered how near she'd come. By heaven, he'd not leave her far behind, even with his fleet mare.

As they rode, she took in the orange moon skimming the treetops in its ascension of the clear midnight blue sky. There would be added light tonight, and possibly a little frost later. Such a beautiful evening, a pity it seemed destined for violence. How she would love to spend it in Vaughan's strong embrace. And how wicked her family would deem such a wish.

Chapter Fourteen

In a drum of hooves, Vaughan cantered La Belle into the yard at Thornton Hall and drew up beside Claire. Admiration welled in him. "We're ahead of the pack, thanks to your outstanding performance."

She dipped her head. "High praise, indeed."

"And deserved." He glanced around. Not a soul in sight. "Anderson!" Bawling for the ensign he'd left to watch the stable and grounds, he threw a leg over the horse and slid to the cobbles in his boots. The instant he dismounted, he reached up to assist Claire. Once she was firmly on her feet, he grasped the reins of both well-trained mounts.

"Herd your family into the cellar as fast as you can."

"Even Grandfather?"

"Mrs. Jenner must help you contain him. We've no choice with the threat of fire." Speaking to her over his shoulder, he strode toward the stable. "Be prepared to slip out of the house at any moment. Don't move Percy unless you must. Leave Ezekiel with him and tell the others to fort up in the kitchen, for now. Except the men. Summon them to shift your horses to the woods and herd the cattle to the back of the field or they'll be taken."

She followed at his heels. "What of Stuart?"

"Warn him what's coming. Advise extreme caution

on his part. Send Lieutenant McCray to me at once."

She caught Vaughan by the arm. "If Stuart's caught?"

Masking his qualms, he pivoted toward her. "I will request your brother be paroled to Thornton Hall."

"But you can make no guarantee?"

"Not with a mob descending on us. Apart from them, if he's taken, the outcome depends on how badly Tarleton desires the contents of that cypher. I'm betting a lot. And I will not divulge the information without assurance of your brother's safety."

"You promise?"

Vaughan didn't need to clearly see her dimly illuminated face to feel her alarm. And share it. If he failed to safeguard Stuart Monroe, it would be his undoing in her eyes. Not only that, he had a grudging respect for the daring young officer.

"Listen to me, Claire. I've done a lot in the course of this war I'm not especially proud of. Let me make amends, at least a little, by helping you."

Then, Vaughan couldn't help himself. Circling his free arm around Claire's waist, he pulled her to him and bent his head, covering her mouth in the hard kiss he'd hungered for all afternoon. No time to savor her yielding lips, or the flame consuming him, an unquenchable fire only she could satisfy. No time for anything, even this stolen moment, though it would be forever printed on his mind…the beautiful Rebel, cold air, starry sky, full moon…

Praying this wasn't the last intimacy they shared between them, he released her. "Now go."

"Have care, Vaughan." Her voice trembled.

He fought to firm his reply. "I will."

Catching up her skirts, she pelted toward the front entrance.

Every window was alight. Mrs. Jenner's extravagance with the candles struck him, and he bet she'd used the special beeswax ones. A pang shot through him. She'd probably planned a special supper in his honor and had no clue what or who was coming to disrupt the festivities. He vowed candles and hearths would be the only light the gracious home glowed with this night. He'd seen too many estates burned. Such a waste.

Truth be told, he'd wearied of serving in an army with a penchant for burning everything. Hadn't General Sir Henry Clinton, Commander-in-Chief of the British Forces in America, said it was impolitic to destroy homes one intended to occupy when they took Charles Towne under his command? Sir Henry, *the shy bitch,* as the quarrelsome general referred to himself, was in New York now, but Cornwallis didn't want civilians needlessly accosted at every turn.

What wouldn't Vaughan give for a return to civility? He'd told Claire both sides in this bitter conflict were guilty of deplorable behavior, and so they were. But when it came right down to it, British forces were the harsher of the two.

Not tonight. He'd die first.

Both mounts in tow, Vaughan strode into the stable, the earthy aroma of hay and horses in his nose. An oil lamp had been lit and hung from a hook casting shadows on the stone and timber walls and dusty beams overhead. Bridles, halters, and ropes dangled along one log wall. Saddles were slung over a low bench. Curry combs and other riding equipment lined a shelf. Here and there, wooden buckets to carry feed and water, pitchforks for mucking out and replacing the bedding, a barrel of oats, and mound of hay filled the crowded building.

Still no one in sight. "Anderson!"

Nickers greeted him in reply from the horses peering over their partitions. He counted two gray cart horses, big sturdy beasts, Claire's mare and yearling foal, plus McCray and Anderson's chestnut geldings. No others remained in the field and all were haltered. Good.

Retaining La Belle's reins, he loosely tethered Bryan. He liked stables and the homey continuity of animals. The sights and scents of the country grounded him. He missed the welcome of dogs and baying hounds, and might be quite happy on the family manor, even adopt farming.

Why, the king himself was so impassioned with rustic life, he'd been nicknamed *Farmer George*. Granted, the monarch was rumored to suffer from spells of madness. But who didn't these days?

Perhaps in their fight for the land and independence they held dear, these stubborn colonists made some sense—

"What happened?" William popped out from a back stall, catching him unawares.

"Apart from my nearly having heart failure at your appearance?"

"With the letter?" the boy clarified.

How on earth did he know about the cypher? He had the ears of a fox and was far too astute for his own good. "Nothing yet." Vaughan waved him ahead. "Make haste to the house."

"Why? I want to stay here."

"This is the first building they'll torch, if we don't stop them."

Eyes wide, his mouth shaped in a large O, he tugged at Vaughan's coat sleeve. "Who?"

"Soldiers."

Vaughan had his full attention. "Make yourself useful. Fetch Joseph and Jim to hide these horses in the woods. Wait there until someone comes for you."

"Yes, sir. I'll get 'em!" For once, the lad was compliant. He hightailed off in direction of the kitchen.

Ensign Anderson stumbled out from a dark corner, rubbing his eyes. He must've nodded off on his field blanket. There was no opportunity to scold him for falling asleep while on duty. At least he was fully clothed and armed with his saber, not pulling on part of his uniform as he'd done earlier today. Men were lashed for less.

He hastened over the floor strewn with straw. "Are we under attack, Captain?"

"By Simmons if we don't look sharp."

Anderson gaped at him in the lamplight.

"The blackguard's got some intoxicated dragoons worked up over this spy I'm accused of allowing to escape."

Every man was aware of the ongoing rivalry between Vaughan and Simmons. He need say no more. "Saddle up. McCray's gelding too. I prefer to face them mounted."

"At once." Anderson fell to action. Metal jangling, he caught up the black double bridles, characteristic of the light dragoons, belonging to his and McCray's mounts.

"What in blazes!" McCray charged through the stable door. The big Scotsman could step lively when circumstances required. "Simmons on the war path again, Captain?"

"In drunken earnest, this time."

"Fellow's never entirely sober."

"No. And Tarleton's off somewhere. Couldn't find him at the Ordinary. Mount up. We'll run circles around Simmons and those ne'r do wells riding with him. I refuse to allow this home to go up in smoke."

McCray scowled. "Not too keen on the notion myself, seeing as I intend on staying the night." Anderson thrust a bridle into McCray's hands and he scrambled to ready his gelding. "Had my mouth all set on that trifle Sally's made. She's roasting a nice joint of beef, too. Smells a treat in the kitchen."

Which is apparently where McCray had been agreeably ensconced. Not that Vaughan begrudged his friend and fellow officer the respite. They'd both endured various circles of Hell serving in the British Legion. Welcome breaks were few.

"I hope these culinary delights still await us after we regain order."

"They had better," McCray growled.

"I like it here. And the food's real good." Anderson was more reserved, but Vaughan never doubted his fidelity. The young dragoon had his horse bridled and heaved the saddle up onto his mount atop the folded blanket on its broad back.

McCray reared his head at Vaughan. "Monroe's hiding out somewhere inside Thornton, you know."

"Yes. Under house arrest. I struck a bargain with his sister."

"Figured as much," McCray said gruffly.

"And I intend to wed her, if she'll have me."

"That so? Bonnie lass, right enough. Mayhap an earldom will tempt her from this confounded rebellion. Is the blasted letter we've heard so much about deciphered yet?"

Vaughan trusted more than his peerage would temp Claire to the altar, but answered McCray while Anderson looked on. "It is. Thanks to Miss Monroe. One final point requires her assistance. I'm not sharing this information with Simmons."

"And let him take the credit? Bloody right, you're not. Good work, Captain. We'll see this through. His Lordship has got to do something about dragoons carrying on like mad dogs."

"Another pack are sacking Halifax."

"Won't impress Cornwallis none. *No unwarranted harassment of civilians were his orders*, as I recall," McCray huffed, tightening the cinch strap on his horse.

"I fully expect him to conduct several hangings before we depart for Virginia."

Joseph and Jim, and an older Negro Vaughan didn't recognize, probably Sally's brother, rushed in with William to relocate the horses. The remaining brother with the limp must be out herding cattle to a secluded spot. Joseph took Bryan's reins. Jim led Claire's mare and its yearling foal. The third man took charge of the docile cart horses. Animals were hustled out the door. Inky figures disappeared into the night, William trotting behind them.

This was as much as Vaughan hoped to accomplish before the clatter of hooves on the cobbles. He heard them cantering on the *alleé*. Lights shone along the drive. "Our guests are soon upon us. And haven't neglected to bring torches."

"Course not," McCray muttered. "But it slowed 'em down a mite."

Torches made from greasy rags wrapped around the end of a stick and set aflame required a little labor, and didn't burn long. But long enough for the men to find their way here with ready fire.

All Vaughan's training and years of service had led to this most unlikely state of affairs. But he'd be damned if Simmons would rule the day. Or night. He swung himself back into the saddle. McCray and Anderson did the same. They rode into the yard and lined up before the house in a defensive posture, Vaughan center front.

Pistol in one hand, his saber in the other, he was ready. The other two drew sabers in silent accord, pistols stowed in the fur-covered holsters at the sides of their saddles. McCray and Anderson had slung muskets over their shoulders, but Vaughan left his in the stable. Even the shorter barreled carbines issued to dragoons were too cumbersome to manage smoothly on horseback, like firing while balancing in a rowboat in a choppy sea. He preferred the dexterity of his other weapons.

Not entirely sure what he was getting himself or his fellow officers into, he attempted to clarify. "It is my hope we may not have to shoot anyone. That threats will serve."

A noncommittal 'humph' from McCray voiced his view. The irascible Scotsman generally considered a trouncing in order.

"Await my signal and follow my lead."

McCray touched his sword to Vaughan's. "Always have done, Captain. Not so bad as facing them damn yelling boys," he said, hearkening back to last summer's violent skirmish with the wild Overmountain men and those chilling war whoops. "But they were fighting on the other bloody side. If we gotta battle our boys and theirs, we ain't never winning this war. Makes you want to pack it in."

"After six years? Hell yes. When I'm lord of the manor, you are most welcome to come help run my estate. You, too, Anderson. Always a place for you in Devon."

"Good to know, sir."

"If we live that long," McCray said under his breath.

Vaughan couldn't assure even the next ten minutes.

The echo of hooves on cobbles announced the initial belligerent arriving in the yard, torch upraised as if to toss it at the first building he saw. By the garish light, Vaughan easily recognized Simmons' girth and surly countenance beneath the flashy helmet common to Loyalists in Tarleton's Legion—one this lout wasn't fit to wear.

Without hesitation, Vaughan cocked his trigger and aimed the pistol at Simmons' heart. "Toss that torch. I dare you."

Even in the diminished light, his fury was glaring. "You would not presume to fire upon a fellow officer."

"I've done worse."

"Aye," McCray grunted. "He has."

Vaughan pinned his antagonist with an unwavering stare. "And I really don't like you."

Sooty smoke encircling his head, Simmons waved

his torch. "Your regard is of no consequence, sir. I am astounded by your threats. We both fight for King and Country."

"So, I had assumed. Appears your loyalty is to yourself."

He'd no doubt Thomas had bought this worthless officer. Shooting Simmons wasn't entirely a bluff, but he'd have to answer to Tarleton. Cornwallis would say good riddance to poor baggage, assuming Vaughan justified his actions.

He could.

Roughly a dozen riders drew in around them. The astonishment in their faces at seeing Vaughan with a pistol pointed at Simmons was visible beneath the torchlight. Almost comical, if Vaughan were feeling amused.

He wasn't.

No sign of his disreputable cousin. Thomas must've lagged behind. None of these men were from Vaughan's particular regiment. A hostile host of green surrounded him, apart from Ensign Anderson, also attired in the Loyalist uniform.

"What the hell are you doing?" demanded a corporal, fuddled with drink. If he'd been sober, those words never would have escaped his mouth.

McCray and Anderson cocked their triggers. "Waiting for you," the Scotsman growled.

"Vaughan!" Simmons bellowed. "You, sir, are harboring a spy!"

He replied with menacing calm. "*Harboring* smacks of treason. Are you accusing me of sedition?"

Stabbing a finger at the house, Simmons sidled on his high-strung mount. "Call it what you will. I'm told the Rebel's holed up in there."

So, Thomas had blabbed his suspicions about Stuart and the hidden passage at Thornton Hall. Vaughan's gut churned, but he masked all emotion except cold disdain. "I am aware of Lieutenant Monroe's whereabouts. He is in hand."

The horse side-stepping beneath an increasingly agitated Simmons required greater effort to contain. Hauling on the reins, he turned his spirited mount in a circle. "Are we to trust you in this matter? The Rebel's sister has charmed you!"

"I am under no enchantment," Vaughan lied, knowing full well he was. "I will not see punishment unleashed on Miss Monroe and her family. But will deliver what is required to Tarleton." He had no choice now, other than to arrange the most ideal circumstance possible for Stuart Monroe's arrest.

Still, Simmons ranted atop his prancing horse. "Fetch the traitor out this instant. And the letter carried by this enemy of the king. I will deliver both spy and cypher to Tarleton before you allow their escape."

"Here, here!" surrounding men assayed.

Vaughan was no reed in the wind. "Not on your life. I shall do as I see fit. If Lieutenant Monroe is harmed, his sister will lend no further assistance. Only with her cooperation can I solve the final riddle in the puzzle."

Hisses and jeers followed. Simmons' disdain was the loudest. "Back at the Ordinary, you said the letter was deciphered!"

"It is. One hurdle remains."

"Enough of this dance, Captain Vaughan. Do your duty and turn over the spy. We can beat the truth from the woman."

"And I can shoot you here and now. Then turn Lieutenant Monroe and the letter over to Tarleton. We shall see who retains his regard. Not that it shall matter to you, anymore."

If forced, he'd shoot first and curry favor later.

"You cannot fire on us all, sir!" Simmons argued.

Vaughan nodded at McCray and Anderson. "Perhaps, we shan't need to. If I take out the head, the rest may scatter like ants. Unless…" He glanced around the nervous assembly, before returning his steely gaze to Simmons. "You wish to settle this dispute between us with a gentlemanly duel."

Onlookers perked up at that suggestion. Dueling let them off without injury or death, while offering entertainment. Far preferable to the formidable and unexpected resistance they'd encountered at Thornton Hall. Simmons had certainly led them to expect an easy assault, and glory.

Clearly, he wasn't taken with the proposal. "Dueling in the ranks is forbidden."

"Not true. It is allowed in certain circumstances."

"Is this that circumstance?"

"Whether it is or isn't the proper arrangement, my honor is thoroughly impugned." Vaughan brandished his saber at the gathering. Uneasy glances exchanged between them. "Who will report us? This lot? It's my say against theirs."

"*Our* say, sir." McCray emphasized his unity with Vaughan.

Greatly appreciated. The gruff Scotsman was a favorite with their superiors.

Apprehension crossed Simmons' eyes, slits in the

mounds of flesh, like a pig faced with the butcher knife. "I am not come to duel, but to capture a spy and intercept his devilish message."

"And I demand satisfaction for the insults hurled at me. Never fear. You may prevail." But no man won over Vaughan when it came to blades.

"I prefer pistols," Simmons attempted.

"Agreed."

"He's a crack shot," McCray reminded the contender.

"Perhaps blades," Simmons hastily amended. "To first blood?"

The coward's way of ending the fight before dire maiming or death. "As you wish," Vaughan affirmed, but made no promise. A point lost on Simmons, now decidedly ill-at-ease. "Or you may offer an apology, leave the matter to me and Tarleton, and ride out of here."

The unintelligible snarl issuing from the scoundrel's mouth in no way sounded like an apology. More in keeping with the guttural rut of an incensed boar.

"Let it be noted, I gave you the chance. You may regret your pride." Vaughan enjoyed a good duel. The last decent match he'd fought was with the Patriot Captain Jeremiah Jordan, a much worthier opponent. The swordfight ended when Meriwether shot Vaughan in the side.

Again, a woman entered into this duel. Besting Simmons would be easy compared to making Claire understand what must follow with her brother. Now that all knew Stuart Monroe hid within the house, Vaughan was required to deliver the concealed Patriot.

Although he intended to request leniency. Even so, would she forgive him?

Chapter Fifteen

Apart from bodily odors of the people huddled in the cellar with Claire, some of whom could use a good scrubbing, and her mother's jasmine perfume, the most pervasive scent came from the barrels of apples and casks of cider stored down here. A hatch in the earthen floor covered by animal skins and more casks of spirits led to the dugout below filled with foodstuffs stored away from prying eyes. Not all their provisions fit in this confined space. Some overflowed.

The lantern Mrs. Jenner hastily lit and set on one of the shelves built against the wall of the stone foundation revealed the faces of the small gathering. Claire ached for her perturbed grandfather, his hands bound and mouth gagged to ensure his cooperation, and was distressed for her frightened mother, partly shrouded under a large lacy cap. Her grim brother, arms crossed over his chest, had endured worse, as had the long-suffering Mrs. Jenner last year in Backcountry.

Not Claire. She'd never been so fraught with apprehension, not only for her family and home, but also for Vaughan outside facing an angry crowd. At least, he wasn't alone. That bulldog, Lieutenant McCray, and green, but loyal Ensign Anderson, would back him up, but there was only so much they could do against an angry crowd. And Vaughan was out in front.

Would he be injured or court-martialed for his

actions? Blackest of all possibilities, killed? If she weren't hunched beside Stuart on the bench propped against the wall, she'd have paced like a pent-up wolf.

The clamor outside mounted. Sounds easily reached the cellar. She nudged her brother. "Now what?"

He lifted a shoulder and let it drop, but his stony bearing was alert. "A lot of shouting. No shots fired yet. I'll tiptoe upstairs and take a look."

"No." She gripped his arm. "You must remain hidden. If you're determined to risk your neck, at least wait until Cornwallis comes."

"Why him?"

"He's less brutal than Tarleton and might go easier on you."

"I suppose his Lordship is preferable to the devil himself. But I will do as I must. I cannot just hide here like a coward."

"You jeopardize our safety if you declare yourself. Captain Vaughan insists you escaped. You make a liar of him."

Stuart wore the look of one who foresaw his fate and didn't relish it. "That ruse won't last much longer. And may, even now, be moot."

Grasping at something, anything, Claire schemed. "If you sneak out the tunnel and head for the trees, you might have a chance."

"Unless I'm spotted. Besides, I'll not abandon my family."

"No. Of course. Best to remain down here."

"Miss Claire's right." Mrs. Jenner was a reassuring lump on the bench across from them that also housed their grandfather. Her petticoats engulfed the greater portion of the rough wood. "Stay in secret as long as may be. Besides, we need yer aid with Mister Monroe and yer poor Mama."

So distressed was their grandfather by news of the impending attack on Thornton Hall, the forceful woman had to tip a swig of Ezekiel's sovereign potion down his throat with Stuart's assistance. Stuart had also contained the elderly gentleman, though Claire was loathe for him to be bound.

Disgust had narrowed her brother's gaze. "Can't have him alerting all to our whereabouts," he'd muttered, and gotten on with the task.

Stuart and Mrs. Jenner were far more practiced in these distasteful matters than Claire. *Needs must* was their motto. Claire would rather gallop her mare in a hundred races and leap as many fences at breakneck speed than face what was happening within this house and out in the yard.

Now and then, her mother sipped from a silver flask clutched in trembling fingers to steady her unstoppable nerves. Dressed in a gown from happier days, with rows of ruffles and bows, and clutching a lace shawl over a second shawl, she sat quavering on an upholstered chair fetched down here for her comfort. She looked anything but, and shook as though struck with cold. One month of wearing widow's weeds was as much mourning as this color-mad woman could abide.

Ill-suited for a hard life, she'd been petted as a girl, lavished with parties and praise. Their father had done his utmost to spare his fragile wife and keep her secure, but all his care had flown with the war, and Stuart had done little to make amends. Still, the woman adored her elder son—high spirited William, not as much.

"Dear God in heaven. What is to become of us?" she wailed.

"Keep faith, Mavis," Mrs. Jenner encouraged her cousin.

Claire reached over and patted the chilled fingers. "Do not despair, Mama. We shall be well." She prayed this was true, and wondered how the others fared.

Sally, Beulah, Minnie, Maddie, and the younger twins, Darling and Precious, were all forted up in the kitchen. They'd pushed furniture in front of the windows and shoved a large chest before the door to block entry by the soldiers. Even if that worked, it couldn't prevent fire from driving them out. The men and boys, except for Ezekiel, who'd remained on the enclosed porch with Percy, had gone to secure the animals.

Claire chafed under the excruciating suspense. "I should take a look outside."

Stuart caught her hand in his callused grip. "Not yet. You may endanger yourself. I still cannot believe Captain Vaughan and those other two dragoon officers are facing down men from their own Godless legion. For you."

"For us all."

At this, Grandpa jerked his head around and made a noise in his throat. Perhaps the medicine was taking effect. The gleam in his eyes wasn't quite as fanatical.

She squeezed Stuart's hand. "I think he's trying to tell us something."

"But at what volume?"

Fingering frills and lace like a child with a favorite blanket, their mother bent forward. "Did I hear a'right?

You say a British dragoon fights *in our defense*?"

Claire nodded. "Three of them, but the senior officer, Captain Vaughan, took charge. He is to be a lord someday, Mama. The only heir of a vast English estate."

Despite the tense circumstances, the frazzled woman cocked her capped head like a bird listening for a worm. A quizzical look came into her hazel eyes. "Is he, indeed?"

"And he wants to wed me."

Stuart snorted. "Our little Claire will someday be a duchess if all goes as she wishes."

"A baroness," she corrected him. "And I do not know for certain what I wish."

The old familiar scheming filled their mother's gaze, like the returning tide. "Consider carefully, my girl."

Claire had done little else.

Creases lined the vestiges of beauty still remaining in the mature woman's face. Setting aside her nerves, like a discarded mantle, to ponder this astonishing development, she mused. "An officer with such a legacy is rare indeed. Such opportunity may not come your way again. Not at two and twenty, in this remote place."

Stuart threw his hands up. "Remote? We have a popular Ordinary frequented by travelers and a growing town."

"'Tis hardly London."

"We are at war with London, Mama," he reminded her.

"This interminable war cannot go on forever," she countered. "If only we could be certain if this officer were true."

"To whom?" Stuart tossed back. "The Legion?"

"My daughter and your sister."

Also what Claire fervently wished to know. At least, this most unusual turn of conversation had distracted the woman from their potentially precarious position in the cellar.

"He may be," Stuart allowed, although he wore his sardonic expression. "One thing I'll say for Captain Vaughan, he's out there fighting for her now."

Again that noise in their grandfather's throat.

Claire was insistent. "I really think we should permit him to speak. He may rave, but he may not. And untie him, for pity's sake."

"Very well." Holding a finger to his lips, Stuart admonished their addled relation. "Pray refrain from shouting, sir, as we attempt concealment. Mrs. Jenner snuffed the candles, but we are easily found and must prepare for flight out the tunnel if need be." He didn't add what they all dreaded, *if the house is set aflame.* Taking the knife from the sheath at his belt, he cut the cords around the old man's wrist, then slid the cloth from his mouth. "What is it you wish to say?"

Those silvery-blue eyes pierced Claire. "If ye wed a redcoat, ye will betray us all."

"But this particular redcoat is fighting for us all. Is that not most exemplary?"

Stuart spoke. "If preserving you, your family, and home are his motive, then yes."

"What else could he want?" she asked.

"The letter."

"He already has it. Deciphered and in his pocket."

Grandfather sucked in his breath. "Do ye not know

what ye do? How could a Monroe lass commit such an unpardonable act?"

"To save Stuart from arrest and possible hanging. Is that not worthy? Have we not lost enough in this family?"

Blotting her eyes with a lace-edged handkerchief, their mother sniffed. "I could not bear to lose my boy, too."

Stuart ran a hand through loose, shoulder length brown hair. "Many sacrifice for the cause."

"The Monroe's have suffered enough. You needn't offer your neck to the noose," the matriarch chastised him, then turned to Claire. "Has this captain all he needs to assure Stuart's safety?"

"Mostly. One clue in Papa's cypher remains yet unsolved."

Their grandfather appeared taken aback by the news. He weighed her disclosure. "Cypher, ye say. What is still wanted?"

"Exactly where the treasure is hidden. We know the place. Bruton Parish. But this part's confusing. 'Where the corbie flies and the fallen lie, there I am. Twice hidden beneath eagle's wings. Beside my brother now I rest.'"

An air of solemnity overcame the older man and his gaze grew distant as if seeing back, back, back. "God forgive me. He lies beside wee Robbie."

Totally unprepared for this revelation, as she might be the ascent of angels, Claire stared at him. "Who?"

"Papa had no brother," Stuart interjected.

The strain showed in their grandfather's careworn face. His voice was faint, but clear. "Our firstborn, Robert, died when little more than a babe. I could not bear to speak of wee Robbie, my lost boy, or hear anyone utter his name. But yer father knew his older brother. They were but a year apart."

Grandfather wiped at a tear with a shaky hand, then dropped his voice even lower. "Sometimes, as a small lad, I heard John whispering to someone when none were there. 'Wee Robbie has come,' he'd say. How I scolded him for tormenting me. So John ceased mention of wee Robbie, as if he never drew breath. But the dead are not forgotten. We carry them with us. How it must have tormented him to deny his brother. They are together now with their sainted mother, God rest their souls."

Goosebumps prickled down Claire's spine. "And Robbie's grave?"

"Bruton Parish."

A chill ran through her. "And the eagle's wings?"

"I know naught of eagles, save for the Monroe crest. 'Tis the cherub on wee Robbie's grave ye must seek."

Something only her grandfather could know. That letter had most surely been intended for him. Had grief over her father's death unleashed a surge of anguish over the beloved son lost long ago? Is this what led to his spiral into madness?

"Grandfather," she prompted. "Are you the one they call the Patriarch?"

He seemed to come back to himself, and his eyes cleared. An expression, more like his former self, displaced the bemusement in their depths. "I recall the name, as if in a dream. Aye, I think I must be him, though the reason for this title is unclear to me."

Claire and Stuart exchanged somber glances. It was

as Vaughan had concluded.

Rocking quietly, the older man softly repeated the line from the cypher. "'Beside my brother now I lie.' My poor boys."

Her eyes dazed from more than the contents of the flask and whatever else she'd sustained herself with today, their mother entered in. "I know nothing of wee Robbie, or this Patriarch you speak of, or much else, but if all you say of the cypher is true, what part did your dear father play?"

Before Claire replied, Stuart spoke. "He contrived it as he lay dying with the aid of someone, we assume a fellow officer. I was given the letter by a courier who said little more than where and when to deliver it. The only thing I'm certain of is Papa's final wish was to conceal a treasure sizable enough to tempt a Loyalist into betraying Benedict Arnold. And now, Claire has revealed all to Captain Vaughan except the last piece of the puzzle."

The accusation cut through her. "To save you."

"Or your darling officer from disgrace."

"Is both so very terrible?

Stuart eyed her as if she'd sold her soul to Satan.

"You do not know what may come of this," she argued.

"I can wager what won't. Arnold hanging from a tree."

She braced for renewed recrimination from Grandfather, but he was lost in thought and no longer decried her as she'd feared. Like clouds chasing over the sky, his mind shifted with an unseen wind. Internal currents carried him back to a time he'd long buried.

Her mother was also deeply pensive. "Your actions

are not terrible, Claire. These are strange times, indeed. You are heavily burdened."

"Aye," murmured Mrs. Jenner, who'd been unusually quiet during this entire exchange.

"The fault is partly mine," her mother wore on, growing weepy.

"None lay blame upon ye, Mavis," Mrs. Jenner soothed. "Ye suffer greatly. Wait until ye meet Captain Vaughan. Sech a fine gentleman. He could provide for our Claire beyond yer imaginings." She gestured at the web-festooned cellar. "And take her away from all this."

"It's not as if we reside down here on a regular basis," Stuart snapped.

Mrs. Jenner wasn't rebuffed in the least. "True enough, but an English manor and grand estate. And our Claire among the gentry. Think of it, Mavis."

Clearly, her mother was. And how Mrs. Jenner worshipped Vaughan. Claire studied the faithful housekeeper. Shouldn't the woman's curiosity be piqued by all that had recently come to light? Normally, she delved for information. Yet, she did not prod them for added details about the mysterious letter.

Unless—was it possible Mrs. Jenner knew more than she'd revealed? If so, there was only one way she could have been enlightened, unless she'd listened at keyholes. And that source was Vaughan.

Aware of how carefully the canny officer conducted himself, Claire surmised he'd only told the housekeeper what he wanted her to know. What else might he have enlisted her to do, apart from acting as a go between for him and Claire? The woman had behaved strangely around him last evening. There was more of an alliance between these two than Mrs. Jenner let on.

Was anyone truly free of secrets? Besides William, that is, who said and did whatever came into his young head.

Maybe Stuart was right. Perhaps Vaughan did battle for the cypher and Claire's help in finding the exact gravesite to dig for treasure, as much as for her safety and the wellbeing of the Monroes. Her heart plummeted from light and hope to the dark depths, like this cellar.

No! Surely not. Everything in her cried out against the appalling charge conjured by her disturbed thoughts.

If ever a man seemed sincere in his profession of devotion, through and through, it was Vaughan. But she'd thought the same thing about Thomas. The difference between the two was that she cared as much for Vaughan as she hoped he did for her. It had been otherwise with Thomas. Her regard for him faded to nothingness in comparison.

Oh, confound it all, she was beyond mere caring and regard with Vaughan. Such faint words paled when passion was wanted. She'd fallen desperately in love with the man behind the uniform, and couldn't just take it back and renounce his claim on her affections. If he wounded her, then she would bleed mightily. If he broke her heart, it wouldn't mend. This was a crazed, once in a lifetime, romance. She must pay the penalty if he didn't return her love.

How could she be certain of him? She had to know.

Bolting from the bench she ran upstairs.

"Claire!"

It was Stuart. "Stay with them! I must learn what is happening!"

And whether Vaughan truly loved her.

Chapter Sixteen

"Captain Vaughan!"

The sharp summons uttered in familiar accents tolled a warning in Vaughan. His gut tightened at the timing of Colonel Tarleton's arrival as the man himself rode into the yard.

By now, the assembly had dismounted and kindled a small fire to better witness the swordplay. Admittedly, Vaughan had dragged it out to teach Simmons a lesson and divert the men from their original purpose in coming. Even without the orange glow, there was no mistaking Tarleton's stocky figure and confident bearing. He feared nothing and no one. And had no need to. He'd make an extremely successful pirate captain.

How Tarleton would view the duel was impossible to predict. All depended on his mood, and any ulterior motives. But why was he here?

Had someone fetched him while Vaughan was absorbed in the clash of blades, and what had they taken Tarleton from? He disliked interruptions, unless merited. Vaughan hadn't noted anyone leave the grounds. Then he spotted that snake in the grass, Thomas, trotting in behind the senior officer. God only knew what vicious tidings this back-stabbing cousin had whispered in his ear.

Arrayed in all the vestiges of the Legion to which

he was fully entitled, Tarleton reined in his latest acquisition, a white-faced chestnut gelding. Hooded blue eyes surveyed the dueling pair from beneath the black leather helmet, the crest surmounted with a rolled black bearskin. Gilt chains adorned the green turban encircling the rim and a clump of black on green swan feathers decorated the side. The headgear hid Tarleton's reddish hair, but not his temper.

Vaughan daren't defy this formidable leader, unless he coveted a painful and dishonorable execution, but could wager carefully chosen words and manipulate him like a skillful game of chess. And he knew Tarleton's likes, dislikes, what he praised and despised, and his driving ambition.

Their commander coolly contemplated him. "Do you intend to run Simmons through?"

Betting on the side of boldness, Vaughan lowered the sword point from his opponents' chest. The slice in Simmons' shoulder oozed blood and his coat was stained. "I had considered it, sir."

Faint amusement crossed Tarleton's ruddy countenance, a move in Vaughan's favor. "I sometimes share that temptation." He scanned the onlookers. "Enjoying the evening's sport, men?"

A hearty assent sounded from the gathering. "We are that, sir!"

Tarleton seemed satisfied. "Captain Vaughan is most skilled with the blade. An exhibition is of benefit. But I am come on another matter." Annoyance in his gaze, he swept a gloved hand at Thomas, then spoke to Vaughan. "I am not persuaded by your cousin's accusations. However, Mister Vaughan insists you harbor a spy and seditious communication. Such a

Beth Trissel

grave charge must be answered. What say you to this?"

Vaughan's mind turned like the wheels of a runaway carriage. "First, I would ask in turn if Mister Vaughan also communicated to you his interest in my betrothed?"

"Y-Y-You liar! *M-M-My betrothed!*" Thomas bounced in the saddle as if he might spring from his mount in a sputtering frenzy.

"Hush, man," Tarleton rapped. "Blathering like a lunatic." A look of surprise crossed his eyes. "Am I to understand, you are engaged to wed Miss Monroe, Captain Vaughan?"

"Rather sudden, I admit. But I was smitten by the fair lady and wrote Lord Vaughan this morning to share my glad tidings. He is most eager for an heir," Vaughan added, rubbing salt in Thomas's wound. "If all goes as my father would wish, Miss Monroe will sail with me to England in the autumn. It is my hope you will attend the nuptials in Williamsburg where Miss Monroe's aunt resides."

Thomas could contain himself no longer. "What nuptials? Nay, sir! Earlier, in the Ordinary, did Miss Monroe not say she was yet considering my proposal?"

A short laugh from Tarleton. "Women profess many things, Mister Vaughan, but will choose a peerage over a merchant any day." He considered Vaughan. "Why all the secrecy regarding your betrothed's brother and the cypher."

"I trust no one with this information but you, sir. And sought you earlier at the Ordinary." Vaughan cast a look of contempt at Simmons. "In no good conscience, could I entrust this drunkard."

Simmons opened his mouth to bellow protest.

Tarleton stopped him. "You reek of ale. Have you downed an entire cask? Pray continue, Captain Vaughan."

Now came the difficult part. "I have exacted your wishes, Colonel. Lieutenant Monroe has been under house arrest since our arrival at Thornton Hall, where I cornered him in the parlor. Miss Monroe obliges me with her cooperation regarding the cypher, which I also obtained. In return, and out of regard for her family, I request her brother be allowed to remain on the premises under the terms of parole. Although a spy, he was in uniform and broke no code regarding conduct during warfare," Vaughan asserted, not mentioning Stuart's skulking in the walls. McCray also kept silent on that point, and Anderson was mute.

Every muscle taut, Vaughan awaited Tarleton's determination. If their leader decreed otherwise, there was nothing he could do other than carry the plea to Cornwallis upon his arrival.

After a nerve-racking pause, Tarleton gave a nod. "I see no harm in granting your request, Captain. If Lieutenant Monroe fails to honor the conditions of his parole, he will suffer the consequences." Elevating his voice, possibly in the event Stuart Monroe were listening from some hidden vantage point, Tarleton added. "Which we all know to be immediate execution upon recapture and ignominious shame for breaking faith with the agreement."

Fair enough, and as much as Vaughan could hope for. He choked back a whoosh of relief.

Tarleton continued in that projected tone. "It may be Lord Cornwallis will desire to exchange Lieutenant Monroe for a favored officer held prisoner by

Washington. If so, your prisoner will rejoin the fray before summer's end. No matter. We can always capture him again. He sounds less than prudent."

"More prudent now, I suspect, sir," Vaughan offered.

A hint of approval touched Tarleton's eyes. "Any chance Monroe will change colors and become a king's man?"

"None, I fear. And request that he not be required to take that particular oath."

A shrug beneath the green coat with its black collar, and Tarleton inclined his head. "So long as he honors his parole."

"He shall." If Vaughan had to lock the hot-headed Patriot in his chamber and give Mrs. Jenner the key.

"Now, what of the letter?" Tarleton pressed.

"One small matter remains, but I know the site we seek. Miss Monroe will assist me in the completion of this mission."

"Will she, indeed!" Thomas rose in the stirrups and nearly sprang from his horse, he was so incensed. "Twisting her arm, are you?"

"Bribing her, more like," Tarleton interceded. "Enough, Mister Vaughan. Pray allow us to proceed," he chided hotly. "Whatever works your will upon the young lady has my blessing, Captain. An ingenious woman, I must say, if she can decipher a missive such as we've intercepted."

"She is quick-witted. And her deceased father composed the cypher, lending her insights," Vaughan disclosed.

Tarleton assumed his speculative expression. "What of the master spy behind so many of these mysterious and vexing communications that have eluded us?"

"The man is as good as dead," Vaughan said truthfully.

Thomas gaped at him. "How can you possibly know that?"

"I have ascertained his identity. He poses no threat."

"You are certain?" Tarleton pressed.

"Upon my honor. He is entirely without reason, sir."

Realization came into Thomas's disbelieving stare. "It cannot be him."

Vaughan frowned at his loose lipped cousin. If he cared the slightest bit for Claire, he would keep quiet about her grandfather. "As I said, the fellow is quite mad."

Another shrug from Tarleton. "One less spy to trouble with, then. Perhaps his madness will even lead the Rebels astray. I leave you to convey the terms of surrender to Lieutenant Monroe. Assuming he remains in any doubt."

"Might his parole include access to the town of Halifax?" Vaughan asked.

"Perhaps as far as the Ordinary, after we depart. So long as he doesn't lift a finger or conspire against the Crown."

"Most generous terms, sir."

"I would not deprive your future brother-in-law of a friendly pint." He leveled a look at Vaughan. "We shall not always be in this wretched country. Someday, God willing, we shall find ourselves back in England. I expect my friends to remember me as kindly as I now do you."

His intent was blatantly clear. "Yes, sir. Lord Vaughan and I will both look upon you with favor."

"Good. I may run for Parliament. Regarding the cypher, we shall speak further later. Without naming the exact location in front of so many, can you say where the clues lead?"

"Williamsburg."

"Most timely. We shall arrive there before many weeks." Displeasure crossed his gaze. A look men trembled to see. "At present, I am encountering more bother with the local militia than anticipated. Cornwallis sends more regulars. They should arrive on the morrow."

"And his Lordship?"

"Soon after. These townsfolk are troublesome. I shall be glad to be done with them and head to Virginia."

"Yes, sir." Vaughan decided it imprudent to advise this senior office on the conduct of his troops at present. He'd been fortunate to secure Stuart Monroe's safety and protect Thornton Hall.

"Have McCray and Anderson patrol this end of Halifax tomorrow. I do not anticipate a militia uprising here, but cannot be certain. Keep close watch and apprise me of any insurrection."

Vaughan saluted. "We shall remain vigilant."

Tarleton's visage lightened, and he tipped a gloved hand to his helmet in turn. "You have done well, Captain. My best wishes for a happy and fruitful marriage. If my duties allow, I should be honored to attend your nuptials. We trust you will serve out your time with the legion as arranged until autumn?"

Much as Vaughan would rather not linger one moment longer than absolutely necessary on this continent, he inclined his head. "I will do my duty, sir."

"As ever. I value your service. It may well be you shall soon be addressed as major. I will have a word with his Lordship, but given your favor, I see no reason why Cornwallis should withhold his approval."

"Thank you, Colonel. I am most gratified."

Vaughan uttered the words, but received this news with a mix of pleasure and dismay. Not long ago, it would have buoyed his spirits. Now, he feared Claire might believe he'd only behaved as he had for an increase in rank and feel herself ill-used.

How enormously she'd impacted his life. Falling in love could be compared to a religious conversion. He wasn't the man he'd been before, but faced the same expectations from his senior officer.

Exasperation flared back in Tarleton's gaze and he rounded on Thomas, still fuming atop his horse in barely constrained silence. "You, sir, have dragged me from before a warm hearth and plenteous provisions, after a most unsatisfactory day, I might add, to attend to this matter when your cousin was fully able. If not for Captain Vaughan's good tidings, I should have you flogged. Back we go, and you shall foot the bill in return for my forbearance and protection of your home and business."

Thomas had lost this cat-and-mouse game. If the inhabitants of Halifax didn't learn of his divided loyalties from the Monroe family, they soon would from his alliance with the infamous Tarleton.

One hand upraised to heaven, Thomas implored him. "I beg your forgiveness, Colonel, and plead most grieved sensibilities. Miss Monroe must be made aware of my continued esteem. It may be my cousin exaggerates their understanding."

Avid onlookers prized every word and gesture of this added drama to a most riveting evening.

"Imbecile," McCray muttered.

A sentiment Tarleton's expression mirrored. He rolled his eyes. "Do you truly believe the lady will choose you over an accomplished officer and future lord?"

Down came his arm and Thomas pointed accusingly at Vaughan. "He has poisoned Miss Monroe against me. And broken the terms of our agreement."

Some of what Thomas asserted was true, but he didn't realize the extent of his fall from grace. "Your initials were discovered in the right hand corner of the cypher, cousin. By Miss Monroe."

Dumbfounded, Thomas stilled in mid protest.

Tarleton spoke first. "Then we must conclude you are a known informant, Mister Vaughan, and of no further use to us with your identity exposed. Nor are you safe here. Better pack your bags and accompany the army to Virginia."

"I am no camp follower!" Thomas thrust back.

"Remain in Halifax at your peril, sir. To linger in this nest of Rebels is the height of absurdity. Until the land is secured, you had best remain close by us. Virginia lies open for the taking." Tarleton glanced at Thornton Hall. "The house is dark and bids no welcome. I am returning to the Ordinary. Simmons, take your men and journey to camp. Ride partway with me. And no more nonsense between you and Captain Vaughan."

With extreme grudging, Simmons grunted an assent.

Scorn in his gaze, Tarleton blistered him with a glance. "Given your conduct and the accusations hurled at Captain Vaughan, count yourself fortunate to escape with no more than a wounded shoulder. I should get a surgeon to stich that cut and a poultice applied before it festers, or you will also be of no use to me."

Spurring his horse into action, Tarleton sprang away.

A glowering Thomas swung his mount around and followed, even cantering to catch him up. When forced to a choice, he'd put self-preservation first. Likely, he'd request Tarleton grant him several dragoons to oversee his hasty preparations for departing Halifax. All the coins he'd squirreled away wouldn't come amiss in his dealings. Bribery would be wanted.

Vaughan did not doubt Thomas would try his tricks against him again in partnership with Simmons. The threat those two posed dangled over his head, a noose he must stay clear of, but there was nothing more he could do to either man unless they gave him cause. And both had been warned by Tarleton.

Seeing the diversion at an end, the remaining men climbed back in their saddles and sped after the departing riders. They'd long since lost interest in burning Thornton Hall and wouldn't dare attempt a reprisal now that Tarleton had given Vaughan the nod and chastised Simmons. Some regarded Vaughan with newfound appreciation and their former favorite with considerably less. Simmons shot Vaughan a baleful look, as if to warn him of impending doom.

Let him. Vaughan couldn't be bothered with the

miscreant. Well, maybe a single gesture, and extended the middle finger in a rude farewell.

McCray snorted. "Well said, Captain."

Turning to both officers, he applauded his faithful followers. They'd dismounted earlier and stood holding the horses, including his, in the event he required their support.

"Well, gentlemen, it appears we are finished here. I thank you for your loyalty. It shall not go unrewarded."

McCray grinned. "Not necessary, but welcome all the same. In the event I run for Parliament."

Vaughan gave a wry smile. "Just be thankful Tarleton was persuaded to my reasoning."

"Aye. An enraged bear is preferable to his temper."

Anderson nodded, then gestured behind them. "We have an onlooker, Captain."

"I thought they had all gone?"

"She's been there awhile, sir."

She? At the hint in Anderson's tone, Vaughan peered into the shadows. Observant fellow. Sure enough, Claire stood half hidden outside the front of the house.

What had she seen? Worse—overheard?

Chapter Seventeen

Divergent emotions coursed through Claire like a swollen stream overflowing its banks. A bewildered, bemused, and volatile tide—especially the latter. Rather than rush at Vaughan with gratitude, she stared up at what she could see of his face beneath the helmet in the light from the fire the rowdy group had kindled.

Accusations poured from her mouth. "Our wedding? You invited Tarleton to our wedding? I haven't even yet agreed to marry you."

His lips tightened, then parted. "You are perfectly within your rights to refuse me, but I strongly suggest you wait until the colonel has left Halifax before making your pronouncement."

The frost in his tone chilled her. "Of course. I do not mean to antagonize you, but am nearly demented from the events of the day."

His expression softened. "Understandable."

She pleaded with him. "I do not know what to think. On the one hand, I am grateful to you for securing generous terms for my brother—"

"And keeping Simmons and his drunken rabble from torching Thornton Hall," Vaughan interjected.

"Yes, and that."

"And insisting your grandfather posed no threat, and concealing his identity."

"Certainly. But—"

"You are vexed because I may receive an advance in rank due to my interactions with your family."

"Yes. Well—no. I mean, I'm not sure." She hesitated a moment, then burst out again. "You were so glib in your conversation with Colonel Tarleton."

"And you fear I am not sincere with you?"

"Part of me is beset with misgiving."

"The part that mistrusts all British, I daresay. Particularly a dragoon captain."

She made no denial.

"One tells Tarleton precisely what he wishes to hear, *must hear*, in order to secure what one wants in return. Or great will be the fall of your house. By this, I literally mean *yours*."

Cringing at the image, she shifted from foot to foot. "I'm not saying I should prefer Stuart hauled off and the estate set afire."

"I hope not, because that is very nearly what happened."

"How near?"

He eyed her as if she'd missed the obvious. "You saw the angry gathering in the yard. Heard the accusations Simmons cast at the Ordinary that followed us here, and gained in strength. Why do you think Tarleton spared your brother and home other than my presence, my battle of words on your behalf? What else have I to gain other than your protection?"

"Besides, the rank of major? You stand to gain a coffin full of goods for Tarleton," she countered.

"I could already do so, given what I've gleaned from the cypher. Yet here I stand, pleading for your good favor."

"You require one more clue from me. I heard you

say."

"A point I exaggerated to emphasize your usefulness."

"Actually, you do need me."

"I know." The softness in his voice imbued the fingers he lifted to her cheek.

While savoring his touch and the intent behind his avowal, she couldn't let go of the argument. "Not entirely, you don't."

"What do you mean?"

"Grandfather had a lucid moment in the cellar and shared the final hint."

"I see. And you're afraid if you confide in me, I shall mount up and ride to Williamsburg?"

"Mayhap."

He dropped his hand from her face as if she'd scorched him. "If this is your opinion of my character, why should you wish me to remain in your presence one second longer?"

She caught his hand. "You know why."

"Less and less." He didn't return the pressure on his fingers.

Letting go of him, she paced in a circle. "I could not believe my ears when you agreed to support Bloody Ban's rise to power in England."

"Another charge? Assuming Tarleton returns to England—that any of us see our home again—his bid may come to nothing. However, I am now in his debt. Apart from that, who do you think aspires to serve in Parliament? He's just the sort. Ruthless, conniving, ambitious."

She stopped and spun toward Vaughan. "What of you?"

"Do you ask if I'm giving an account of myself?"

"In part."

"In truth," he amended, and had the right of it. "Admittedly, I have been guilty of such behavior. But my inclinations dwindle more and more as I am in the company of a certain young lady."

Pleasure warmed the swell of emotions engulfing her, but she fought to keep her head above water. "What of Parliament?"

"I have no interest."

"Not even an appointment to the House of Lords?"

"Assuredly not."

"Then to what end will you apply your powers?"

"You fear I shall grow bored?"

"A man of your abilities? Yes."

Mirth hinted in his face. "I rather fancy the notion of farming. Breeding superior horses and hounds, anyway. And fathering exemplary children. That should hold my interest, at least until the next war."

She flushed and sought refuge behind a quip. "If it's fought over here, I do hope you will sit that one out."

"Oh, I dare say the French will get up to some further mischief and embroil England."

"Seems there's always some war or other."

"I weary of them." His voice reflected his fatigue.

"As do I." Feeling a little more relaxed with him, she couldn't resist asking. "In regards to the children you speak of siring, will they be ours, or will any wench do?"

"Ours. Most certainly."

"Yes. I heard you fling that heir issue in Thomas's face. Was that wanted?"

The faint humor in Vaughan's expression faded. "Do you pity him?"

"A bit."

"Were you also aware my cousin is the reason Tarleton knew Lieutenant Monroe was within Thornton?"

Stunned, she shook her head. "No."

"Yes. Thomas forced my hand when it came to admitting your brother's presence and declaring him under house arrest."

Another strike against the reprobate.

"Did you think I only divulged that information to impress Tarleton?"

"I did wonder," she admitted.

"And still do, I wager."

Again, she made no denial.

Jaw rigid, his mouth a tight line, he parted it. "A rather wounding silence."

"I cannot swear the thought hasn't crossed my mind."

"Fills it, more like. Could your opinion of me plummet any lower, Miss Monroe?"

With that, he turned and strode across the yard and into the house, leaving her to stare after him with a growing sense of having erred rather badly.

Chapter Eighteen

"And leave him there for the duration of our stay!" Vaughan admonished Mrs. Jenner, entrusting her with the large brass key.

He'd locked the recalcitrant Stuart Monroe in his bedchamber with plenteous provisions, even hot water for bathing. Nothing was denied him, except freedom to do as he liked. Still, he ground his teeth. Ungrateful wretch.

Let him. Vaughan wasn't about to risk the hothead breaking parole on a foolhardy treasure hunt in his determined pursuit of General Arnold. Time to let that matter rest.

He spoke from the other side of the door. "Would you prefer a real prison, Lieutenant, or the black underbelly of a frigate where privateers are held? Poor wretches never get out."

"No," came the unwilling reply. "I suppose I owe you some measure of thanks for the terms of my surrender."

"*Some*? You are fortunate not to be hanging by your neck while your house burns to ashes. As it is, you have all the comforts of home." And brandy, which Vaughan hoped his prisoner would generously imbibe and succumb to oblivion until morning.

He spoke again to Mrs. Jenner, standing with her brows arched and mouth agape. "Lieutenant Monroe may exit his chamber when the Legion leaves town in a day or two. If he ventures any farther than *Person's Ordinary* thereafter, he is in danger of prompt execution should a Loyalist retake him."

"And I will not be here to save your neck," Vaughan warned the sullen man on the other side of the door.

These Patriots were a galling lot. Everlasting work fighting to subdue and subjugate a people hell-bent on rebellion. If the choice were his, he would cease striving and sail home on the next tide.

"Maddening," he muttered to Mrs. Jenner, who dipped her head in acknowledgement.

He strode down the hall to the parlor allotted to him for his night's repose. Such as it was likely to be. But the state of Stuart Monroe wasn't what truly troubled him.

For one who'd carried the day better than he could possibly have expected, Vaughan had lost the battle for Claire. Dwelling on the unhappy exchange with her earlier that evening did nothing to improve his spirits.

Damn and blast. He set his plumy helmet on the low table, deposited his scarlet sash, coat, and waistcoat beside the headgear, and undid his silver gorget and black neck stock. He flung them atop the pile, stripped his shirt, and added it to the heap. Then pulled off his boots and set them aside. His stockings and breeches joined the rest of his uniform.

After sluicing his bare body with the hot water Mrs. Jenner had sent to his room, he lathered with the soap and rinsed off the rich suds. Fresh linen awaited to towel himself dry, also thoughtfully provided by the housekeeper. He shouldn't have been short with her after all she'd done. It wasn't her fault she dwelt in such a cantankerous household.

Exhaustion came over him. He was bone tired, and heavy spirits dragged him down. He exerted himself enough to fish in his portmanteau for the tooth powder and small brush he carried and cleaned his teeth. Then undid the queue at his neck, ran a comb through his hair, and left it loose around his shoulders. Pulling on the fresh shirt doubling as his night attire, he lowered himself into the armchair before the hearth.

Supper awaited him on the stand beside his chair, but he scarcely heeded the food, preferring to scowl into the flames. The ale didn't go untouched, though. And he managed a portion of the trifle McCray had praised so highly.

The knob turned and the Scotsman entered. On seeing Vaughan's black countenance, he stopped short. "Believe I'll find it a mite more cheering out in the stable with Anderson and the lad following at his heels like a whippet."

Vaughan glowered in reply and McCray crossed the room. Catching up his bedroll from the corner, he stumped off to join the pair. Ironically, Anderson seemed the big brother William never really had. Maybe Stuart Monroe would take a hand in rearing his sibling while under confinement. Lord knows, the boy needed direction. The entire family would benefit from Stuart's enforced stay at Thornton Hall, for as long as it lasted.

No doubt, the brash officer would be released in a prisoner exchange all too soon and Vaughan would encounter him in battle. The thought didn't cheer him. His standing was low enough in Claire's esteem, possibly irreparably. He didn't solely blame her for their heated encounter in the yard, and hadn't expected vociferous praise, but more gratitude and less recrimination wouldn't have come amiss.

Well, that was that. He'd pleaded his case and she'd passed harsh judgment, making no overtures toward him since.

'Retired to her bedchamber, sir,' Mrs. Jenner had offered. Not that he'd asked about Claire's whereabouts, but the all-seeing housekeeper must've noted his glum speculation. And she had to realize something untoward had occurred between the couple, given his dark mood and Claire's withdrawal.

Despite this piercing thorn in his side, Vaughan was glad he'd spared Claire and her family the further ravages of war. If only his efforts had meant more to her and not been interpreted as pure selfishness. He was the first to admit he could be self-centered, and strongly inclined toward this direction in the past, but on this occasion he'd battled for Claire. Confound it.

Sunk in frustration, he sat listening to wood pop in the hearth and the noises of the household. At last, the home grew still. The unsettled members trundled off to bed with a late supper must've succumbed to a stupor, likely induced by an herbal elixir. Stuart Monroe was quiet. Finally. What was he like when not obsessed with rebelling against the king?

Quite amiable, possibly. War didn't bring out the best—

A rap at the door jerked Vaughan from his internal rant.

Mrs. Jenner sailed in with more food and drink on a tray. Brows arched, she looked from him to the stand at his side. "You've scarcely touched yer supper, sir. And I feared it mightn't be enough."

"Plentiful. Leave what you've brought. I'll eat it later."

She set the tray on a high-backed chest. Plainly, she wanted to inquire into his melancholy, probably his and Claire's, but he was in no temper for a chat.

"Will that be all, sir?"

"It will." Probably all that would transpire between them apart from a civil farewell.

He intended to return to camp in the morning and rejoin Tarleton. He'd grow as addled as the rest of this household if he remained here, tormented by Claire's distant presence. "I am not to be disturbed before dawn. Only a light breakfast."

"Yes, Captain. Until the morning, then."

"Thank you for your service, my good woman."

"Happy to oblige." Eyeing him in consternation, she dropped a curtsy and skirted out the door, closing it behind her.

Blast it all. He badly wanted to resolve matters with Claire. Why did she have to overhear him in the yard and take such offense?

Getting to his bare feet, he walked to the couch, tore the bedding from the plush upholstery, and spread it before the hearth. He'd sleep here. The floor was still more comfortable than the hard ground he'd spent many a night on, and brooding into the flames suited him.

Red coals blurred before his eyes. Weighted with cares, he succumbed to the realm of nothingness. How long he dozed, he didn't know, only that a light tap sounded at his door.

Who the—? It had better not be the well-meaning Mrs. Jenner again. A frayed temper could only stretch so far, and he wasn't among the most patient of men.

"Yes?" he asked, an edge to his tone.

"It's me."

Claire? His heart leapt like a horse at the start of a race. "One moment."

He scrambled to his feet. His shirt barely covered the essentials and the neck hung open, but he didn't pause to pull on breeches and hastened to open the door.

What on earth, or heaven? A vision stood before him.

Gowned in a white shift, and only a shift, Claire hovered outside the entryway. Even her feet were unclad. The linen cloth fell just below her knees, leaving her shapely legs exposed, and the sleeves only reached her elbows. The drawstring neckline was a tug away from temptation. Hardly proper attire for paying a call, nor was the hour or place. Nothing about this was seemly, but roused him to the core.

Before someone spotted them and jaws dropped, he took her by the arm and drew her inside, then quietly shut the door. Utterly improbably as this seemed, she stood before him. He had yet to ascertain why.

"I am elated to see you," he said, in lowest tones. "But what in God's name are you doing here?"

"I came to apologize for doubting you." Her voice the barest whisper.

He ran his appreciative gaze over her. "Dressed like that?"

"I couldn't sleep."

Strangely, he had been. No longer. "What is the

hour?"

"Midnight."

"The witching hour, and an enchantress visits me."

Firelight played over the appealing flush in her cheeks, and she dropped her eyes, a demure gesture out of place with her appearance and arrival. And she was met with his barely covered thighs, his shirt nearly transparent in the orange glow. The curve of her breasts showed through the shift and he didn't dare glance any lower. They might as well be naked.

The exhilarating image made his blood run hot. So much for obscuring evidence of his manhood.

"You best be glad your brother is locked in his chamber, and the rest of your family senseless," he chided under his breath, feeling anything but sorry she'd come.

The hint of a smile at her lips, she glanced up. "I had considered that."

"Had you? Well, consider this." Clasping her shoulders, he gazed into her face. "What am I to do with you? Bear you to my couch, invite you to lie with me before the hearth?"

She looked him straight in the eyes. "Would you like to?"

He almost choked. "Beyond description. But I should have to marry you on the morrow."

"All right."

"What? Make love to you or wed you?"

"Both."

His chest pounded wildly. "So, despite everything, you are accepting my proposal?"

"I am."

"Even if we discover the town of Halifax sacked in

the light of day, you will not hold me accountable?"

"Not if I may hold you now. Please, Vaughan."

Her plea cut through him like molten fire. Dropping his hands from her shoulders, he caught her to him, savoring her womanly softness. "My dearest."

"I cannot bear to let you go," she whispered.

"Nor I, you."

Burying his lips in the delectable arch of her neck, he trailed kisses up her smooth skin, spreading goosebumps as he went. She shivered in palpable enjoyment and sighed, the sweetest sound this side of paradise.

He nuzzled her ear. "I adore you, and have from the moment I laid eyes on you."

"The second moment," she said breathlessly. "Being vexed with me at the first."

"Must you argue everything I say?" Covering her lips, he settled the debate with a kiss tender, yet heated with the passion surging inside him. If he were a forge, he could meld white hot iron into steel.

How fervently she returned the pressure on her mouth, willing, wanting, withholding nothing. But she must. He must. Battling desire with determination, he released her—a terrible wrench.

No. He couldn't do it. Enfolding her in his arms again, he returned for yet another searing kiss. He could linger hours at her lips. But he mustn't.

Hard evidence of his need couldn't be hidden, crushed as he was against her shift, but masculine desire didn't seem to frighten her in the slightest. This was the woman who'd kissed him earlier, at her initiation, and the one who'd gone on that breakneck ride with him. This was his bold Claire. But would she still feel this way tomorrow?

So winded he could scarcely speak, he strove to preserve her honor. "Sweetheart, I want you more than I can say. But you must be my wife."

"I shall." She laid her cheek against his chest, the warmth radiating through the cloth.

"It cannot be tomorrow, my darling, unless we find a most tolerant priest with a devotion to the Crown."

"Most all the inhabitants of this town are Patriots."

"I had noted that," he said drily.

"What of the courthouse? Mightn't a clerk do the job?"

"I would hold the man at knife-point, if he would accomplish the deed. But do you still have a functioning courthouse?"

"We did. I think."

"All is chaos now. Any clerk with a bit of sense is in hiding while troops prevail."

She tilted her face and fixed entreating eyes on him, rendering him nearly mute with the yearning in their depths. "You will soon be gone from me. I do not know when I shall see you again."

He groaned. "Precisely why I mustn't compromise your honor and leave you to suffer rumor and ruin."

Lifting her hand, she stroked the loose hair at his shoulders. "My darling, we haven't the time or means for the usual courtship, engagement, and church wedding expected of a young lady. The world is topsy-turvy."

"I cannot argue that," he conceded.

"All we truly have are these stolen moments. If you desire an heir, now is the hour to conceive it."

Had he heard aright? Regarding her through the red

haze of need warring with reason, he strove to comprehend. "How can you possibly know?"

"Female intuition."

"Not a state I am versed in. But if I lie with you now and you do, indeed, conceive, you will be well along when we sail for England this autumn."

"Then I shall arrive in the *interesting condition* that will most please your father. As the only remaining son, he must accept your choice or let Thomas Vaughan inherit."

"That is out of the question. A beautiful young bride carrying his grandchild will gratify the old curmudgeon."

Vaughan made up his mind in the decisive way years of leadership had prepared him to execute. "Very well. You have persuaded me. But first, please accept this token." Taking the ring embellished with the family crest from his little finger, he slid it onto her thumb. "Wear it on a cord at your neck for safekeeping."

Her eyes glistened. "Always."

"In the morning, I shall write you a letter swearing my allegiance and asserting you are my wife. Keep it with you. And promise you will journey to Williamsburg as soon as may be and remain with your aunt. I hope we may formally wed there."

"I promise."

"Do not breathe a word of this, but I expect the Legion will remain in Eastern Virginia once we arrive. If we journey to New York, you will accompany me, and we shall sail from that harbor."

She nodded.

"You must hasten from Halifax with all possible speed after my departure. Resentment shall be heaped upon you for your bond to me. At least in Williamsburg, the power of the Crown is greater."

Tears filled her eyes, and he smoothed them with his fingers. "You realize what you are forsaking? Your people may never forgive you."

"In time, they shall. And if not, you are my choice."

"So long as we do end as *Romeo and Juliet*."

"Never. Neither of us will take our own lives."

He caressed the tendrils curling at her face, shorter than his locks, yet charming. "Agreed. And I shall battle like the devil to stay alive."

"Pray God, you do." With a shaky breath, she pressed her lips back to his famished mouth.

He drew her down with him onto the bedding before the low flames in the hearth. A chill was in the air, but he was too afire to notice. Was this truly real? If he dreamt, he wished never to awake, and drank her in as she undid the tie at her neck, slipping the shift down over her creamy shoulders.

How smooth and round were her breasts, and perfect, blushed with rose. It seemed wealth enough to gaze upon her, let alone touch such purity. Divine, to cup his hands over the mounds swelling beneath his palms, and to cover each pert nipple with his lips. She trembled, but not with fear. Nor when he slipped his fingers between her thighs. Only a breathy gasp escaped her.

Heat flooded them both, in a washing wave. He felt her wanting, and there was no possibility she could miss his pulsing need. Still, she made no effort to repel him. If she had second thoughts, she hid them beneath rapturous sighs, quivering at his every touch.

But must be absolutely sure. "Claire, are you certain this is what you want?"

"Yes." A husky affirmation.

One final try. "'Twould require great strength of will to cease now, but I shall if you so decree."

"Proceed with my consent."

A sublime utterance. Rolling her over in his arms, he poised above her, his hair brushing her face. "I feared to lose you after our falling out this evening. Now, here you are offering yourself to me."

"Everything I have is yours." She circled her arms at his neck, exquisite breasts pressed against his chest, voluptuous curves to his hammered hips, and kissed him long and hard. Then paused to gaze into his eyes, a hint of mirth in hers. "What more invitation do you require, sir?"

The implication that he, a former rake, had to be coaxed into intimacy, sent him into paroxysms and he buried his face in her neck to muffle the laughter. Tears streaming down his eyes, he managed a muted reply. "Nothing.

"Then get on with it."

Too much. He was off again, with her squirming delightfully as he smothered his guffaws against her perfumed skin. She giggled softly. And he prayed none overheard the euphoria in his chamber.

"Do you know what you invite?" he whispered in her ear.

"I await discovery, sir."

Without another word of protest in his effort to spare her virtue, he eased his shaft into her oiled warmth. A charge of desire surged through him. Too jolting. Too fast.

Reining himself in, he forced himself to slow down and proceed with care. She was a novice at lovemaking. He mustn't spoil her first foray into a wondrous new world. But he needn't fear she'd cry out and bring someone running. She took all he gave and urged him in even further.

A gasp, and a tremor shot through her. She gripped his upper arms and hid her face in the curve of his shoulder.

Breathing deeply, he halted. "All right?"

After a few gulps, she nodded. "Yes. Go on."

Mindful of her every exhalation, each tremor, he moved rhythmically within her. The hands clamped at his arms relaxed and she recovered her stride.

This passionate woman would make one hell of a wife. And he loved her so; he could hardly bear the thought that this single union might have to last them for a lifetime. If something happened to him, or more forbiddingly, to her.

Somehow, someway, he would prevail and take Claire home to England. For now, he throbbed with the desire to simply take her. All of her. And she freely gave.

Chapter Nineteen

The pale light of dawn and Mrs. Jenner found Claire tucked next to Vaughan on the bedding before the hearth. She glanced around drowsily at the housekeeper poised in the doorway, a tray in her hands. For once, she wished the hard-working woman had overslept and given them a few more precious, undisturbed minutes.

What bliss to slumber in his arms, pressed to his muscular chest, after the thrilling intimacy shared between them. The morning was chill and the fire had died down to red coals in the grate, but she was warm under the covers in his embrace. If only the world and all its clamor would fade away and she might always be with him.

The adept Mrs. Jenner summed up the situation at a glance. Blocking view of the couple with her well-swaddled figure, she spoke over her shoulder to whoever trailed behind, probably Jim. "The captain don't want kindling now," she said, and hurriedly shut the door. Her expression hovered between the unruffled acceptance of a plain woman accustomed to such matters, and the protective demeanor of a mother hen wanting to scoop Claire under her wings. "I daresay you two made up that quarrel."

Claire answered with a smile.

Vaughan rolled over, his glorious chest bare, blond

hair brushing his shoulders. The blanket concealed the remainder of his magnificence. He truly was her golden knight.

"If this good woman says, 'Your lady mother is coming to your chamber,' that is not a good omen." He referred to the quote from *Romeo and Juliet*.

Suddenly alarmed, Claire appealed to Mrs. Jenner. "Is she?"

"Yer mama? Nae." Mrs. Jenner bore the tray with the steaming cup and corncakes dripping butter and molasses to the stand at one side of the hearth. "But Mrs. Monroe asks to meet the captain at dinner. And Mister Stuart is more amenable this morning. He requests permission to join the family in the dining room."

Which meant Stuart hadn't overheard Claire's outrageous deed in the night. Or worse—he had, and wished to confront her. "What of Grandfather?"

"Quiet. Poor man's scarcely spoken since the cellar," the housekeeper replied, with a meaningful glance at Claire.

"Oh. Yes."

Pushing up on his elbows, Vaughan rubbed his chin, thoughtfully. "I find myself inclined to entertain the notion of a family dinner. If you would convey these tidings and see all are invited, Mrs. Jenner."

"Indeed I shall, sir. 'Twill please them. Perhaps—it might be best—if I quietly fetch Miss Claire's day dress?"

"I think it might. I trust we may rely upon your discretion?"

"Not a peep from me, Captain. And I'll take care no one sees me bring 'em."

What an odd twist to imagine the housekeeper furtively fetching her clothes.

"Excellent," he said. "Perhaps some warm water for bathing and a second cup of whatever passes for tea when you're able?"

"And you might find a cord for this." Claire waved her hand, the impressive black onyx ring on her thumb catching the light, the stone in the broad gold band emblazoned with the head of a stag. "'Tis large for my finger. I shall wear it at my throat."

"Oh my." Mrs. Jenner covered her mouth to stifle an outburst, then withdrew her palm. "The heavens be praised. He's given you his ring."

"And will write her a letter avowing my intent which you shall witness," Vaughan interjected. "Lieutenant McCray and Ensign Anderson, as well, until more can be done by way of marriage. I shall also pen a copy for her kin."

Both hands clapped to her face, Mrs. Jenner did a little caper. Unlikely for one of her girth. "Oh, that is worthy, sir."

"Did you fear I would ravish her and go?"

Flushed like one burnt by the sun, she paused in her jig. "Such has been known to happen."

"So it has. Thus every effort shall be made to assure her rightful place at my side. Any child who may be borne of our union is proclaimed my issue."

"Most gratifying to hear, Captain." Grasping the hem of her apron, she blotted her eyes.

Tears also filled Claire's.

"Turbulent times, my good woman, or I vow I should have wed her first."

Mrs. Jenner bobbed her head, then flew into action.

"My—I've much to see to. And this young lady will catch her death." Snatching up the shift Claire had left on the floor, she advanced on her.

Nothing for it, other than to oblige the determined female. Vaughan redirected his gaze as Claire sat up and stuck her head through the neck and pushed both arms into the sleeves, amusing, given all he'd seen in the night, but she appreciated his decorum. Mrs. Jenner did the ties at her bodice, as if she were five-years-old. With a satisfied nod, the preoccupied woman swept from the room. Though she assured the door was shut tightly behind her.

His lips twitched. "I am surprised she didn't dress me as well."

Claire was flabbergasted. "What a notion."

He chuckled. "Shall we dine on our provisions, Madame?"

"Not *Miss*?"

"No longer." Reaching out, he clasped her hand and pressed a kiss to her palm. "I regard you as my wife."

Words couldn't begin to express the emotion welling inside her.

He slipped his fingers through her tousled hair. "After breakfast, I'll send McCray and Anderson to patrol this edge of town as Tarleton directed. Other dragoons may join them."

"Will you go, too?" Her heart ached at the thought of parting with him for a single second.

"Not unless I am summoned. The war can conduct itself without me for a day. We shall spend this time together. It's little enough to ask. And I have letters to write."

She studied him through the blur in her eyes. "You still have not inquired about the cypher."

"Nor shall I, until you are willing to impart whatever it is you gleaned from your grandfather."

"Only this." Blinking hard, emotions running high, she decided to confide all. "You were right. Papa did have a brother."

Vaughan was instantly alert. "Let me guess. He's buried at Bruton Parish."

"Yes. My late grandmother was from Williamsburg, the Carter family."

"Prominent," he mused. "Your mother also hails from there."

"The Randolphs, another old family. But in regards to 'Wee Robbie,' as Grandfather referred to the boy, he must have died when they were visiting his wife's home and was interred in the parish yard. Grandfather could hardly bear to speak of his lost son and kept him a secret all these years."

The intensity in Vaughan's expression reminded her of a fox on the scent. "But your father knew?"

"Oh, yes. Grandfather was adamant Papa did."

"This may alter everything," he said quietly.

Her stomach knotted. "What do you mean?"

"I must consider the implications."

The gravity in his manner sent a tremor down her spine. "Dear Lord. Please don't tell me you have changed your mind."

His brows arched. "In respect to us? Never, dearest."

"What, then?"

"I speak of the cypher."

Still, she didn't grasp his meaning and shook from

the chill and uncertainty.

"Here. Mrs. Jenner was right. You grow cold." Closing the blanket around Claire's shoulders, he held her close. "Have you not yet realized you did not solve this mystery alone, nor can you see it through without me?"

"But your loyalty is to Tarleton."

"True. And his chief wish is to prevent the treasure from falling into Rebel hands to be used against General Arnold. Nor would he object to obtaining it for the Crown, but I have another scheme. One not yet contemplated by anybody."

"Will you share it?"

He pressed his lips to her head. "When it's time."

Puzzled beyond description, she had no choice other than to wait for revelation. In a peculiar reversal, he now possessed the remaining clue.

Chapter Twenty

Vaughan extended his arm to Claire. "You would outshine every lady at any ball you attended."

Tingling at his admiration, she laid her hand on his crimson sleeve. "You flatter me, sir."

"Not in the least. You deserve every syllable."

His praise made the two hours she'd spent apart from him laboring in preparation for this dinner worthwhile.

Mindful of the esteemed occasion, and prodded by her mother, she wore a sumptuous flowered gown from prosperous days, sunk low at the bodice above the boned corset pinching her waist and bosom cruelly.

"No beauty without price," her mother had cajoled her.

Three petticoats, the outer one of beribboned and embroidered azure taffeta, made a sky-blue background for the floral fabric, and the gold silk shawl borrowed from her mother lent a sunny accent. The crowning feature, and one Claire detested, was the coiffed and curled powdered wig atop her head. Iridescent feathers fluttered from the jewel-studded comb affixed to the false hair. Although the jewels were paste, they shone like real gemstones. She liked the comb and feathers, impossible to anchor in her short locks, and Mama had declared the impropriety of 'deporting oneself with shorn tresses', so she wore the white wig. But if

Vaughan approved her appearance, then all was right.

Skirts rustling, Claire walked by his side into the elegant dining room. Candles shone from the long sideboard, high cabinet, and every possible surface. Even though it was early afternoon and sunny out, the scent of beeswax wafted sweetly from the many tapers. Mama wanted the room to glow like Christmas. The green paneled walls reminded Claire of holly leaves, and the red chair railing of its berries.

A pang cut through her. This might be the first and last time Vaughan ever graced this chamber. Tomorrow might well find him gone. Surely, the day after.

One comforting thought; they could be at his home by yuletide. Farfetched as that seemed, it was possible, despite the war and vast ocean lying between them and England. Autumn would come, and they would depart as he'd promised. She must hold to this shining beacon, or sink in despair.

For now, he was here. His presence filled the brightly lit space around them. Even though his coat was scarlet and he fought for the Crown, he was so handsome she could scarcely breathe—also partly the corset. She proudly accompanied him to the petite woman in mauve taffeta waiting to greet him.

"Madame." Offering a short bow, he took her mother's hand in his and pressed his lips to the dainty, gloved fingertips. "I thank you for your kind invitation."

"Captain, we are honored you can join us." Her mother spoke clearly, no evidence of the slur that often accompanied her speech. She'd put aside her brandy and nostrums for the important occasion.

Fan in hand, preening beneath the lace cap, she

gazed at Vaughan with the esteem she bestowed on the higher ranking members of society. To be in the presence of landed gentry, albeit a British dragoon captain, was the height of achievement. For all her support of the revolution, when it came right down to it, wealth and nobility impressed Mrs. Monroe. Highly.

"We offer our gratitude to you for your service to our family and the preservation of our home, sir."

"I am glad to be of service, Ma'am, and hope you will visit Hartford House soon after my return to England." He paused and smiled at Claire with such dizzying appeal she felt giddy, and would have even without the snug stays.

"*Our return*," he amended. "Your lovely daughter and mine. Lord and Lady Vaughan would welcome you, and my sisters should be gratified by your company. The younger girls are ever eager to attend social occasions and in want of a proper chaperone."

Rapture crossed her mother's face and years fell away. She almost looked pretty again. Doubtless, visions of dinners, parties, and the balls she sorely missed, even grander in England, floated before her mind. Claire was happy for her, and realized she'd been lost in her own misery for so long, she hadn't fully considered the ravages upon her mother. This likely accounted for her recourse to elixirs and strong drink.

Enthralled by the mental image he painted, the grateful woman seemed buoyed above the perilous seas upon which she'd been cast. "There is nothing I should like more, sir."

The roll of Stuart's eyes and unintelligible mutter voiced his view on the matter. Claire was well-versed with his disdain for aristocratic privilege, another cause of the war. That Vaughan was the future Earl of Carbery did not impress her brother in the slightest. The flint in his narrow gaze could strike sparks. He resembled the severe ancestor in the portrait mounted above the glowing hearth. Not reassuring.

Out of uniform, and appropriately attired in a dove gray coat and fawn breeches, Stuart leaned his lanky frame against the corner of the carved mantel. She hoped he didn't contemplate grabbing the poker and attacking their guest, and was tempted to remind him of his promised behavior.

Their beaming mother was the opposite of her stormy son. She snatched at any opportunity offering a rise in class distinction and had latched onto Vaughan's proposal to her daughter like the answer to her prayers. Perhaps it was. The matrimonial minded woman was besotted by the signed letter, witnessed and sealed, stating his intent, and the crested ring suspended from the black velvet ribbon around Claire's neck.

She fluttered her gilded fan. "I should take much pleasure in visiting Hartford House, sir, after your safe return to England, as my health allows."

"Good. I have written Lord Vaughan regarding my attachment to your daughter and shall acquaint him with your desire. Perhaps Master William might attend school at Eton? I can vouch for its excellence having gone there myself, and smooth his path."

If he'd offered her the keys to the kingdom, she couldn't have been more awe-struck. "Might you render that possible?"

"Readily. By providing tuition for his schooling and passage for you both aboard a merchant ship."

"Over my dead body." This time, Stuart was quite

clear.

Vaughan ignored his caustic comment. Claire shot her brother a warning look. One more utterance like that and she'd advance upon him, ludicrous in her attire, but she would. And he knew it.

Curling his lips in a mock smile, he bit back any further remark. At least, for now.

Their mother feigned deafness, a common ploy. "What a blessing that would be, Captain, and exceedingly hospitable."

"No service is too great for those Claire holds dear."

"She's our darling girl, but William—" Mrs. Monroe waved at the window, indicating the boy in the distance. "You see how he is, outdoors at all hours, running wild like a pony. And equally as unruly." She colored, clapping a hand to her mouth, and released it. "Of course, you're aware. My apologies for his behavior in wounding your guide."

"An unfortunate accident, Ma'am."

"How fares the poor fellow?"

"Mending, at the hands of your skilled healer."

Relief crossed her eyes. "Oh, yes. Ezekiel possesses a marvelous knowledge of herbs."

Heads turned as Mister Monroe entered the room, dressed in black and leaning heavily on his cane. Unlike her mother whose age had magically diminished at Vaughan's coming, her grandfather had added years, seemingly overnight. How was it possible this man had wielded a sword with the skill and strength he'd displayed only two days ago?

Was his medicinal dosage too great, or had recalled grief overwhelmed him, or a combination of both?

Yesterday, he'd been in the throes of despair over the threat to his home and memories of past loss. Vaughan had saved Thornton Hall, but Claire had no idea how he now stood with this unpredictable relation. She could better foresee the weather than Grandfather's mood, and hastened over the polished floor to meet him.

Taking his arm, she gestured at the repast. "Please join us at the table, sir. We are about to be seated."

"Aye, lass. No need to make a fuss over me. I'm just a bit stiff."

"The weather, perhaps?" But the damp chill alone didn't account for his evident weakness. Was this the same man who'd wrestled Lieutenant McCray and stout Mrs. Jenner and given them a rough time of it, not long ago?

He acknowledged Vaughan with a nod. "Captain. You are to dine with us, I trust."

"Yes. Thank you, Mister Monroe."

"The womenfolk tell me the house wouldn't be standing without yer intervention on our behalf. Yer entitled to a decent meal and a bit of hospitality."

"Most welcome, sir."

Claire raised her eyebrows at Vaughan, who lifted the gold braid on one scarlet shoulder and let it drop. Despite Mrs. Jenner's insistence her grandfather was much calmer today, neither of them had expected a cordial greeting.

The old man indicated the seat to the right of his place at the head of the table. "Sit ye there, Captain. Claire at my left. Stuart bring that sour countenance and sit alongside yer sister. You could curdle milk with that scowl. My daughter-in-law will grace her usual place. Will ye not, Mavis."

The matron inclined her head. "I shall do my utmost."

A rare occasion; one of Grandfather's clearheaded days. Grateful he had the presence of mind to give sensible direction and recognition, Claire accompanied him to the table. Each person stood behind their chairs, an unspoken truce between Stuart and Vaughan as they bowed their heads.

Grandfather repeated the familiar blessing offered before a meal. At its conclusion, he waved a trembling hand at the assembly. "Pray be seated."

No ranting? No raving? She could scarcely believe this was the madman she'd dealt with far too often, and exchanged glances with Vaughan.

Bending low, he pulled back the walnut splat-back chair for her and pressed his mouth near her ear. "Keep watch on both men," he whispered, then stepped to the aid of her grandfather who appeared particularly shaky.

"Allow me, sir." Vaughan assisted him.

"My rheumatics are flaring up, and I'm a wee bit poorly is all. Nothing a tonic will not put right. Need some sassafras for a good blood cleansing. Mayhap some mullein for m' chest." He carefully lowered his bent frame onto the chair.

His demeanor alarmed Claire. "Shall we send for Ezekiel?"

"Nae, lass. After dinner will be soon enough to down one of his potions."

With that, she must be satisfied. Creating a disturbance by summoning the healer, coupled with Stuart's ill humor, would distress her mother.

Stuart seated the matron at the other end of the lengthy board covered in snowy cloth and laden with the best blue and white china and gleaming silver, a bowl of punch in the center, then settled beside his sister. They'd excused William from joining them. He was bent on patrolling the grounds as his newfound friend Ensign Anderson was off doing in town. Given that the two fought on opposing sides of this raging conflict, Claire wasn't certain whom the boy guarded the estate from, unless he intended to shout an alert upon spotting anyone he deemed a threat.

Delicious fragrances accompanied the tread of feet. Mrs. Jenner sailed into the room followed by Joseph, Jim, Minnie, and Maddie, each bearing the first course. The mingled aroma from the tureen of barley soup, platters of smoked ham, roasted pigeon, seasoned beefsteaks battered and fried in ale, and eggs in croquettes made Claire realize how hungry she was.

More dishes and desserts would follow this initial round, and a stream of spirits liberally poured forth. The kitchen had hummed with activity for hours, both cook and housekeeper eager not to be outdone by any other home Vaughan visited in the colonies. The expectation he would carry back a favorable account of Thornton Hall was reflected in Mrs. Jenner's face.

He tipped his hand to her. "Splendid. My compliments."

"Thank ye, sir." Well-satisfied, the housekeeper scuttled out the door. All but Jim followed. The youth remained to wait at the table, while the next culinary conquest was in the making.

Meanwhile, the gentle clink of cutlery sounded. Claire was torn between enjoying the appetizing fare and scrutinizing the assembly. Stuart ate in silence, but appeared on the verge of bursting forth any moment.

Several glasses of punch on top of the ale, wine, and brandy, might tip him over the edge. Her mother summoned a smile when Vaughan caught her eye, though she darted apprehensive looks at her elder son.

Vaughan's composure was honed with the innate awareness of danger he wore like a mantle, epitomized by the sword hanging at his shoulder. He might dine with the household, glossed in the veneer of good breeding, but he didn't trust them, nor could she fault him for his extreme caution.

Undeterred, their hostess attempted conversation. "In regards to your home, Captain. What age is Hartford House?"

"It's difficult to say for certain, Ma'am. The original structure was built in the fifteenth century and has been expanded at various times since. My father also has an estate in Wales, and a home in London. For the season, of course."

"Of course." Her mother hung on his every word, as if spoken by an oracle.

Not Stuart. Claire nervously sipped her wine.

"Do you hunt?" their hostess ventured.

"Often," Vaughan assured her. "We have excellent horses and hounds at Hartford. Do you ride, Mrs. Monroe?"

"No. Though my daughter will heartily enjoy all the sport you have to offer. The girl relishes a thumping good ride."

Choking on the last swallow she'd taken, Claire coughed behind her hand. A faint smile played at Vaughan's lips. Stuart eyed his mother as if the effusive matriarch had taken leave of her senses and rumbled disapprovingly.

What would follow? Claire hadn't long to wait. They were finishing the first course when her brother laid down his fork with the manner of one about to cross blades.

Dismissing his flighty mother, Stuart appealed to their grandfather, seemingly more of sound mind today. "Will you not speak, sir? Are you aware of your granddaughter's engagement to Captain Vaughan, their *matrimonial bond*, as avowed in his letter? Is this outrage to be borne?"

Claire gripped the table. Her mother's face creased in horror at Stuart's renewed intrusion into her desperate attempt at a dinner party. With the watchful eye of a herd dog, Vaughan shifted his gaze from one man to the other.

His eyes thoughtful, Grandfather chewed and considered. He swallowed, stroked his beard, and gave a nod. "Aye. I am aware of her betrothal. Not deaf, mind you. But will not stand in her way."

Stuart reddened. "You cannot possibly bestow your blessing on the pair. Have you no issue with her wedding an officer in the British Legion?"

Grizzled brows drawn together, the older man fixed narrow eyes on his grandson. "I have every objection to the lass wedding him, save one. 'Tis plain enough she's smitten by the captain."

"She must come to her senses," Stuart argued.

"And you to yours," their mother flung back. "The war will not go on forever. We shall not always be at odds."

"But we are now." Stuart thumped his fist down on the boards, rattling the china.

"And you would be hanging from a tree were it not

for Captain Vaughan's intercession," the perturbed woman reminded him. "Honestly, your interference is vexing enough to request he escort you back to your chamber."

"Gladly," Vaughan growled.

Steel glinted in both men's gaze. Stuart sprang to his feet. Vaughan rose. Claire recoiled from them coming to blows. Especially here and now. Her poor mother. She'd be back in bed imbibing her nostrums again.

"*Wheesht*, Stuart," Grandfather hushed him, frowning at the males on verge of battle in the dining room. "Sit ye down, gentlemen. Do not spoil the dinner. The ladies have little enough pleasure these days."

Still bristling, the two men lowered themselves to their seats. 'Twas a narrow escape. No true cessation of acrimony.

Laboring to speak, as though from the effort of uttering each word, Grandfather wore on. "Hear me, Grandson. At two and twenty, yer sister is of age to give her own consent. And she need not remain under this roof when you are master. As to Captain Vaughan, he can give her what we cannot, a grand home free from warfare and children raised in safety."

"England is also at war," Stuart argued.

"Not invaded. Not torn with strife," Vaughan interjected. "Most folk live peaceably."

Stuart rounded on him. "Isn't it enough you wish to take my sister to dwell among those whose yoke of tyranny we struggle to shift from our necks, but also my mother and brother? They will be scorned."

Vaughan shook his head. "Englishmen and women are not so vehement about the war as are the colonists.

It is of passing importance to most. With the backing of Lord and Lady Vaughan, your relations will be eyed with curiosity and then accepted in society. Apart from my wife, who will remain with me, your mother and brother may return to Thornton Hall whenever they wish. I desire only to be of service to your family."

His voice wheezy, Grandfather spoke again. "Decent of you to offer, Captain." Then he addressed his grandson. "Whether they go or stay, yer duty is clear. And lies here. Heed the terms of parole as befits a man of honor. If ye are exchanged, fight for the cause. But do not fall. You and the lad are the last of the Monroe line. Wed a genteel lass and fill this home with children. Praise God for each who draw breath. Too soon—they may cease." He eyed Stuart with solemnity. "Give me yer word you shall do this. Let your sister choose as she will."

Stuart grudgingly nodded. "As you wish."

Approval touched the older man's gaze. "Good. War consumes all if ye have no care—like grass before a scorching—" He broke off as a spasm seized him. Bent forward, he struggled in the hold of an unseen force, hands fisted, every muscle tense. And gasped, alarmingly.

The gathering sprang to their feet, Vaughan first at his side. He supported the stricken man, twisting in pain, then as he slumped in his seat. Breath rasped in his throat.

Claire stared in the shock gripping them all.

"Mister Monroe. Is it your heart?" Vaughan asked.

"Aye." His head lolled and his eyes closed.

Vaughan pressed his fingers to the feeble man's throat. "His pulse is thready."

"I'll fetch Ezekiel." Jim spun around and sprinted through the door.

Claire feared the gifted healer would be too late. Stunned by her grandfather's collapse, she and the others clustered around him, though she had no notion what to do.

Vaughan waved them back and loosened the black neckband and white cravat at his throat. She saw Stuart wanted to push the intruder aside, but Vaughan's air of authority held sway.

Supporting their grandfather in his arms, he gently lowered him to the floor, his head elevated. "We need a pillow. Someone get a blanket."

Her mother snatched up her skirts. "I'll go."

Stuart stripped his coat and handed it to Vaughan who folded the velvet cloth into makeshift support and slid it beneath their grandfather's head. The vital spirit that was Robert Monroe seemed to be slipping away. Wordless prayers welled in Claire.

"Lay me to rest wie my lads and sainted wife. Wie Wee Robbie," he panted, in a faint voice.

Though dazed, she wondered how his wishes could be honored. His sons were buried in two different cemeteries.

Stuart swiveled his gaze at her. "His mind wanders."

The only explanation. Grandfather was often confused. Oddly, he'd been more lucid today than he had in weeks.

Through her alarm, she met Vaughan's eyes. A knowledge in those blue depths told her he suspected something they didn't.

She couldn't imagine what.

Ezekiel hurried in as rapidly as his arthritis allowed, a small glass vial in his black hand. He knelt beside his charitable master, one gray head bent over the other. "Don't you go through them pearly gates yet. You hear? I'm gonna give you some foxglove to quicken yer heart. I mixed in willow bark to ease yer pain. Tastes a might bitter."

The barest nod. How pale Grandfather looked. His lips were bluish.

Vaughan lifted him while Ezekiel tipped a little of the brownish-green tincture into his mouth in careful sips. "Can't give you too much," he explained. "What can cure, can kill."

Claire feared death was imminent, either way. She knew foxglove was poisonous, but efficacious too. Potent willow bark tea, she'd had for aches and fever. Vile tasting stuff, but effective. She could but trust Ezekiel.

He trickled the tiniest bits into Grandfather's pallid lips, then pulled back his hand and set the bottle aside. "Now, we wait, and pray."

Claire was. Fervently.

The old man's arthritic knees couldn't long endure kneeling on the floor. Vaughan motioned the elderly Negro to a chair and continued to support her grandfather while the cluster stood in rigid tension. Mama swept back in with the blanket and dropped beside them. Her rustling skirts engulfed the floor.

"Don't you leave us, Robert," she pleaded, wrapping the woolen cover around him.

Was it wishful thinking, or had his labored breathing eased a little?

No. Not her imaginings. He did inhale more easily,

and a tinge of color lessened the deathly pallor in his face. He unclenched his hands, relaxing the coil he'd knotted himself into. Exhalations of relief ran around the anxious circle.

A slow smile spread over Ezekiel's wrinkled face. He rose from the chair and bent over the prostrate man. "Told you it weren't yer time yet, Mister Monroe. You rest up, and I'll take right good care of you."

There had always been a special bond between these two. Grandfather weakly lifted his hand and clasped the healer's.

With careful nursing, he might yet recover. Hope made Claire as weak as fear had and she slumped against Stuart. "Thank God," she murmured.

"And Ezekiel." Stuart closed his arms around her, and she knew, even though he was unhappy over her choice of husband, he wouldn't forsake her.

Vaughan clasped Ezekiel's arm. "You possess more skill than any physician I've encountered. Have you an apprentice?"

"I'm thinking on training young Jim, Captain. He's the only one with a ha'p'orth of sense."

"Maddie has potential, too." The words were scarcely out of Vaughan's mouth before Mrs. Jenner flew into the room, her plump cheeks flushed, ample bosom heaving.

"Oh, Mister Monroe, sir. I wouldn't have had this happen for all the world. We must bear ye to yer chamber." She paused in her headlong rush to assist the invalid and turned to Vaughan. "Captain, Lieutenant McCray's in the yard. He says to tell you to come. Yer wanted in camp."

Now? Claire's heart plummeted.

Chapter Twenty-One

Everything in Vaughan hated leaving Thornton Hall and Claire, like spiraling down from heaven to journey into purgatory. They stood hand in hand in the yard, her cloak and skirts tossing in the wind. The breeze sent clouds scudding across the late afternoon sun and darkened the sky. The somber mood suited him. La Belle was saddled and all in readiness for his departure. Thoughtful Mrs. Jenner had wrapped up some of the food from dinner for him to take and share with McCray and Anderson. All that remained was to bid farewell to this woman he'd fallen inextricably in love with. Impossible.

"Claire—" Speaking was difficult.

McCray cleared his throat. "I'll just wait over here, Captain." He rode his gelding a discreet distance from the couple and halted, allowing them a moment.

The Scotsman's gruff sympathy touched Vaughan more than he cared to admit, and he was already engulfed by powerful emotion. Unstable ground. He fought for footing.

Catching Claire to him as if it were their last embrace, and well might be, given the uncertainty of war, he buried his face in her hair, freed from the white wig. The scent of roses was sweet in his nose. "Nurse your grandfather and come to Williamsburg as soon as he's better."

"I will." Her voice quavered.

"I am entrusting Percy to you. When he's mended, he can drive the coach and see you safely there. If any demand to know your business or accuse him of running away, declare him free and in paid service to you. I will see he's reimbursed. Be my bold Claire. Accept no other alternative than him remaining in your keeping until we are reunited."

"No one shall take him from me."

He smiled faintly. "No. They won't. Promise, come what may, he shall be a free man."

"I promise."

"If you encounter British troops or Loyalists, showing them the letter and my ring will serve you well."

"But not Patriots." Even now, her wit was apparent.

"Not remotely. I know not how long it will be until the Legion reaches Williamsburg. If able, I shall write and alert you with instructions. Or seek you out upon our arrival."

"Percy and I will be there."

Clasping her shoulders, Vaughan gazed into her eyes and spoke in profound earnest. "Food may be in short supply. Bring provisions with you, conceal them under bedding in the carriage, and in your aunt's home. Percy is crafty and will aid you."

She gave a nod.

"I shall endeavor to send word of my whereabouts. Speak nothing of what I confide to anyone except Percy, or we may both be accused of sedition. Much is uncertain."

Shortened hair streaked blond and brown ruffled

about her face in the breeze. "I understand. Before you go, what of the mystery behind the cypher?"

He knew this tormented her. "Do not press me, sweetheart, If you force my hand, I must inform Tarleton. Matters are best left as they are for now. More is yet to come, I trust. Do not use a spade without me."

A tremulous smile, and she inclined her head. "I will undertake no grave digging without your leave."

"How odd that sounds. And now, my dearest, I must go."

She wrapped her arms around him. "'When you depart from me sorrow abides and happiness takes his leave.'"

A quote from Shakespeare's *Much Ado About Nothing*. At least, the couple were happily joined at the end of that play.

He replied with a quote from the same work. "'I love you with so much of my heart that none is left to protest.'"

Covering her lips in a kiss both tender and heated enough to sear this moment into their memories, he held her to him and then broke away.

The wrench was terrible, like pulling out a blade sunk in his chest. But he had no choice other than to touch her damp cheek and swing himself up into the saddle. Tarleton required every man to rebuff the obstinate militia forted up across the river. Anderson was already in action. The army would leave Halifax tomorrow, or soon thereafter, and Vaughan must stay with his regiment.

He gazed down at her, fixing her liquid eyes in his mind.

She lifted her arm in farewell. "Godspeed. And

may the Lord keep you in the hollow of his hand."

Vaughan could scarcely speak. "And you."

With that, he turned La Belle away and urged her into a canter. The faster he left, the sooner they might meet again. Pray God, it wasn't in the next world.

Chapter Twenty-Two

Late June, Bruton Parish, Williamsburg, Virginia

Finally! Vaughan was coming. After interminable days stretching into long, hot weeks, they'd be together again. At least, for a while. Holding fragrant nosegays of rosemary, lavender, and mauve phlox, Claire stood in the walled yard beside the imposing brick church quivering with anticipation. She wanted Vaughan all to herself these first precious moments and hours. But Percy shook his head.

He wiped a white sleeve across his beaded brow. "I best stay with you 'til the major comes. I don't like leaving you on your own with the army in town. Bad enough you don't have a proper chaperone. What would your aunt say?"

Shading her gaze from the sun, strong even beneath her wide-brimmed straw hat, Claire looked into his brown eyes, crinkled with concern. "She thinks I'm at the church to pray for the cause and honor the fallen. I can well imagine the scolding I should receive if she knew otherwise."

He clucked in imitation of a hen. "The little biddy scolds you like a broody bantam."

Claire smiled at his comic imitation. "Aunt Millicent feels it her duty to dissuade her misguided niece from wedding a British officer. No matter how influential. She doesn't share Mama's admiration for the gentry."

"Mayhap the major can charm her. Pity that nice Miss Smith went to Thornton Hall."

"Yes. I sorely miss her cheerful spirit, but our loss is Thornton's gain." Cousin Ethel, the older spinster who'd hung on with Aunt Millicent, was a dour soul, though the Negro cook was pleasant and reminded Claire of Sally. "Where should we wait? Vaughan said to meet him late afternoon."

Percy adjusted his black tricorn. "'Bout time, then. Let's find us some shade."

"Let's. 'Tis scorching hot."

Claire was sweltering even in her lightweight linen. She'd be as wilted as a plucked daisy when she met Vaughan if she didn't get out of this heat. And she'd taken pains with her toilette, choosing this gown so he might admire how the green hue complimented her eyes. The flowers sprinkling the skirt lent an airy feel, and she'd tucked lavender into the pale green ribbon encircling the crown of her hat.

"Maybe he's here before us somewhere," she suggested.

"We'll soon see."

The bell tower cast a shadow, and there were nooks in recesses along the church. She peered closely into any place that might hide a man and continually glanced over her shoulder as she strolled with Percy along the brick path winding through the parish grounds behind the church.

A low chuckle escaped him. "The major ain't gonna leap out at you like a startled deer."

"True. Foolish of me."

"I understand your eagerness, Miss Claire. I'm right keen to see him again myself. He liberated me from a cruel master."

"And you saved his life when William fired on him."

"And he saved mine again by seeing my wound was well-tended. But it's more than repaying a debt that keeps me loyal to Major Vaughan. He speaks to me like I've got some sense, not thick in the head just cause my skin's black."

"One of his many admirable qualities."

Percy's high esteem for Vaughan buoyed her spirits when she was low, a frequent occurrence. Strangely, with most of the town hostile to the man she loved, the former slave was her only friend. She'd made it clear to anyone who inquired that Percy was free and in paid service, but his circumstances in Williamsburg were trying.

"Governor Jefferson should have included slaves in his Declaration of Independence," he muttered.

"And women, as Abigail remonstrated her honorable husband, John Adams. I know the revolution cannot accomplish all we might wish, but I still hold the cause dear."

"And the major dearer," Percy said.

"Always. When we sail to England, would you like to accompany us?"

A smile spread over his dark face. "Believe I would."

"Good. We should welcome your faithful service." She hesitated, knowing he'd rather rejoin Vaughan and the British Legion. "Might you also remain with me until we rendezvous with the major this fall, and see me safely there, wherever that might be?" Percy was an excellent guide.

"I could do that, Ma'am."

"Thank you. We should be mightily grateful."

Still alert, but less overt about her watchfulness, Claire walked with Percy through the churchyard. She paused by two graves, one dug not many months ago. He waited as she knelt and laid rosemary, the herb of remembrance, lavender and phlox on the older grave marked by a weather-worn headstone carved with cherub wings and the words, 'Committed to God. August 17, 1735.' The adjoining grave sported a headstone etched with eagle's wings and the date, April 3, 1781, the day her father died. No name was chiseled on either memorial, as if both awaited the carver's hand.

Chills ran through Claire as she laid the second nosegay by this stone. At Vaughan's request, she hadn't done more than discover the site where Wee Robbie was laid to rest, and the companion grave noted in the cypher. She hadn't attempted to dig for treasure. Nor had she breathed a word of this secret to anyone save Percy, who'd accompanied her earlier and already knew the significance of her visit.

Vaughan would spot the fresh bouquets and know. This observance done, she rose and continued with Percy to the shadowed corner beneath a sweeping catalpa tree. Widespread branches with large, heart-shaped leaves created an inviting bower. The air wasn't exactly cool, but less sultry.

He leaned back against the silvery gray bark. "This is better. Major Vaughan said the churchyard, and here you are."

She could hardly wait to lay eyes on him. The holiness of this sanctified ground seemed a fitting place for their reunion. Seeing Vaughan again was sacred. Her chest fluttered as though a host of butterflies winged within her.

"Look at that one." Percy pointed at the most impressive memorial, an ornately carved above ground chest. These opulent table tombs, and the accompanying statuary, paid tribute to the wealthiest of society. "It's fancy enough for a duke."

"Or an earl." She dearly prayed her noble knight wouldn't be laid to rest here.

"Reckon that would do for me." He indicated the simple wooden cross marking many graves, all most folk could afford.

"No one is dying," she whispered furiously. "Not Vaughan, not Stuart, and not you."

But they both knew men fell every day. Civilians got caught in the confusion or felled by disease. And it frightened Claire to death.

Cattle bawling in the distance broke into her morose thoughts; it must be feeding time.

Percy blew out his breath. "I never saw as many cows as I did yesterday." He gestured beyond the brick wall curved protectively around the church. "Drovers herded them over the street. Flocks of sheep, too. Wagonloads of shelled corn, bacon, and too many gallons of rum to count went through. Lord Cornwallis aims to feed his army."

"I heard some of the uproar from my chamber, but Aunt Millicent was determined I not venture out. I hope his Lordship leaves some provisions for us. Our food rations are ample, but I fear running short. His burgeoning army are raiding Virginia like Scottish reivers."

"Not all behave like reivers, Miss Claire."

"No. But enough do that the damage is felt. The young Frenchman, General Marquis de Lafayette, Washington's new right arm, has been unable to keep them at bay. The revolution seems fated to fail, and folk are war weary."

"To the core. You can't have it both ways, the Patriots winning this war and Major Vaughan coming out on top."

She sighed. "I'm torn between agony over the state of the colony and dread for his welfare. I cannot lose him to this endless bloodshed, Percy. But we're standing in a place that clearly says I can. When will it all end?"

"For us, when we sail. For the rest of this country, Lord only knows. Take heart. Only a few months yet to go."

The tread of boots caught her ear. She looked around and there *he* was. Her heart leapt into her throat.

How magnificent Vaughan looked striding toward her in his uniform, as vibrant as ever. He didn't wear the helmet. His gold hair, pulled back at his neck, shone like a halo in the sunshine, and his eyes were vivid. Had they always been that blue? It hardly seemed possible he was here.

No grime streaked his face or his attire. He'd turned out in full regalia. He hadn't come straight from the saddle and must've taken time to bathe before meeting her.

"Vaughan!" Snatching up her skirts, she rushed at him.

He caught her up, whirling her around in a swirl of petticoats, and clasped her to his chest. Whispering her name, he covered her lips and kissed her as if he were famished and could never be satisfied. And so was she. For a long moment, it was just the two of them, the world and its endless squabbles forgotten. Then he seemed to recall himself. Before she grew giddy from breathlessness, he drew back.

Running his eyes the length of her, he smiled. "How are you, my dearest?"

She smiled back, knowing what he wished to learn. "Quite well, thank you, sir."

"Indeed. Like the fairest rose, you are abloom. Might there be a reason for this?"

"There might."

He frowned in mock vexation. "Claire, do not keep me in suspense. Tell me, are you with child?"

Her lips twitched. "I suspect I am."

The glow in his eyes made up for all their time apart. "Then we had better get you to the altar promptly." He gestured behind him, beckoning at unseen figures.

From around a brick corner, strode Lieutenant McCray, Ensign Anderson, and the devil himself, Banastre Tarleton. She nodded warmly at the first two men, who returned her acknowledgement with the utmost cordiality, while regarding the senior officer with dry-mouthed misgiving.

Then, drawing on the decorum bred into her, she curtsied. "Colonel."

Tarleton bowed, lifting his reddish head with a hint of amusement in his astute gaze. "You needn't be alarmed, Miss Monroe. We are come to witness your nuptials."

Vaughan explained. "I assumed your aunt wouldn't approve, so we shall proceed and inform her once the deed is done." He gestured toward the church. "The priest awaits."

She eyed him in wonder. "You arranged all of this?"

"It's little enough for you, my darling."

"And readily done, given we've overrun the town. The good father could hardly refuse," Tarleton pointed out.

"I suppose marriage at the point of a sword is better than none at all," she offered hesitantly.

"I really don't think he objects. His family is from England and has ties to ours," Vaughan assured her.

"Ah. Another connection."

"Valuable, as you see."

"Indubitably," agreed Tarleton.

Vaughan hailed Percy who sprinted to them with a grin.

"Welcome, Major."

He smiled and clapped his former guide on the back. "I've missed your keen senses, my friend, but she couldn't be in better hands. Come, make haste to the wedding."

Almost too flabbergasted to speak, Claire allowed Vaughan to escort her across the churchyard. It crossed her mind to wonder, as they passed the site where Wee Robbie lay, what he'd confided to Tarleton.

Spotting the nosegays, he slowed with her at his side. "Allow us one moment, Colonel. Please go ahead, and we shall catch you up."

A nod and faint smile from Tarleton, who took the

lead. The others followed him toward the sanctuary while Vaughan spoke to Claire. "There's something I must tell you."

"I'm listening."

"With the arrival of Cornwallis, General Arnold has been relieved of his command in Virginia and sailed for New York."

"We heard rumors. So, the traitor got away, despite everything."

"Do not berate yourself. Even the crafty Frenchman, General Marquis de Lafayette, could not catch the sly fox. A hunted man is a cautious man, and Arnold's among the most cagey. He is beyond reach now."

"The devil protects his own, I suppose. What of that other backstabber, Thomas?"

"Skulking among the camp followers. Likely biding his time and seeking opportunity." Vaughan held up a hand before she could caution him. "I am ever watchful of him and Simmons."

Relief swept over her. "Good. Now, tell me what you know of the cypher."

Vaughan gestured at the yard. "Do not dig here, or you will unearth your father."

Her jaw dropped. "But how?"

"Ponder carefully. 'Beside my brother now *I* rest,'" Vaughan quoted, emphasizing I. "The brother only he and your grandfather knew of. The brother concealed all these years. Captain Monroe was sending a message. *This* is his real grave. The reference to the *corbie* and the trickster the crow represents, and him being twice buried, are clues to the treasure hidden in the second site at Halifax."

"You mean, it's been there all along? How did we not realize at his burial? I heard no clanking."

"Likely the goods were muffled in cloth and the casket weighted with stones, if necessary, to imitate the heaviness of a body. You never opened the box, did you?"

"No. Too many days had passed since his death for a viewing."

"As your father anticipated. The price for Arnold's head was already accumulated, and a hiding place wanted when Captain Monroe was mortally injured. The rest fell into place with his ingenious wit."

"Papa truly was a genius. And he dearly loved riddles. Does Tarleton know the truth?"

Vaughan smiled wryly. "He does now, and thinks it a merry joke on the Rebels."

"I suppose it is, in a way. Though not to us. Will he order the site dug up?"

"By whom? We have no plan to return to that hornet's nest in the near future." Vaughan bent his head to whisper in her ear. "Here's my thought. When the time is right, confide in your brother. He can unearth the false coffin. No one knows to whom the valuables belong. This legacy may save Thornton Hall from financial ruin."

"A strange legacy, yet it might prove timely. Stuart is paroled and back in the fray," she added, somberly.

"With La Fayette. I know. Come along, my lady. We have vows to speak."

"And a long life to honor them, I pray."

"With all my heart, darling."

"Wait." She held to his arm. "How long will you be in Williamsburg?"

"A few days. Will your aunt agree to host me, do you think, or would she prefer some other officer? We are staying in homes all over town."

"Given those terms, I suspect she'll prefer your company. After your stay here, can you say where you shall be?"

"Not much. There's talk of fortifying a hamlet with a command of both the river and Chesapeake Bay called Yorktown."

With a happy cry, she threw her arms around his neck. "But Yorktown isn't far. We could see each other."

He held her close. "As often as possible. Though nothing will satisfy me until you lie each night by my side away from this wretched war. Meanwhile, I want you here with your grudging aunt and Percy, at a distance from the army. I think it safer. Disease spreads among the camp followers."

Sudden dread. "What of you?"

"I am hale. You carry our child and future heir and must take every care."

"What makes you think the baby will be a boy?"

"I simply know. But I would also be delighted with a girl." Then he laughed and swept her up in his arms, to the shock of passersby. "Will you cease your chatter, Madame, and hie thee to the church?"

She giggled as he bore her to the door. Just think, he'd be close by in Yorktown. What could be better? Other than sailing away on the next tide.

Chapter Twenty-Three

October 3rd, Gloucester Point on the York River across from Yorktown

"Tarleton's down, Major!"

Vaughan wheeled La Belle around at McCray's shout. Through the blur of riders in green and red coats and high spirited horses, he spotted Tarleton sprawled on the grass beneath his mount. The horse struggled to right itself.

What on earth happened? Tarleton was an expert horseman, and his gelding among the finest in the Legion. Had a dragoon careened into them, hurling the pair to the ground?

The timing couldn't be worse. Not far up the tree-lined road, an advance guard of French hussars led by the flamboyant Duc de Lauzun galloped right at them. How many cavalry were under the French duke's command Vaughan had no idea, but suspected a lot, given the cloud of dust rising in their wake. Behind this first wave, would be more. And then the infantry.

A grim prospect with their leader down. That left Vaughan one of the highest ranking officers still standing and the only one in sight.

"See to Tarleton!" Shouting direction, he converged with other dragoons of the British Legion and Queen's Rangers.

Several Rangers sprang from their horses and rushed at the senior officer, now freed from his mount and staggering to his feet. He could barely stand and must be dizzied by a blow to the head in addition to the pronounced limp. Supporting Tarleton between them, they dragged him back behind their lines. His badly shaken gelding followed.

With Tarleton out of enemy reach, at least, for now, Vaughan turned his attention to the oncoming riders. Saber upraised, shouting "Huzzah!" he led his men in a charge.

Possibly his last.

Claire's sweet face flashed through his mind. He prayed he might see her again. Nothing had gone as planned and he'd scarcely laid eyes on her since their hurried wedding. They should have been happily together abroad ship by now, sailing for home on swift currents, sped by a favorly wind. Instead, he was stuck here fighting for his life and the Crown.

Thundering hooves, the high whinny of horses, and clash of men engulfed him in a tumultuous swell. Musket reports burst on every side, accompanied by the anguished cries of the wounded. The dead lay where they fell. Acrid gunpowder clouded the clear air of what had promised to be a fair autumn day.

Dodging the blade coming at him, Vaughan pierced the Frenchman in the shoulder, loosing a bloody stream. The man's wail was lost in the confusion. He spun La Belle around and attacked a second rider. Knocking the pistol from his hand, he countered with a ripping slash across that hussar's arm.

Another howl, and he wheeled away to see Duc de Lauzun in the melee, regally attired in his striking blue and gold uniform.

Damn. The duke was afire.

Vaughan could wish Tarleton hadn't taunted Lauzun by leaving a message with the pretty widow at Seawell's Tavern, five miles up the road, saying he was anxious to shake hands with the duke. The jibe insinuated the meeting between the two would occur at Lauzun's defeat. No doubt, the Frenchman had whipped his forces into a frenzy to give Tarleton the satisfaction of his iron grip.

With the determination of a man bent on avenging an insult, Lauzun waved his sword and shouted indistinct commands. Even if Vaughan's comprehension of French were better, he couldn't have discerned the directives over the din. But the hussars understood and Lauzun's cavalry divided into two lines.

Bloody hell. He surmised there were several hundred riders forming each flank—more than the combined cavalry in the British forces. They might be outnumbered, but not yet outmaneuvered. And to Vaughan's credit, he had plenty of battle experience.

Fired with equal zeal, though fueled by a very different source—the desire to be with Claire again—Vaughan signaled his men to attack Lauzun's front. A second force of dragoons charged the Frenchman's flank, a tactic discussed earlier with Tarleton. Like hounds going in for the kill, the Legion and Queen's Rangers rode at the French Hussars with fierce cries. British infantry took to the woods on either side.

In the smoky chaos of battle, each maneuver carried the potential for life or death. Knowing which dragoon was where and whether injured or remaining in the saddle was impossible. Only that they must press the French. If they lost the field and the day, they would be pinned down in camp. Or worse.

Vaughan spotted McCray's face twisted in a wrathful mask. He was glad not to be on the receiving end of that brawny arm. Then he charged La Belle after a French cavalryman—caught off guard when the man whirled his mount around, a barrel aimed at Vaughan.

A loud blast sent the hussar flying to the dusty turf. He glanced around to see Anderson, smoke escaping his short barreled musket, one he'd skillfully mastered while on horseback. He waved at the loyal ensign in acknowledgement of his providential intervention and sprang away on La Belle.

"Huzzah!" The cry circled the British ranks. The French were falling back. Despite Lauzen's outrage, this furious assault was more of a challenge than they cared to meet.

Before Vaughan could further rejoice, he sighted a swarm of Continental militia, Virginians among them, under the command of the young officer, Colonel Mercer. *What the*—

Doing the unthinkable, Mercer dismounted on the field. "Forward, my boys!"

Shouting encouragement, he led his seasoned militia into battle at a run. His courage stunned all present.

The difference between these oncoming soldiers and the French—they fought for their homeland. Nothing roused a man quite so much as the defense of his land and family, his way of life, the independence these stubborn Rebels refused to relinquish. They charged as fearlessly as the best trained British regulars. Clearly, these were a picked battalion of grenadiers, chosen for their strength, skill, and resilience.

Half the militia fired on the Legion and Queen's Rangers, striking all too many, while the other half attacked the British infantry in the woods. Royal Welsh Fusiliers took cover and fired back with all the outpouring of courage anyone could require of a soldier. And more. The air was white with the pungent smoke. It filled Vaughan's nose and his parched throat.

Still, these stalwart grenadiers came—on foot or horseback, with the ferocity of an injured grizzly. And the hussars were reforming.

The sinking realization that they were not going to win the battle, weighed Vaughan's gut. He could stand his ground alongside fellow dragoons and fight to the end for king and country. Or surrender the field and live to fight another day. Over the explosions of muskets, clash of swords, and ever-present roar of men came the sound of fife and drums signaling retreat. Tarleton must've regained his senses and directed their actions.

Much as their commander hated to lose any fray, particularly this one, sacrificing his force wasn't wise or in his nature. Plus, he'd go down with them. Problem was, these Rebels had no intention of simply letting the British forces get away. They'd have to fight for retreat.

Vaughan reared La Belle, shod hooves pawing the air. Her loud whinny in his ears, he swung the warhorse around. She kicked at any man who drew too near and he struck out with his saber. Between her lethal hooves and his deadly steel, he beat a howling path through the insurgents, then bounded ahead.

With crack Virginia sharpshooters taking to the trees, the dragoons were more dependent than ever on the Welsh. His father's, and his own, heritage.

Continual firing from the brave fusiliers allowed the Legion to head for camp.

Dear God. No!

A sharp pain tore through him like a lead ball when he saw Ensign Anderson go down. Shot through the chest, he tumbled from the saddle to the grass. His frightened gelding bolted ahead.

Perhaps he still lived! Vaughan swung La Belle toward the spot where his loyal companion of these many months lay on his side. Reining the mare in, he scrambled from the saddle. She stood faithfully amid noise and confusion as he knelt in the stained turf. He gently rolled Anderson over, then pressed his fingers to the wounded man's throat—the dead man. There was nothing even Ezekiel could do.

Damn it all. Anderson wasn't the only one among the fallen. Others were going down all around them. But next to McCray, Anderson was his closest comrade. And he wasn't bloody leaving him here lying in the field.

"Steady, girl." Fighting back hot tears, he boosted the fallen man onto La Belle and laid him across her neck. The mare seemed to understand what was required of her and made no protest.

Vaughan was preparing to mount when an unpleasantly familiar voice growled. "Pity you didn't survive this either."

He swiveled his head. Simmons was poised above him on his horse with a pistol pointed right at Vaughan. So, this was it. Once Lord Vaughan died, Thomas would triumph and inherit the family estate through the deed of his spiteful henchman, amply rewarded, no doubt.

Unless—the child Claire carried was a boy, as Vaughan sensed. If she made it back to England, the inheritance would still pass to his son.

Terrible thought. What if she were their next victim? If Thomas intended for Claire to meet with an equally unfortunate *accident*, Vaughan could do nothing to protect her. He'd find her and the baby, or send Simmons.

Fury surged through him in a fiery tide, but he couldn't grab his pistol from the fur-covered holster on La Belle's side fast enough. Damn! Why hadn't he carried it?

"I believe you have that barrel aimed the wrong way, Captain Simmons. You can shoot him or me, but not both."

Stuart Monroe? Vaughan peered up in wonder at his brother-in-law's stern regard. Of course, he'd be among Virginia's elite grenadiers. No longer a lieutenant but a captain, he noted, and seated astride Bryan, the horse Claire had left behind for him.

Simmons shifted the barrel toward the Virginian.

Without hesitation, the swifter man fired, sending a lead ball through his heart. Vaughan stared from Simmons, toppled face down in the grass, back to Stuart. "Marvelous shot."

"If I find the scoundrel, Thomas is getting the same," he informed him.

"My wily cousin has a way of landing on his feet."

"He'd better land far from here."

"He made for New York before the siege."

"A rat abandoning ship." Stuart nodded at the body of the young Loyalist lying atop La Belle. "I'm sorry about Anderson. He was kind to William. The lad will grieve his loss." Waving other advancing militiamen aside, he gestured for Vaughan to mount. "Claire would never forgive me if I didn't help get you back to camp."

Vaughan swung himself up into the saddle and gazed into eyes the same hue as Claire's. "Give her my love."

Stuart extended his hand. "She doesn't want it from me. Do your utmost to live and lavish my dear sister with affection yourself."

Moved by this unexpected gesture, Vaughan clasped his firm grip. "I will. Thank you."

"You spared me. We're even. And Vaughan, if we're both alive at the end of all this, I will bring her to you."

Too overcome to speak, he gave a nod and turned from one of the most remarkable occurrences ever to transpire on a battlefield. Then sped after fellow dragoons with his sad burden. All the while, the Royal Welsh Fusiliers fired to cover their hasty retreat, or even less would return to camp. And he realized, today's failure to break through the French and Virginia line had left them trapped.

The fortified hamlet where Cornwallis's army was entrenched across the river was rapidly becoming a disaster. Rather than the ideal defensive position to maintain seaborne lines of communication with the larger British army in New York, Yorktown was cut off. Allied troops had them surrounded by land and the French fleet under Count De Grasse was anchored off shore in the Chesapeake Bay. The forces closing in on them were larger, better armed, and tenacious.

A premonition, like someone walking over his grave, ran through Vaughan. He remembered Mister

Monroe's rant when they first arrived at Thornton Hall about fire and brimstone awaiting them. 'Twill rain hellfire on ye all,' the old man had prophesied.

At the time, Vaughan discounted his threats as pure madness. Now, he feared the worst was yet to come. Yorktown wasn't going to end well.

Chapter Twenty-Four

October 22nd, the Chesapeake Bay

Seagulls called overhead and waves lapped along the shore where Claire waited in the morning sunshine with Stuart and Percy. The brine in the breeze carried a nip of fall, and she hugged her wool cloak against the chill air.

"It's finally over, Claire. The end of the revolution and victory in sight," Stuart repeated, as though he still couldn't grasp the amazing events at Yorktown four days ago.

Neither could she, or that she'd soon leave these shores, possibly forever. "Return to Thornton Hall, as soon as you're able. Convey my deepest affection to all and hopes Mama will visit in the new year. Send William too, if you like."

"I shall. And carry glad tidings of Cornwallis's surrender."

Ahead of them, at water's edge, some British officers were already in the smaller boats that would row them out to the French ships anchored in the bay. The gracious Count de Grasse had agreed to carry the defeated officers, under flags of truce, to New York City. Lieutenant, now Captain, McCray, was among them. More gathered in preparation for departure, but Vaughan lagged behind. Every moment apart from him was agony, heaped on days of dread for his safety.

Circling one arm around her, Stuart swept his other at the men making ready to depart. "It's difficult to believe after a short stay in New York, you will set sail for England. Unlike the regular troops headed for prison camps, poor beggars," he added. "Seems General Washington also approves the privilege of rank and aristocracy so esteemed by the British and Europeans."

"For which I'm grateful," she said hoarsely, her voice husky from tears and worry. "If he paroles British officers and allows them to return home, what quarrel should you have? Vaughan requested the same for you."

"True enough, and I'm happy for your and Vaughan's sake. Though many Americans find Washington's terms too generous and object to him regaling Cornwallis and his senior officers at dinner parties these past few evenings. There's a brotherhood among the gentry that survives warfare. Bitter enemies one day, amicable dinner companions the next. It makes no sense."

"To our way of thinking, no," Claire agreed. "But a boon for us that Washington honors this tradition, and he's allowing a few servants aboard ship."

Stuart clapped Percy on the back. "You are in luck my sister and the major have you in their employ."

His dark brown eyes alight with hope, he nodded. "That I am, Captain."

Regarding her brother anxiously, Claire gripped the sleeve of his blue and white-faced Regimentals. "What's keeping Vaughan? Are you certain he's all right?"

Stuart patted her fingers reassuringly. "As well as

Beth Trissel

any man can be who endured days under siege with scarce rations. At least he was pinned down at Gloucester with the Legion and not in Yorktown itself. The town is nothing but rubble after all that shelling."

"Still, he had to hear the continual bombardment."

"Oh, yes. He heard. Night and day."

"The cannon fire unleashed on Yorktown hardly bears thinking about. And we're told pox is spreading among the slaves who sheltered with the army."

"Their plight is most pitiable. Disease is bound to spread." Stuart hugged her to him. "Neither side got off lightly, Claire. We have our injured and dead, too. How you endured the deteriorating conditions in Williamsburg, I don't know. The hospital is overflowing."

"Aunt Millicent forbade me to set a foot out of doors for weeks. I've practically been under house arrest all fall."

"An old curmudgeon she might be, but she kept you safe from disease and the wrath of your neighbors."

Claire nodded somberly. Marriage to Vaughan hadn't endeared her to the Patriots in town, but she made no apologies for the leadings of her heart. "I'm grateful you fetched us, Stuart. Otherwise, it mightn't have been safe for Percy and me to travel here."

"I hope they wouldn't attack an expectant woman, but the mood of the people is volatile. These are unsettled times."

Didn't she know?

The light tread of boots and low nicker of a horse caught her attention. Her spirits soared. There was Vaughan, thinner than she remembered and worn, but alive. His lean frame showed no signs of injury. He'd escaped relatively unscathed.

Rather than the customary scarlet uniform and helmet, he wore a dark blue tricorn on his head, the same shade as his coat and waistcoat. White ruffles showed at his neck from the fresh shirt and cravat, and charcoal breeches fitted his well-muscled legs above shoes, not boots. Someone, General Washington or Count De Grasse, had seen this nobleman's son was properly attired. The cherished sword hung from the leather carriage at his shoulder, as officers had been allowed to keep their side arms. And he led La Belle.

Breaking from Stuart, Claire hurtled herself at Vaughan. Though smudged from fatigue, his blue eyes hadn't lost their gleam. Laughing, he caught her to him, but made no effort to swing her around. Rather, he held her close, as though she were the dearest being in the whole world.

"Dear Lord, you are a vision for sore eyes. An angel I feared never to see this side of paradise."

Heart pounding with the unbridled joy of finally being in his arms again, she fought the urge to break down and weep. Battling to force the words from her tight throat, she choked out an assurance. "I am quite real and my belly too swollen for a celestial being."

He chuckled. "No angels have your rounded form." Pulling back, he looked into her face. "But they would trade heaven for your eyes." The kiss he covered her mouth with was but a foretaste of the delights to come.

They broke off as Stuart strode to them. "Major, I am glad to see you safely arrived."

Vaughan shook his hand, then passed him the reins. "Look after La Belle for me, a great favorite of mine and one of the finest mounts I've ever had the privilege to ride. If you feel inclined to make the journey to Charles Towne, she belongs to Captain Jordan."

"I've heard of him."

A wry smile, and Vaughan nodded. "No doubt. Jordan's reputation precedes him. I suppose now he can abandon that godless Backcountry he rules like a king and make a proper life at his lovely plantation with his fair wife." He undid the portmanteau from behind the mare's saddle and set it on the sand. "I regret leaving La Belle behind."

Stuart patted her gleaming neck. "I should very much like to keep her, but ought to compensate Captain Jordan. Alas, at present, I could never afford such a horse."

Claire considered her brother. "Actually, Stuart, you can. There's something I've been meaning to tell you about the legacy Benedict Arnold inadvertently left us."

"*You*, to be precise," Vaughan interjected. "Whenever you wish to dig for it in the family plot at Halifax."

While Stuart weighed this startling revelation, Vaughan closed his arm around Claire. "Arnold left us a rather different sort of legacy than goods of worldly value. If it weren't for him, my darling Claire and I never should have met. Despite Arnold escaping the noose, I think your father would approve the legacy he bequeathed his children."

With that, she wholeheartedly agreed.

The smile spreading over Stuart's face spoke his consent. "I suppose there's no use trying to return all that stuff now. No telling to whom it belongs."

"None. Make good use of it. Now, we must take our leave of you." Vaughan clasped Stuart's shoulder in farewell, and picked up his portmanteau. Percy shouldered Claire's trunk.

A quick hug for her brother, promises to write, and she walked through the sand at Vaughan's side toward the rowboats. "How long until we're in England?"

"With a good wind and the blessing of Providence, we should celebrate Christmas at Hartford House."

She gazed at his handsome profile. "Then for that blessing I pray."

"We've come this far, my dearest. I expect we shall complete our journey in good time and with the greatest contentment. I know, I shall. Just to be with you, and eat and sleep without cannons bursting through the night will be the greatest of plenty. Shall you be content, sweetheart?"

"Blissful. A lifetime isn't nearly enough to give you all the love I have."

"Nor I. But I shall endeavor to fill you to overflowing."

She patted her middle. "You already have, but I'm eager for more adoration."

Wind, waves, and the shouted greeting of men excited to depart muffled his chuckle, though not the smile in his eyes.

Beth Trissel

A word from the author...

Married to my high school sweetheart, I live on a farm in the Shenandoah Valley of Virginia surrounded by my children, grandbabies, and assorted animals. An avid gardener, my love of herbs and heirloom plants figures into my work.

The rich history of Virginia, the Native Americans, and the people who journeyed here from far beyond her borders are at the heart of my inspiration. In addition to American settings, I also write historical and time travel romances set in the British Isles, and nonfiction about gardening, herbal lore, and country life.

For more on me visit:

http://bethtrissel.wordpress.com/